PRAISE FOR OVERKILL

"I finished reading in three sittings and was almost late for work one day because I couldn't tear myself away. It gave all the feels of watching Buffy for the first time, but now with characters like me!"
- **V.S. Holmes**, Author of *Blood of Titans*

"Overkill has everything from vampire hunting to mystery, romance, twists and turns, and pristine descriptions. There are even some pop culture references sure to give the reader a chuckle or a smile."
- **Cynthia Brubaker**, Author of *Gomada Academy*

"Buffy who? Eric and Tony are the vampire hunters you want to be reading about! Wilham has a way with words that completely immerses you in a fictional world. The characters are so relatable, diverse, and *real*, that it makes it so easy to fall into the storyline."
- **Whitney L. Spradling**, Author of *These Dangerous Fates*

Hunters of Ironport: Book Three

Kill Your Darlings

Lou Wilham

This book is for you. Yeah, you. Shit's tough right now, I hope this helps you get through it.

CHAPTER 1

THE ENTIRETY of Ironport was tucked into their beds. Sleeping peacefully, safe and warm. Likely dreaming of sugar plums, or fluffy bunnies, or some shit. Something better than the blood and pain that had haunted Eric's dreams since he was thirteen and his Venator gene activated.

Most of his students. His family. His friends. And even his boyfriends.

All tucked in, safe and sound.

Not Eric Marcelino though.

Never Eric Marcelino.

There was no time for sleeping, no time for rest, when Ironport was inundated with vampires. He'd thought for a while there that things couldn't possibly get any worse, but Eric should have known better. Things could always—*always*—get worse. Hadn't his life proven that to him again and again? Every shift of the season, every tick of the clock, every turn about the sun, things seemed to get *worse*.

His friends died.

A vampire took his boyfriend.

The vampires grew in number.

His body aged and ached.

And still, the vampires kept *coming*.

With a grunt, Eric leapt backward, avoiding the swipe of clawed fingers and fanged teeth dripping in saliva and venom. He perched atop one of the decrepit monuments of the old graveyard at the center of Ironport, arches aching from pushing all his weight onto his toes. His shirt stuck to his spine from a heat that refused to release its grip on Ironport even as they moved into fall.

"Seriously though," he muttered, mostly to himself because he knew the vampire wasn't going to answer, "where the fuck do you guys keep coming from?"

"There's evidence to suggest," Bert said, his voice crackling through Eric's earbud, "that this one in particular was the victim of a hit and run on—"

"Now is not the time, Bert!" Eric teetered on the toes of his tennis shoes as the vampire all but ran headfirst into the monument in their attempt to get to Eric. There was something strange and mindless about the current crop of vampires. Almost rabid. Like they'd given over entirely to the bloodlust, but different. Even a newly turned vampire starved for blood knew enough not to run headfirst into stone. Especially at full speed like that.

The vampire shook their head, stringy hair falling into their face, as if dazed by the blow. But it didn't slow them down. They reached for Eric's ankles, although far out of reach, nails scraping loudly against the stone and leaving behind tracks of drying brown blood in the moonlight.

"I'm just saying that it looks like this little horde came from—"

"We'll talk about this when I get home, Bert." Eric hissed, spinning on his toes to get a better view of the graveyard. There were at least two more vampires clawing their way out of the ground. If Bert was right, then they'd been turned as recent as last night, possibly this afternoon. Fresh corpses were never in short supply, but on this scale? It hinted at a connection to the morgue that Eric hadn't previously considered.

"How many is that this week?" Bert asked, relentless in

his need to fill the silence between them with something more than Eric's labored breathing.

How long had he been at this? An hour? Two? He'd lost track. He hadn't expected this fresh crop of vamps to cause so much trouble. They were fresh dead—they should be uncoordinated and unwieldy. And they were to some extent, but they were also brutally quick. Vicious, they homed in on him in a way Eric hadn't previously experienced. Like someone had given them his scent specifically and sent them on their way.

"Twenty." And it was only fucking Wednesday. Goddess, Eric was so fucking *tired*. Spread too thin. He almost longed for the time when he'd thought Dash was up to something because things were too quiet. He should have taken that time to rest when he'd had the chance. If only he'd known . . .

"This isn't sustainable," Bert said. Eric tried not to think about the strain in his words as he leapt down from the monument to face off against the vampire now that he'd caught his breath. He couldn't think about the anxiety, the growing concern, he saw on everyone's faces when he came home bloody another night. Couldn't let it slow him down.

This was not sustainable, Bert was right about that. But Eric Marcelino was going to try anyway. What other choice did he have? Let the kids come out here and put their lives on the line?

Ducking away from seeking hands, Eric came up behind the vampire and took the opportunity to slam his stake through their back and into their heart. It was harder than going through the front, even with the way a vampire's body was brittle and easier to break apart. But a moment later they burst into ashes, and two more took their place.

There wasn't a chance in hell that Eric would let the kids come out here and do this. Sure, they were all Venator, all of age, all much older than he'd been when he was thrust into the battle against the undead, but that wasn't the point. The point was they were *his* kids, and if no one else was going to protect them from the harsh reality of vampire hunting, he'd do it himself. Provide them the safety no one had ever bothered to offer him.

"How many signatures are you seeing?" Eric asked, kicking one vampire in the stomach to get himself some breathing room to deal with the other, as he struggled with the long chain around his neck. Their claws scraped at his skin, cutting through the thin T-shirt he'd chosen to wear out hunting today, leaving behind a bloody trail Hunter would no doubt fuss over.

"Five."

Fuck. Hadn't he already put six down? He didn't know, he'd kind of . . . lost count at some point. It was hard to keep track of the bodies and the ashes when they wouldn't stop coming for him. When every moment could be his last. Plunging a stake into the vampire who had him by the collar, their head tilted to go for his neck, Eric stumbled back, his foot catching on a bit of uneven ground. He just managed to get the pendant his Nonna had gifted him—his Cross—out in time to put some distance between himself and the vampire. An invisible bubble protecting at least his neck and face.

It gave him the distance from the next threat to get his feet back under him. "Please tell me it's five total, not five more."

"Wish I could, buddy." Bert didn't sound as sorry as he likely should about that, but Eric didn't have a second to spare to think about it as the next vampire lunged at him.

They got close. Too close. Their fangs snagged at his forearm. He hissed at the burn of fresh blood welling to the surface and the sound of rumbling from somewhere underneath him. A hand burst from the ground and grabbed his ankle, nails digging in so deep he swore they'd tear through muscle and tendons. Eric yelped, nearly dropping his stake.

Thank the Goddess for Venator balance. He stamped down hard on the wrist of the creature below him, somehow managing to keep the one at his front at a distance. He could do this. He didn't need to bring the kids into this. He didn't need to bring Tony into this.

Tony, who should be at home, resting, trying to wrestle his wolf into submission. A process that was taking far longer than they really had time for. But Eric would give him the space, and the time, and the understanding that someone like Tony deserved. Change was hard. Even harder when it was on a cellular level. Plus, he wasn't a Venator anymore. He was a werewolf now. That made this not his fight.

The creature below Eric burst further from the earth. They let him go long enough for him to lunge forward and push the vampire at his front with his body weight until he could shove them and stake them. That was the thing about hand-to-hand combat situations, Eric had learned early on: They were close range, yes. But not so close that the only thing he had available to him was his own teeth. That distance would work for a vampire, but not for a Venator.

Spinning, he slammed the stake into the vampire still struggling from the ground before they could fully pull their torso out. That just left one.

"Now. Where are you?" Eric murmured softly, crouching low and ducking behind another monument to give himself cover while he caught his breath.

"There's another signature incoming," Bert said, but he didn't sound worried about it.

"Vampire?"

"No. Something else."

Great. Just great. Eric flipped the stake in his hand and longed for the baseball bat he'd left in the trunk of his car. It hadn't seemed smart to bring his entire kit out on patrol. It would slow him down. A mistake he'd made once already this week. Whoever said Eric was a slow learner wasn't paying attention. Still, he clearly needed some middle ground on that. The duffle was too much, but his jean pockets were too little, especially in the warmer weather where he worked up a sweat too quickly to wear a coat with pockets for supplies.

If he lost the stake in his hand, he had one extra jammed into his back pocket, and once that was gone, he was fucked.

He'd have to chat with the kids about a better method once he made it back home. The little shits were good at stuff like that. They didn't have the instincts and reflexes yet to go out into the field, but they were good at tactics. Good at providing a new set of eyes when Eric was unable to get out of his box. He'd been doing this too fucking long, he knew that, longer than any Venator in history, and it made him set in his ways sometimes.

"Human?" he asked, ducking another swipe from the vampire and coming up swinging. With the blunt end of the stake clutched in his fist, he slammed it into the vampire's temple, leaving behind a long cut that leaked blood for about a second before it closed up.

"No." Bert huffed, and Eric could hear typing in the background. The kid was probably pulling up data or statistics, or something that Eric would get hopelessly lost in if he tried to sit down and read it. Good thing he had the kids for that too. Dyslexia was a bitch and a half when part of your job was reports and procedures. Bert made a soft sound low in his throat, curious and thoughtful. "Supernatural."

"What kind?" Not that it really mattered. He'd have to do something about whatever was coming for him. Hopefully it was a lower folk who'd gotten curious by the scent of blood and could be chased off. That happened sometimes. Goblins or fairies lured in by the promise of easy prey. Or maybe some folk out on a walk near the graveyard. That happened sometimes too. He sent up a silent prayer to the Goddess that it wasn't someone he'd have to fight, and he grunted under the force of the vampire grabbing him by the collar and slamming him bodily into the monument he'd been standing on a few minutes before. His ears rang, and Eric was sure a migraine was incoming after that, but it didn't slow him down. Not this time.

"Eric," Bert said, patiently, but also frustrated? Eric wasn't sure how that worked. Only Bert seemed to be able to express both emotions at once. It was the warning call of a Bert-style lecture. "You know very well that I can't tell what *kind* of folk it is."

Eric didn't know that, but in all fairness it probably wasn't because no one had told him. It was probably because he hadn't been paying attention when they did. It was hard to focus on the technicalities of the tech they were using when Eric just wanted the shit to work.

"A vampire is a negative force," Bert droned in Eric's ear, and Eric head butted the vampire when they got close, hard enough to make his own skull scream in pain. But it dazed them, giving him the advantage. "A human is a neutral force. They show up on the radar but really don't leave a lasting impact. They're tiny by comparison. A folk is a positive force. But the radar doesn't differentiate between . . ."

Eric tuned him out after that because Bert had descended into what Eric could only describe as jargon. Lots of technology terms and magical knowledge Eric didn't have. He only knew one thing, and that was the hunt. The slay. He hadn't had time to become educated on the wider world of magic like his students had.

Lucky them.

With the vampire still trying to shake off the way Eric's head had slammed into theirs, Eric managed to jam his stake into their sternum. They burst into dust a moment later, and Eric coughed, doing his best not to inhale more of it than he had to.

"Eric," Bert said, his tone cautious.

"What?" If Eric sounded annoyed, it was because he was. He was tired, and sore, and his head hurt. He wanted to go the fuck home and curl up in his bed. "What the fuck do you—"

Something slammed into him, taking him to the ground. Eric choked, the wind knocked out of him, his vision momentarily darkening before it cleared again, albeit with stars dancing before his eyes. Tony's face hovered above him, lips peeled back to reveal sharp teeth, a feral look in his glowing green eyes as every breath left him in a hard puff.

"Eric! Eric, are you okay?! Answer me! Eric!" Bert's voice went unbearably high when he panicked, and Eric had to resist the urge to rip the earbud from his ear and fling it across the graveyard never to be seen again.

"I'm fine, Bert. It's just Tony." Eric grunted, shoving Tony off him so he could sit up. Then he removed the earbud, stuffing it into his pocket, before Bert could freak out further. "What the fuck are you doing here, man? I told you to stay home."

Tony shook himself, the manic expression clearing a bit as he tamped down on whatever struggle he was having with his internal wolf. "I smelled blood. I got worried."

"You didn't smell blood all the way from home." Eric narrowed his eyes on Tony, a disapproving note to his voice.

Tony shrugged, running his fingers through sweat-slicked blond hair. He wasn't going to give any reason why he was in this part of town when he was supposed to be safe on campus with the kids and Hunter, and Eric knew that. He knew it because this wasn't the first time in the last couple of months that Tony had crashed one of Eric's hunts. Usually, he got there earlier and made a mess of things. Small mercies he hadn't this time.

"I don't know how many times I have to tell you," Eric grumbled, rolling to his feet and straightening his clothes. He frowned when he looked at the dirty and slashed shirt he'd been wearing. Thankfully it wasn't one of the nicer ones. But still, buying clothes only for them to be ruined out on patrol was getting prohibitively expensive. He wondered momentarily if Ava could patch it for him and then promptly discarded the thought, shaking his head. He couldn't deal with his best friend and her shit right now. "You don't have control of the werewolf yet, and until you do, you're no good to me."

"I have control!" Tony snarled, baring pointed teeth from where he sat amid the browning grass of the graveyard.

"Sure you do, pup." Eric rolled his eyes and offered Tony a hand up. "Come on, let's go home. I've got to call Kalla."

"What the fuck for?" The annoyance about Eric calling his ex was entirely unwarranted, Eric and Kalla were just friends now, but Tony had a jealous streak a mile wide.

"Because she's the Sheriff, and I need to talk to her about her contacts at the morgue." Eric yanked Tony to his feet and started back toward his car. "Did you drive?"

"Took the bus."

Eric sighed, pinching the bridge of his nose. That was so fucking dangerous. With the moon hovering heavy over them, all that would have to happen for Tony to lose control was for someone to piss him off. A task that wasn't exactly *hard* to do when it came to Tony McMahon.

"Great." Eric exhaled and forced himself to start moving again. He needed to get home. That was it. Just get home. And then he could spend time with Hunter and hopefully wind down. "C'mon."

Chapter 2

THE URGE TO CLAW. To tear. To rip. To break.

It sat heavy in Tony's chest. Pushing at his ribs. Threatening to take over every other thought he had. He had always been the destructive sort, but this knocked that up to an eleven. Driving the desire—the compulsion—so high that every second he spent holding it back was a lesson in endurance.

How long could he hold out? How long before he let the wolf free to do what it pleased? He didn't know. And the not knowing sent a shiver down his spine.

Eric was right. He shouldn't have come out tonight. Not with the way the moon sat heavy above them. Not full. But too close, too close, too close. A few more days? A week? He was sure there was an app for that, but he couldn't be fucked to bother, honestly.

Putting himself on a bus with the wolf so close to the surface wasn't smart, but what was impossibly *less* smart was sitting in a car with Eric. The air circulating from the outside wasn't enough to muffle the scent of him.

The sharp bite of blood. The smokiness of his hair products. The clean, crisp scent of laundry detergent. And the subtle smell of skin and sweat, tangy with a rich undercurrent of something Tony might have called woody. But he was no expert on scents, and even with his enhanced ability as a werewolf, he still hadn't learned to pick a person's scent apart down to the cellular level.

It was overwhelming, and the wolf wanted to get at Eric. What it would do once it did, Tony didn't know, and he didn't want to find out. He knew that Eric could handle himself. He'd proven that time and again. But that didn't mean they should test his mettle against the beast living in Tony's chest.

"Hey," Eric called, gentle, reaching halfway across the center console, but stopping before he touched Tony. Like he was afraid of what Tony would do to him if he was caught by surprise. That was fair. But the thought of it had him grinding his teeth. "You good?"

"'m fine, sweetheart. Why wouldn't I be?" Tony asked, forcing a smile. How long had he been zoning out there? He squinted out the window, trying to gauge how far they were from campus now, but he didn't know Ironport the way Eric did. Six months wasn't enough time to know a place, not really. It would take a lifetime, and honestly, Tony was starting to wonder if he even had that long ahead of him. Not with the way the vampires were constantly knocking at their door.

Eric's hand dropped back to the gear selector that rested between them. "Right." Why did he sound disappointed? Maybe he thought they were about to have a heart-to-heart there in the middle of the highway. They weren't. Tony wasn't the type, and honestly, he didn't think they had time for something like that. Not with so much coming for them. Eric cleared his throat. "Anyway, I think we need to have a discussion about something I noticed tonight."

"Shoot." Tony didn't like the tone in Eric's voice now. It was businesslike, but there was an edge to it. Fear, maybe? Tony didn't know him well enough, not yet, to recognize all his shifts in mood. Hunter was better at that, and likely always would be. Tony tried not to be jealous. They were *sharing*, and Tony had said he was okay with that. Said he was fine splitting Eric down the middle like the last piece of pie. It was just . . . Well, Tony had never actually gotten that sticker in kindergarten.

"I know we've talked about this a little bit," Eric hedged, his hands flexing on the steering wheel in the dark as the car slowly climbed the winding road back up the mountain to Moondale U campus. "But there's something wrong with these vamps."

"Wrong how?" What could be worse than being a bloodsucker? As far as Tony was concerned, they were all beasts, getting exactly what they deserved at the pointy end of a stake. But he'd never been the sort to overly examine the creatures he was sent off to slay. Eric had. Eric had the capacity to feel for them, to want to know why they did the things they did. Likely to want to help them, if he could.

Before Ironport. Before Eric. Before the kids, and the school, and that whole thing with Dash, Tony might have looked down on Eric for it. He might have snubbed his nose and been disgusted by Eric's ability to see the undead monsters they spent their lives fighting as something other than what they were. Now he just . . . *marveled* at it. Eric was something else.

"It's like they're mindless."

"That's what happens when you die and all the blood dries up in your brain." Tony snorted. That probably wasn't what really happened when someone was turned, but Tony didn't know anything about vampire physiology, and he was fine with that. It wasn't his job to know how they functioned. It was his job to make sure they turned to dust.

"That's not—" Eric cut himself off, and although Tony couldn't see him in the dark of the car, he knew Eric had rolled his eyes. He huffed out an annoyed breath. "Anyway," Eric continued, clearly deciding it wasn't worth it to argue— he was right in that respect. "Even freshly turned vamps aren't usually this mindless. Their hunger drives them, sure, but they don't act like fucking lemmings."

"Lemmings?"

"You know, that computer game from when we were kids with the critters that would walk right off a cliff? Or run into shit without any thought to the damage it would do?"

Tony didn't know. He hadn't had access to a computer at home growing up. It wasn't until he'd left home, and gone out on his own, that he'd been able to afford things like that. And by that time, he'd had other things to worry about. Like how he was going to pay his bills. How he was going to keep Lu fed, and clothed, and in school when he'd almost dropped out himself. Couple that with the fact that he was seven or eight years younger than Eric—he wasn't sure exactly, Eric was always cagey about his age—and there were some references he didn't get.

"Sure," he said instead of voicing that. He didn't particularly need the wounded look from Eric that always came with the reminder that the man had been born with a silver spoon in his mouth, and maybe other people didn't have those same life experiences. "So what you're saying is . . . ?"

"What I'm saying is I watched a vamp run headfirst into a granite monument at full speed." Eric shook his head as if trying to clear the image away. "That's not normal behavior for even the hungriest of vamps."

"They're extra thirsty right now. What of it?"

Eric grunted, his frustration clear in the sound. "They're not just thirsty," he said, shaking his head again. "It's like all their instincts have been turned off. And the way they keep going after me . . ."

Tony's skin prickled in something that might have been fear at those words, gooseflesh and hairs raising all along his arms, legs, at the back of his neck. His stomach twisted in anxiety. He liked Eric too much to think about him being in danger like that. He wasn't sure when it had happened, or how, but it was a fact of life now.

The sky was often a cloudy gray.

It snowed in the winter.

And Tony McMahon *liked* Eric Marcelino.

Liked him enough that the thought of something happening to him made the creature in Tony's chest growl a warning. Liked him enough to share him with someone else when Tony had always been a grasping, greedy, possessive sort.

"What are you saying?" Tony asked, pushing everything else from his mind and focusing on the fear. On the reminder that Dash was still out there, somewhere, watching and waiting. It hadn't been easy to forget about him, but in the few months or so since he'd disappeared in a literal puff of smoke, so much else had happened. Some good. Some mixed. Some bad. But still enough to give Tony more distance and perspective on everything Dash had—

No. He wasn't thinking about that right now. Right now, his focus was on Eric and what Eric had noticed about the vamps tonight.

But Eric was biting his lip, his eyes fixed on the road in front of them, refusing to look at Tony. He was scared too. Worried about what all of this meant for them. Tony could practically smell it on him.

The turn signal was loud in the silence. Click-clacking. Making Tony's ears cringe.

"Eric. Baby." Tony pressed gently because he had to know. As much as Eric might want to skirt the question, to keep those around him from worrying, Tony had to know. He had to prepare himself for what was coming. For the danger Eric was putting himself in. He'd do anything he could, anything at all, to protect Eric. Even if that meant going against Eric's wishes. "What are you saying?"

"I don't really know what I'm saying," Eric admitted

softly. "Or rather . . . I don't know what it means. They're after me specifically. Dash has implanted some kind of compulsion that they can't deny. Their sole existence once they're turned is to find me and get as close to killing me as they can. What that means, I don't know. I mean . . . we know Dash wants me dead. He wants to stop the prophecy. But . . ."

"But wouldn't it be quicker for him to come after you himself?" Tony hated that he could finish that thought. Hated that he knew exactly where Eric's head was at. But he hated the truth of the sentiment even more.

"Yeah."

"Well." Tony bumped his head back against the headrest on the seat, letting out a long, slow breath. He wished he had a joint on him, something to calm his nerves and put the world at a distance. But he hadn't smoked since he was turned, too afraid of what the wolf would do if his defenses were down. "That bit's easy. He's a fucking coward. He knows if he comes at you head on, he can't beat you. And why bother fighting fair when he can keep making minions to do his bidding?"

Licking his teeth, Tony turned to look at Eric through the dark of the car and the silence of the mountain road around them, and he had to push the next words out through a throat gone tight with despair. "He knows you're going to get tired eventually, princess. He knows you can't keep this up forever. It's been, what?"

"Nearly four months." Eric's voice sounded like a croak. And like that, Tony could see the way his shoulders slumped more than normal, weighed down by exhaustion instead of poor posture. His lids were heavy with it. The furrow to his brow hadn't been there when Tony first came to Ironport.

Goddess, maybe if he'd never come. Maybe if he'd stayed in fucking Miami, far away from Eric Marcelino with his pretty eyes and sharp tongue, maybe then Eric wouldn't have to face this. Maybe then Eric wouldn't be so fucking *tired*. But that was what destiny did, wasn't it? It fucking forced a person to do things they wouldn't normally. Shoved them into impossible situations that either made them, or broke them. Tony was on the verge of the latter. All he could do was hang on with everything he had and hope Eric wasn't on the verge of breaking right with him.

"You need to let me come out there with you," Tony said, fighting every instinct within him to keep his voice level, reasonable. To not let his desperation show. His frustration and anger at being told to sit in the corner and wait his turn. Getting into a fight now wouldn't help either of them, but Goddess, that's what he wanted. A fight, even one with Eric, would at least make him feel like he was doing *something*. Not sitting on his hands waiting for someone *else* to take care of him. "If you did, I could have your back. I could make sure that—"

"We've had this talk, Tony." Eric held up a hand to silence him. "You can't. Not until you have better control over the wolf. Not until—"

"Fuck that! You *need* my help! You need someone who can—"

"It's too dangerous. Not just for you, but for me too. And for anyone who happens to be within spitting distance of us if you were to—"

"FUCK YOU!" The wolf roared in his chest, his eyes flashing a glowing green as his nails grew to claws and dug into the door panel so deep, he left grooves behind. His breath came in hard pants, puffing out of his nose loudly. Blood flooded his mouth as his elongated canines cut into his lower lip.

"Okay." Eric pulled the car to a park outside of the dorm at 1106 Moonshadow Way. Most of the lights were off, aside from the soft warm glow of the one above the stove in the kitchen that Tony had left on, and a lamp in a window upstairs—Hunter's bedroom, Tony's mind supplied.

Hunter was waiting up for them. No. Hunter was waiting up for *Eric*. Tony wasn't sure how he felt about that, and honestly . . . it didn't matter. Not when compared to the rage still making his claws dig into the upholstery.

"Okay," Eric said again, his voice soft, gentle, kind. Without a single trace of fear. He should be afraid. He should be very afraid. He should heed the warning growl that rumbled up from Tony's chest when Eric reached for him again. He stopped mid movement but didn't pull his hand back. "Take a breath."

Tony's eyebrow twitched, irritation flaring sharp and hot in his chest again, but he forced himself to listen to Eric's soothing voice, forced himself to follow the order. It settled something within him. His chest loosened. He pulled his hand away from the door and frowned at the gouges he'd left behind.

"I'll fix that."

"You better." Eric laughed, the sound strangled, but he shook his head. "Can we talk about this more tomorrow?"

"Yeah." Tony nodded, taking another deep breath. "Yeah, we can."

"Cool." Eric smiled at him, tentative and sweet, and Tony melted.

"Cool." Tony laughed, then leaned over to press his lips to Eric's, sighing at the gentle, warm pressure. Eric returned the pressure, a soft, happy murmur rumbling in the back of his throat, curling in the air around them. It sent a shiver down Tony's spine, and he caught himself scooting in closer, near climbing over the center console to get to Eric, even if he knew it wasn't a good idea. Even if he knew this too might make his control snap. Especially with the wolf already so close to the surface. He didn't care. He didn't *care*. He bit into Eric's mouth, hands reaching for his hips, needing more. Needing to be close to him. To pry apart Eric's ribs and fucking live in his chest.

Eric pulled back, putting a hand to Tony's shoulder, lips a little swollen, a dazed look in his eyes. "Let's get inside. I've got to shower and look at these cuts, make sure they don't get infected. And I think—" He paused, eyes flicking up to the window that shone like a beacon in the night. "I think Hunter is waiting for me."

"Right." Tony swallowed around a sour note of jealousy that sat heavy on his tongue. "I'll umm . . ." He took a deep breath. *You agreed to this. You said it was okay. Nut up and be a good partner, Tony. You can do it.* "Why don't you two sleep in tomorrow, and I'll be in charge of getting the gremlins fed and out the door."

"Really?" Eric's eyes jerked back to Tony's face, a smile threatening the corner of his lips. It was enough to soothe any ruffled feathers at the thought of Eric letting Hunter, not Tony, care for him tonight.

"Yeah. Really."

"Thanks, Tony. You're the best!" Eric leaned in and brushed another quick kiss to the corner of Tony's mouth, then he was all but rolling himself out of the car, and Tony was helpless but to follow.

# Chapter 3

COUNTING stitches was supposed to be soothing. Supposed to help distract Hunter from the weight of everything happening. The influx of vampires. The danger his boyfriend, his brother, and his friends were in. The pressure the Council of Creatures was putting on him to release his latest reports on the vamp activity in Ironport.

It was supposed to help clear his head after his visit to the graveyard to look after Britt's headstone left him raw.

At least, that was the absolute bullshit lie Ava sold Hunter about a month ago when she finally taught him how to crochet. She'd fed him some line about how soft crafts were relaxing. How the repetitive motion of his hook looping the yarn over and over again would help him find his center.

What she hadn't told him was how fucking *frustrating* it could be when he didn't count for a few rows, calling it good, then twenty rows later realized somehow the thing he was trying to make was shrinking in size.

What the fuck.

He huffed, leaning back against the headboard, and held the bit of fabric up to glare at. "What the fuck even *are* you?" He hissed at it.

It didn't answer.

"Are you a blanket? A scarf? A tablecloth?"

Still no answer.

It didn't help that he hadn't given it any thought before he'd started this project. He'd just picked a yarn from Ava's shop that he liked, chosen a stitch he thought was easy and functional, and got to work. Part of him thought that it would reveal itself the way Ava's projects did sometimes. But he was no stitch witch. He was just . . . well. He still didn't know *what* he was, much like the slowly shrinking crochet project.

Rus said she had some theories, but she wasn't telling him. She said something about wanting to wait until Moondale revealed more to her, whatever that meant. He assumed the ceremony at the Heart in a week or so would give them some answers. But that didn't help him *now*.

Huffing, he dropped the material to his lap again, his ringed fingers twitching around the soft yarn. It would make a good blanket. But did he have the yarn he needed to make it large enough for all three of them? He couldn't tell. He didn't know enough about crochet. Damn it.

"I'll have to frog it all probably," he muttered to himself, already reaching for the ball of yarn he'd created a couple days ago. Why did he have to ball the yarn when he had a perfectly acceptable skein? It was all about aesthetics, okay?

It was almost too easy to start unwinding the yarn, wrapping it back around the ball. All his hard work undone. But there was something cathartic about it too. This bit was almost more relaxing than the making itself. The unmaking. What did that say about him? Nothing good probably. He slid his glasses further up his nose and pushed it from his mind.

A creak on the stairs drew his gaze from the ball of yarn in the basket at his side to the door. The house alerting Hunter to someone coming home.

It had taken some doing, but slowly, Hunter could tell that 1106 Moonshadow Way was warming to him. At first, he had thought the house was just a house. A tired old dorm building that had housed one too many co-eds through the years. But over the last few weeks he'd been noticing things the house did. Little things. Putting things away, but not where he'd expect them to be stored, like 1106 was being petty about having to clean after its residents. Which, honestly, having housed young adults for this long? Hunter could see why it'd be a little pissy and less likely to show itself. But Hunter thought perhaps he and 1106 were coming to some kind of understanding.

A shadow moved in the hall, then another as two people walked past the nightlight on the stairs, and Hunter frowned. Eric came into view a second later, his form slumped heavily against the doorframe. There was a slash down the front of his shirt, blood glinting in the low lights of Hunter's bedside lamp.

"Hey," Eric said, his voice rough, likely from the vampire dust he'd no doubt inhaled while on patrol.

A smile twitched at the corners of Hunter's lips, soft and slow. He couldn't seem to help himself. The idea of Eric coming home to him? Curling up with him after a long night of hunting? It made something warm settle in Hunter's chest. He just wished Tony would let him in enough to be that safe harbor for him as well. But he was so closed off. A veritable Fort Knox. And no matter how hard Hunter tried, he couldn't seem to bridge that gap. He knew they'd agreed to share Eric's time. Knew that the understanding was that they would be an unconnected triangle, but there was . . . something. Hunter couldn't quite put his finger on it. Something that made him want to shift that. Tony just wouldn't let him try.

"Hey," Hunter replied, stuffing the half-frogged maybe-blanket and the ball of yarn into the basket and dropping it off the side of the bed. When he turned back, he saw Tony hovering in the hallway behind Eric as if perhaps he wanted to join them but refused to allow himself to ask.

Hunter gave an awkward wave, and Tony nodded back

before continuing toward his own room. Hunter's shoulders drooped and he sighed at the rejection.

"It's okay," Eric murmured gently, as if he had read Hunter's thoughts. He probably had. They'd been friends for so long at this point, the only one who could read Eric better than Hunter was Ava, and they had some weird kind of mind meld he couldn't even begin to explain. It was like the moment they'd become friends, their brains had merged into one. Freaky, but endearing all the same.

"It's really not." Hunter shook himself and rolled off the edge of the bed, pushing to his feet so he could scuff his bare toes through the plush rug. "But it will be." It was a promise, one he wasn't sure he could keep, but he'd do his best. What other option was there? It wasn't like the way his breath hitched every time Tony dismissed him would go away.

He reached for Eric, his rings glinting in the low light as his fingers settled on Eric's hips. "Let's get you cleaned up," he whispered with a gentle tug on Eric's belt loops. "Bath or shower?"

Eric hummed thoughtfully, almost tripping over his socked feet as he followed Hunter toward the bathroom. "Bath," he said after a moment, his voice soft and hazy, dipping into that tone he took when he handed over the reins.

It took a lot of trust for the caregiver Eric Marcelino to let someone else look after him for once. And Hunter felt privileged to be the one that Eric let see him this way. All soft and yielding.

"Could you wash my hair?" Eric tilted his head back to look at Hunter through his lashes, a sleepy smile spreading his lips.

"Yeah, hon, I think I can do that. Come here, baby, let me take care of you." Hunter nudged the door shut with his foot and continued tugging Eric slowly across the messy floor of his bedroom to the bathroom. With careful maneuvering, he settled Eric against the sink and spun to start the bath. The tub was a small freestanding clawfoot thing with nowhere near enough room for someone of Eric's height, but he'd make himself fit.

"Clothes go in the hamper," Hunter reminded as he grabbed the Epsom salts from the shelf and dumped a healthy scoop into the slowly filling tub.

Eric grunted as he stumbled out of his jeans, dropping them into the wicker hamper along with his socks and under-wear. When it came to the T-shirt, Hunter watched him glare at it as if it had personally offended him, then throw it into the small trash bin in the corner.

"I'll get the first aid kit too." Hunter shuffled across the bathroom to the sink and pulled a plastic box from beneath it, his fingers already twitching at the thought of looking after Eric. Steam rose, making his glasses fog up, and he pushed them into his hair, the nose pads catching at the strands and drawing a wince from him.

"Let me." Eric's fingers were careful as he untangled Hunter's glasses from his hair and set them on the counter gently. The cut on his chest looked worse without the shirt to hide it from Hunter's keen eyes. He hissed when Hunter reached for it, shying away from his searching touch until his back hit the countertop.

"Sorry."

"No. No. It's okay. It needs to be taken care of. I know that." Eric shook his head, dark hair falling into his eyes. He didn't bother trying to swipe it out of his face, just tilted his head back and shook it, the strands stuck to the still-cooling sweat along his temples.

"We'll get it clean first. Then I'll wrap it. And if you're a good boy, maybe I'll give you a treat."

A visible shiver raced up Eric's spine, and he leaned in closer. "I can be good."

"I'll bet you can." Hunter chuckled gently. "Do you need anti-venom?"

"One bite. My arm. But there was no venom. The rest are just claw marks."

"Okay." Setting the first aid kit on the floor so it'd be within easy reach, Hunter slowly led Eric to the tub and helped him in.

The water, hot enough to turn his skin pink on contact, made him hiss, but it didn't stop him from sinking deep enough that Hunter had to shut it off lest it overflow the tub.

"Wash up first," Hunter instructed, reaching to the caddy hung over the shower head to grab Eric's favorite shampoo and conditioner. He couldn't remember when they'd started all but sharing Eric's room, but it didn't really matter at this point. That might have been why Tony was so standoffish with him still—because he'd all but moved into Eric's bed and left no room for Tony. A thought that was just foolishness. If Tony wanted to join them, they'd make it work. Not that Hunter had ever said as much.

The water sloshed as Eric rubbed a loofa over his body, clearing away the grime and the blood from the hunt. By the time he was finished, what was left behind was a muddy gray color.

"Should have had you shower first." Hunter sighed. "I'm not using that water to clean your cut. You'll need fresh."

Eric whined but didn't fight him when he unplugged the tub, letting the dirty water drain away before he started refilling it. He did shiver, though, as his skin was hit with the slightly cooler air of the bathroom.

Refilling the tub took a few minutes. In the meantime, Hunter pushed the sleeves of his long-sleeved shirt up to reveal arms covered in so many tattoos, his brown skin was nearly unrecognizable through the black and the colors. Then he wet a rag in the sink and started on the cut on Eric's chest, doing his best to be gentle.

"It'll be gone by the morning," Eric complained, but he'd tilted his head back over the edge of the tub, his arms open wide, leaving Hunter room to work. His eyes closed.

"Doesn't mean we should leave whatever shit was under that vampire's fingernails embedded in it. Do you want to get blood poisoning or ringworm or something?" Hunter clicked his tongue softly.

"I don't think that's how that works."

"You're not a doctor."

"Neither are you." Eric laughed softly, peeking one eye open to watch Hunter work. "Tony said he'd take care of the kids in the morning, so we can sleep in a bit."

"That was nice of him." The water had reached Eric's chest by that point, and Hunter dipped the washcloth into it to ring out the blood before going back to cleaning the cut.

"It was," Eric agreed.

Hunter wasn't fooled. Eric had brought this up for a reason. He wanted to talk about it. Hunter did too, but now wasn't the time. He didn't have the energy or the emotional bandwidth to deal with Tony's drama and take care of Eric at the same time, so he let the silence stretch. Eric was kind enough not to push the matter.

With the scratches on Eric's chest taken care of, the rest was easy, soothing in a way Hunter's crochet project hadn't been. He took his time, massaging first shampoo and then conditioner into Eric's scalp and neck until he was practically boneless. He sank down so far into the tub, the water touched his chin, and his feet poked out the other side near the faucet.

"All right," Hunter said after a while. "Bedtime."

Eric grumbled, letting Hunter pull him from the tub and dry him with a fluffy towel while the water drained. That done, they stumbled back into the bedroom and Eric flopped onto the bed while Hunter found him a pair of boxers to sleep in, and grabbed some fresh bandages. When he turned back, Eric was sitting on the edge, his feet on the floor, his head tilted back in something Hunter could only describe as pleading.

"What is it?" Hunter asked with a fond but exasperated sigh.

"You promised me a reward if I was a good boy." His honey-brown eyes were wide and puppy-like, his brows drawn together, his mouth pressed into a soft pout.

Hunter's heart flipped over in his chest, a warmth spreading outward to every extremity. Eric knew exactly what he was doing, he always did. He was a smart man, for all he liked to pretend that he wasn't. Especially when it came to how to twist Hunter up inside and wrap him around Eric's little finger. Fucker.

"And *were* you a good boy?" Hunter asked, already knowing full well that he was going to give Eric whatever he wanted. How could he not?

"Mm-hmm." Eric nodded, a smug smile spreading across his face.

Brat.

"I see." Hunter crossed the room, slow, and measured, tossing the boxers and bandages onto the bed beside Eric before he fell to his knees between his spread legs. "Won't argue with that," he murmured, pressing a kiss to the inside of Eric's knee, drawing a soft murmur of contentment from his lips.

He left a gentle trail of kisses along the inside of Eric's thighs, and a grumbled moan rolled up his throat when Eric's fingers twisted in his hair, trying to urge him closer, sooner. It wouldn't do. Hunter would work at his own pace, and Eric knew that. He bit Eric's thigh in punishment, and Eric whined before ceasing his attempts to urge Hunter along. Hunter pressed an approving murmur into the crease to the side of his half-hard cock, nudging Eric's legs wider at the joint.

Eric spread to accommodate him, his breath rasping softly

in his chest from where he sat above Hunter, and Hunter didn't give him any time to catch his breath. He swallowed Eric's length down in one quick movement, ripping a keen from Eric's throat as he sucked him gently into full hardness before he set to work.

The pace was slow, languid, measured. Exactly the way Hunter preferred to be with Eric. He understood Eric's need for frenzy and roughness, but Hunter had always liked him best like this, slowly taken apart bit by bit.

Pre-cum was bitter on his tongue, but it didn't slow Hunter down as he stroked his tongue over Eric's tip, lapping at the fluid and drawing a shiver from him. Eric's hands tightened in Hunter's hair, and Hunter's own cock twitched in interest. He'd have to take care of that later. After he'd turned Eric into a puddle and put him to bed.

It didn't take long, Eric's hips jerking up as he lost himself to Hunter's lazy rhythm, his tip brushing against the back of Hunter's throat once, twice, three times and then he was coming undone. It burned down Hunter's throat, and he swallowed what he could before pulling away and finishing the rest with his hand, spitting what he hadn't managed to swallow into the trash beside the bed.

"Should have warned me," Hunter grunted.

"Sorry," Eric muttered, muzzy with sleep.

He must be really tired. He usually had the courtesy to at least tug Hunter's head away. "All right." Hunter sighed, grabbing some tissues from the bedside table and cleaning them both before he helped Eric into his boxers, wrapped his wounds, and nudged him into the bed, the covers up to his chin.

"What 'bout you?" Eric asked. His blinks grew longer and longer as sleep pulled at him.

"I'm good, hon. You get some rest. I'm just going to clean up the bathroom, then I'll come to bed."

"Mm-kay." A second later, Eric was out like a fucking light.

Hunter shook his head, leaning to brush a kiss to his forehead, carefully carding his still wet hair away from his face. It would be a fucking mess in the morning, but they could worry about that then. In the meantime, Eric needed his rest.

CHAPTER 4

THE LIGHTS OVERHEAD BUZZED, the sound drilling into Eric's ear, making the headache that much worse. It was quickly becoming a full-blown migraine. His stomach turning. His vision tunneling. He breathed through it and tried to focus.

Sleeping in should have helped. At least, it used to help. But that was before the stress of everything else. Before Dashfield B.M. Chadwick. Before the knowledge that the prophecy given to him at birth wasn't just about the annihilation of everything he knew, it was also about his assent to power.

Power he didn't want. He could barely keep track of his students, much less an entire city. He didn't have the fucking energy to be the head of an organization, to step up to the plate when the Huntsmen fell apart.

He shook himself, focusing again on what Hunter was saying, his voice a low rumble with something hanging off the edge of the words. Regret. Guilt. He said, "I need to send in my report."

Eric's stomach twisted painfully again, and he had to look up at the lights, breathing deeply, focusing on the pain in an effort to quell the impending panic. It didn't help. Nothing was helping. He felt more than heard Tony shift closer, his fingers brushing lightly over Eric's hand where it hung at his side.

"You can't," Eric said after a long moment of letting the buzzing lights burn his eyes. It didn't help. Nothing helped. He was going to be sick. Maybe not right this second, but at some point soon. "You know you can't. You know what will happen if you do."

They'd talked about this—*a lot*—over the last few weeks. But even Eric wasn't foolishly hopeful enough to think they could keep the Council of Creatures at bay for long. Especially now that they'd filled Janet's seat as acting mayor, and Huntsmen representative with another prominent member of the Huntsmen community. He didn't know who they'd chosen, but he had his suspicions.

"They're going to subpoena me for it. Any day now." Hunter twisted the ring on his thumb around and around, not meeting Eric's eyes.

Goddess, why couldn't anything in Eric's life be easy? Why did everything have to be an uphill fucking battle? And why was his own bad luck somehow rubbing off on Tony and Hunter? It didn't seem right, or fair. Maybe he should have distanced himself from them weeks ago, gone off on his own when the shit really started to hit the fan. It would have kept them safe.

That was the least he could do for the men he loved, right? Keep them safe. Keep them away from this fight. *His* fight.

Not that they would have stood for it. Stubborn assholes that they both were.

"What will happen if they find out about the increase in activity?" Tony asked, but he had to know the answer to that question already, didn't he? There was no way he was so devoid of the facts to escape from the truth of their predicament.

"They'll send the kids into the field." Eric had to push the words through a throat half strangled with fear, half with grief. If his kids were forced into the field, they'd die. He would lose them. He had no doubt about that. They weren't ready. Not for the threat they were currently facing.

Maybe—*maybe*—a few months ago when the attacks were fewer, and there were less vamps in every one, they could have handled it. But now? Eric had faced eleven vampires last night. *Eleven.* Even with their numbers, his kids couldn't have handled that situation.

They weren't ready. They might never be.

"Just tell them no." Tony shrugged, rocking back on his heels and crossing his arms over his chest. Putting up a front of toughness that Eric didn't believe for a single second.

Eric sighed heavily, his shoulders drooping. "If I do that, they'll take the kids." He didn't even have to think about what the consequences of such an action would be. He knew. "They'll take them. They'll shut down my program. And the kids will be forced into the field anyway. Without my protection. Without my ability to send them in groups. They'll be thrown into the battle with nothing more than a pat on the butt and a *good luck, kid.*"

"How do you know?"

"Because that's what they did to me."

It hurt more than maybe it should have, so many years later. The wound was old. The betrayal and the reminder of how no one—not even his parents—had cared enough about Eric to try to protect him when he'd been thirteen and thrust into this fight, *ached.* He'd been abandoned. By his friends. By his family. By his community. And he wouldn't let that happen to his kids.

Tony growled softly, the sound a rumble in his chest that he probably didn't even realize he was doing. His wolf instincts grew stronger every day, slowly becoming a part of him. Eric wondered sometimes what would happen when the wolf finally took over. Would there be anything of Tony left to love?

"We won't let that happen," Hunter said, his voice firm. Although Eric knew well enough that Hunter had no plan to keep it from happening. Because what could they do? Their options were few: give the Council of Creatures what they wanted and risk the kids' lives under controlled circumstances, providing them with Eric's continued supervision, or don't give in to the council, and lose any ability to protect them.

"Just falsify the reports," Tony suggested, and both Hunter and Eric turned to blink at him. "What?"

"Lying on paperwork for the Council of Creatures is considered treason." Hunter's face had paled, his twitching stopped entirely, which was worse. Terror replaced the worry. "Do you know what the punishment is for treason?"

"They can't punish you if they never find out."

"But they will," Eric said, running his fingers through his hair. It was a complete mess, just like his life. Yay. They matched. "They will find out."

"How? Who's gonna tell 'em?" Goddess, Tony's view of the world was so simple. Oh, that Eric could live in a world like that. Where everything was so clear cut, and lying to a ruling magical body wasn't a quick recipe for death.

"Because they always do!" Eric threw his hands in the air, his heart kicking in his chest.

"How?" Tony pressed, his lips pursing.

Eric could see from where Tony was sitting how this would make sense. Just lie. No one would ever have to know. But Tony didn't know how Ironport worked the way that Eric did. He hadn't been born here. Wasn't raised here within the community of Huntsmen that were deeply entrenched in Ironport's roots. He didn't understand.

"If they need reports to know about the activity—"

"They don't need the reports," Hunter said, shaking his head and taking off his glasses so he could pinch the bridge of his nose. Maybe he was developing a headache too. Honestly, it was surprising they all weren't laid up in bed from the sheer stress of this situation.

Tony stopped, frowned, his jaw working as he chewed the inside of his cheek. "Then why are you writing them?"

"They *do* need the reports." Eric shook his head. "But if you think for a second that Hunter's reports are the only method they have for gathering information on the vampire population, you're sorely mistaken. And even if that weren't true, they're not fucking stupid, Tony. Anyone within spitting distance of this town can see some shit is going down here. The only ones who seem oblivious to the fact is the humans, and that's only because they see what they want to see."

"The only method to slow them down is to waylay sending in the reports at all," Hunter confirmed. "The council doesn't need them to know how large the threat is, but the formality of them will allow the council to act. Having the numbers on records will give them the evidence they need to make changes to the current Venator system."

"So . . ." Tony stuffed his hands into his pockets, and Eric could tell he was keeping his posture carefully casual, calling on what control he had to make himself seem calm when he was anything but. *Join the club.* "So just don't send them in? What're they going to do about it?"

"I don't know, honestly. I've never held on to them this long."

And that was worse. Eric got how that was so much worse.

"Whatever they do about it, it won't be good," Eric concluded. He could picture it now, the Council of Creatures sending some of their goons to Hunter's lab to raid his filing cabinet. To rip the place apart in search of the information they wanted. They wouldn't even need a warrant since technically the entire place was funded by them and belonged to them anyway.

"Then . . . what do we do?" Tony's green eyes flicked

between Hunter and Eric, unsure. He was the youngest of them. The least knowledgeable in Ironport politics. But Eric appreciated how he included himself in this. How he'd become a part of their team. Even if it was just because his sister was one of the Venator likely to be affected by any decision made by the Council of Creatures.

"I might be able to buy us another week." Hunter ran his fingers over the hairs that had wiggled loose from his bun, taking a deep breath. "Maybe two. If I give them the reports from the first week or so after Dash disappeared. The numbers were high then, but not as high as they are now."

"Any theories on that?" Not that it mattered. Whatever the reason, they were fucked.

"Desperation probably." Hunter tapped his fingers on the table, his rings clacking lightly against the wood. "He thought you'd be easier to kill at first. The numbers have gone up steadily every week since then. Early on, we didn't have as much information either. Their frenzied, rabid behavior only became evident in the last couple of days or so."

"They'll seem less dangerous."

"Theoretically."

"And in the meantime?" Tony pressed in closer as their voices lowered.

"In the meantime, we figure out how the fuck we're going to find your ex and put an end to this once and for all." It sounded simpler than it was, Eric knew that from experience.

"Any chance we can alter the Ghost Tracer's algorithm again to make it look for him?" Tony chewed on his lower lip thoughtfully. The idea was impressive, not something Eric expected. But then, there was so much about Tony that Eric still didn't know, wasn't there? It hadn't even been a full year since the day they met, and they'd spent a portion of it separated because of Dash's abuse.

"Maybe." Hunter slid his phone across the table and pulled up the app. The screen turned black, full of text that made Eric's vision swim. So he looked away from it, focusing instead on Tony as he came to lean over Hunter's shoulder. "We'd need a way to track him."

"Right." Tony tilted his head, his brows drawn together in thought. "Some way to differentiate him from all the other vampires and spirits."

"Exactly."

Eric smiled to himself, watching them both inspect the code, speaking softly. Working together. A team. This was what he wanted for them—for all of them. The ability to lean on one another.

"Let me think on it," Tony said. "I'm no tech whiz like you are, but we should be able to come up with something between the two of us."

"We should get Bert involved too." Hunter had his own grin twitching at his lips, making the stud in his lip glint in the low light. "And I'll need to talk to Rus about a spell to tie it all together."

"Okay." Tony nodded. "Do you want me to come with you?"

"Yeah, that might be nice. Let me just clear it with her first. Rus is kinda . . ." Hunter shifted his head from one side to the other. "Well, she's a wildcard. I can never tell how she'll react to certain things."

"Sure. I get that." Tony grinned back at Hunter, a warmth flooding his cheeks that dusted his freckles in pink under the lights of Hunter's lab.

"All right." Eric clapped and winced when it made his boyfriends jolt and his own ears ring. He hated having to break up this little love fest. Especially when it was the first time it seemed they were getting along, but they had work to do. "Sorry." He scrubbed at his face.

"'s fine, pretty boy." Tony shrugged, but whatever companionable air had been between them had fallen away. Damn it.

"Just . . . happy to have a plan finally?" Eric's shoulders scrunched up near his ears, uncomfortable with the attention. "And I umm . . . I've got to get to class?"

"Right. I'll walk you." Tony nodded and moved away from Hunter. "See you later, Delacroix."

"Yeah, later." Hunter snorted, turning back to his work.

Chapter 5

TONY WAS on the edge of sleep when he heard his door creak open. It could be anyone. None of the residents in this house seemed to have any respect for a closed door. Whoever it was knocked timidly on the frame as if that would excuse the rude behavior of not asking if they could come in first.

Tony cracked his eyes open, glaring at the blurry figure through his lashes. Short dark hair—not his sister or Fin. Short in height—not Eric or Hunter. Pale skin—that too marked off a number of the kids including Bert, Kate, and Nik. Thank the Goddess. That only left Chase, Hunter's kid brother.

"What do you want, kid?" Tony croaked, scrubbing at his face as he reached for his phone on the nightstand to check the time. It had to be early still. The light through the curtains was milky like pre-dawn, or it was being filtered through the clouds. He grunted when he saw that it was already almost noon. Rain then, not early. "Shouldn't you be in class?"

"I stayed home." Chase shifted on his feet, his blurred shape moving one way and then the other where he still stood in the doorway as if afraid to enter Tony's space without permission. So he had some manners then.

"Why?"

"Didn't feel good."

Tony frowned, sitting up, and reached for the glasses he

sometimes wore when he couldn't be fucked to bother with his contacts. The prescription was wrong these days, anyway. Turning into a werewolf affected a person's vision, who'd have thought. He caught himself squinting through the lenses, his eyes straining, a headache settling in quick. But it was better to be able to see Chase for the most part.

The kid was shorter than Hunter, by a lot. He probably hadn't hit his last growth spurt yet, but even with that, Tony wasn't sure he'd ever be tall technically. He was still in his pajamas, a flannel set complete with a button-up shirt like a grandpa would wear.

But that wasn't what made Tony sit up straighter and take a closer look. It was the way Chase was curled inward. His arms were crossed over his stomach, his shoulders hunched forward as if to make himself as small as possible. A thin sheen of sweat coated his pale face, and his lips had lost much of their color.

"What is it, kid?" Tony asked. Already he was rolling to his feet, his own grogginess long gone. "You shouldn't be out of bed if you feel this bad. C'mon. Get back in bed." He shooed the kid back into the hall gently and toward the collection of rooms that belonged to the kids.

"I thought—" Chase swallowed thickly as if willing down his own nausea, breathing heavily through his nose. "I thought it was just a stomach bug."

"Did you take anything?"

Chase shook his head, then seemed to realize that was a bad idea when he let out a soft groan of pain.

"I'll get you something. I dunno what, but I'll see what we've got in the cabinet downstairs. Is it cramps?" He knew Eric kept an extensive first aid kit in the kitchen for the kids with everything from aspirin to period supplies. Hopefully there would be something there for whatever this was.

Chase groaned, his form almost crumpling, and Tony had

only a second of warning to catch him before he collided with the wall.

"Whoa there, kiddo." Tony shifted, helping to support Chase's weight as he breathed through whatever was going on in his body, his breath coming out in hard huffs through his nose. "Is it cool if I pick you up? This'll go a lot faster if I do."

"Mm-hmm." It came out more as a whine, but Tony didn't wait for further agreement before he scooped the kid into his arms.

It wasn't far to get to the door marked with Chase's name on a little whiteboard. It looked like the writing was Eric's, and underneath it was a message from Eric himself, likely written that morning before he headed out for class.

Feel better soon! Call me if you need anything. - Eric

Tooth-rottingly sweet is what that was. Tony clicked his tongue, shaking his head as he pushed the door in. Chase's room was the same size as all the kids' rooms: small. But tidier than Tony had been expecting of one of Eric's gremlins. There was a fluffy area rug spread across the floor that looked like it might have been vacuumed in the last week versus the last decade like in Lu's room. The chair to the desk against the window was pushed in, the surface clear of anything apart from a cup with pens and pencils sticking out of it. And all that was on the nightstand set beside the twin bed in the corner was a glass of water and Chase's plugged-in phone. The only thing out of place among the tidiness was the covers on Chase's bed, which looked like the kid had been tossing and turning all night in them.

Tony settled him carefully onto the bed and pulled the blankets up around him again, doing his best to straighten them as he went. Chase was still breathing hard, his body curled into the fetal position the moment he was on the bed, his knees so close to his stomach they might have been doing more harm than good.

"Okay, kid," Tony said, keeping his voice soft so as not to add to Chase's distress. "You need to tell me what your symptoms are, so I know what to grab for you."

"It's like—" Chase panted through another wave, his face scrunched in pain, eyes squeezed shut. "It's like my veins are frozen. Like there's—" Another harsh click of a swallow, and the kid turned green about the gills but managed to not hurl, which Tony was grateful for. "But like not cold. Like fire. Like it burns. Like when—" He gasped, curling impossibly tighter on himself. "Like when you've been outside too long in the snow, and you start to warm up, and it hurts." Chase whined. "It hurts so bad."

"Okay." Was it just him or did his own voice sound faint? He took a breath and tried to settle the racing of his heart, tried to ignore the way it pounded against his rib cage so hard, it might leap free. He knew that feeling. And he knew exactly what it meant.

"So," he said, his mouth suddenly dry, his throat tight. Eric was going to fucking freak when he heard about this. "I know what's wrong with you."

Chase made a pained, questioning sound but didn't uncoil himself from where he was still wrapped so tightly around his stomach that it looked like he was trying to hold himself together when all his body wanted to do was fly apart. Scatter to the wind. Tony knew that feeling too. The unmaking that came before the remaking.

He had to take another deep breath before he spoke. Gear himself up for this. Because he knew what this meant. "Your Venator gene is activating."

"Wh–what?" Chase blinked up at him through eyes blurry with pain, and fear, and unshed tears. Poor kid. This was only the beginning of all the shit he'd go through now that he'd won the worst lottery in the history of the world.

"You tested positive that you had it, right?" Tony spoke slowly. He knew for a fact that all of Eric's kids had. It was why they were there, trying to learn what they would need should their gene ever activate. Why Eric had taken them in —to protect them from the Council of Creatures, who would send them out into the world to die without any guilt. That's what Venator were for, right? Tin soldiers for a war Tony was rapidly coming to wonder if they didn't need to be waging at all.

"Yeah." Chase whimpered again, another wave rolling over him, and Tony waited for it to be over. He wanted to reach out. He wanted to offer his hand to the kid. To provide some small bit of comfort. But Chase wasn't his sibling, and he didn't know how okay Chase was with being touched, especially by someone who was essentially a stranger.

"Okay, so." Tony tried to keep his words slow and easy to understand. Tried to channel Eric and his patient teacher energy. It was harder than he'd thought it would be since he'd never actually been to any of Eric's classes. Maybe he should sit in on one of them. Maybe he'd learn something. "Just testing positive doesn't mean your gene will ever activate. Plenty of Venator go their entire lives without it activating. I tested positive when I was born, but mine didn't activate until I was a teenager, with puberty. Which royally fucking sucked, let me tell you. I was already going through so much shit and then—"

"Tony," Chase hissed, impatient.

Fuck. Right. Now was not the time to get sidetracked. He cleared his throat. "Anyway, point being, it doesn't activate right away, if at all for some. But when it does, it's like this." He gestured to Chase on the bed. Chase, for all his quiet, calm nature, seemed irritated by the movement but didn't say anything. "I mean, upside? You'll heal real quick once you get over this hump."

"And what's the downside?" Chase asked through gritted teeth.

"You're gonna be sick for a bit." Tony didn't add that if the council found out, they would put Chase into the field no matter what Eric said. That was simply the rule of law for people like them. Their gene activated and it didn't matter how ready they were, how young they were, how untrained and untested. The Huntsmen sent them out to fight the vampires. Tony himself had barely survived his first night out on the hunt. Coming home to his father after, without any fangs to show for his efforts . . . that had been worse. He shook himself.

"You can't tell him," Chase begged, his eyes fixed on Tony again, the soft, warm light of his bedside lamp glinting against the tears now appearing along his lash line. "Please. You can't tell him."

"Tell who?" Tony had a feeling he wasn't going to like the answer, but he had to ask anyway.

"You can't tell—" Chase screamed, his face losing all its color as he thrashed against the next wave of fire in his veins.

Tony reached for him, took his hand. "Squeeze," he ordered. "Squeeze as hard as you can. Channel all that pain into me. I can take it."

It wouldn't do much. Tony knew that from experience too. But it was better than nothing. And so what if he had to sit by this kid's bedside all day to help him through this? It was more than he'd ever been given. It was also exactly what any kid deserved. They deserved to have an adult in their life willing to take the pain for them if they could. It was what Tony had always provided to Lu, and what he was quickly realizing he'd do for any of Eric's little brat pack. Weird how family could be born of almost nothing at all.

The pain passed, and Chase didn't let go. He kept a firm

grip on Tony's hand, and Tony didn't even try to shake it, or ask him to release him.

"Who can't I tell, kid?" Tony brushed Chase's dark curly hair away from his face. He'd have to let go eventually, to go and grab the kid some painkillers at the very least. Not that they'd put much of a dent in what he was feeling, but it would be better than nothing, and it would make Tony feel useful at the very least.

"Hunter." Chase shifted in his bed, what might have been guilt making his eyes jerk away from Tony to look over his shoulder at the wall behind him. "You can't tell my brother."

"Why not?" Tony didn't like this. Not at all. If someone kept information like this from him about Lu, he'd be absolutely fucking livid. He might not know Hunter super well, but he knew him well enough to know that he cared for Chase more than he cared for almost anything else in his life. That included Eric. He'd want to know about this. He *should* know about this. It was his right as Chase's sibling and guardian.

"He'll have to report it." Chase's eyes returned to Tony's, and the sheer fear, the pleading, made Tony's blood freeze in his veins. When Eric had said the Council of Creatures was a danger to the kids, he hadn't bothered to wonder if the kids knew that. If Eric kept his fears of what they'd do away from his family. But he supposed he shouldn't be surprised; Eric was the honest type. And his kids were geniuses, the lot of them. "And if he does . . ."

Chase didn't have to finish that sentence. Tony knew what would happen if Hunter reported his activated gene to the Council of Creatures. "Okay," Tony said, letting out a long, slow breath to try to calm himself down. "Okay, we won't tell Hunter. Not yet anyway."

Chase relaxed.

"But we need to let Eric know."

"But—"

"No buts. I can't cover this up for you all on my own. I'll need help, and Eric is the best person to do that." Tony gave Chase's hand a squeeze, comforting. "You trust him to protect you, right?"

"I do."

"Good, then we'll tell him when he gets home. And between he and I, we'll come up with a game plan. Till then, you need to get some rest. All right? It's gonna get worse before it gets better."

"Okay." Chase let go of his hand, pulling the blanket over his shoulder and shimming in the bed to get comfortable. "You won't— You're not going to leave me, are you?"

"Just to run downstairs and grab you something for your fever, and the pain. Then I'll be back. Promise."

Chase nodded and let his eyes drift closed, leaving Tony to do just that.

CHAPTER 6

ERIC BLINKED at the text on his phone. People didn't usually text him. They knew better. They knew how the words would swim sometimes before his eyes if he was having a bad focus day. How just looking at letters could exhaust him. But he'd felt his phone vibrate during class and when he pulled it out there was a text from Tony:

TONY

You need to get home

Now

Eric didn't like the sound of that. He sighed, scrubbing at the wrinkle between his brows, trying to smooth it away, but it was no good. It seemed to be permanently etched there these days. And he was so fucking *tired*. Even with the extra rest he'd been gifted by Hunter and Tony.

He briefly considered texting back. Asking Tony, *What now?*

But it would be easier to head back to the house and see for himself. Wouldn't it? He was done classes for the day. No sense lingering in the lecture hall or his office when he didn't have office hours today, and most of his paperwork was on his desk back at the dorm anyhow.

The house was quiet when he got there, and Tony wasn't

waiting downstairs for him like he'd been half expecting. His stomach gave a sickening twist, a warning. The air about the place was charged, tense, making the hairs on Eric's arms and legs prickle like they did right before a vampire attacked.

Kicking off his shoes at the door, Eric pulled a stake from his messenger bag and settled the bag carefully on the floor against the wall. Then he crept slowly through the house, skipping the creaking stair right before the landing on his way to the second floor.

The long hall that held all their bedrooms and bathrooms was silent, but not oppressively so, and that at least allowed Eric to relax. Not much, but a little.

A light shone from under one of the kids' doors. Fourth down on the right.

Chase.

Eric's fingers tightened around the stake, wood grain digging into his palm.

He was a couple of doors down when a soft, rumbling voice called, "Pretty boy? We're in here."

Tony.

Eric let out a breath, his shoulders loosening, unhitching from up around his neck. He was still holding the stake when he nudged Chase's door open further to find Tony sitting on the floor, his back leaning against the bed while he scrolled through his phone. Chase was curled up, passed out under at least five blankets.

It was sweet, almost. The way Tony had posted himself next to Chase's bed and not left. The picture of care Eric hadn't ever thought he'd seen Tony in. He wasn't the nurturing type. And that had been okay. But there had been some concern over what would happen when Tony moved into the dorm. Over how he'd fit into their weird family unit.

Eric supposed he shouldn't have been worried at all. Tony was a good man. A caring brother. A partner worthy of Eric's admiration. And here he was, proving it again.

Tony looked up from his screen and frowned, his eyes flicking to the stake and back to Eric's eyes. "On edge much?"

Eric looked at his hand and wrinkled his nose, almost confused at the sight of the stake even though he knew he'd pulled it from his bag. He bent to set it just outside the room. If his jeans weren't so fucking tight, he'd probably have tried to tuck it into one of the pockets. But if he had, he'd have likely ripped his pants. Not something he was in any mood to deal with.

"Can you blame me?" Eric asked with a shrug.

"S'pose not." Tony locked his phone and dropped it to the floor beside him.

"What's happened? Do we need to take him to see a doctor?" Crossing the room, Eric reached for Chase, fumbling with the blankets so he could get a better look at the kid. Chase hadn't been with Eric as long as some of the others, certainly not as long as Bert, but he was still one of Eric's kids. And that made him important.

"No. No doctor," Tony said cryptically. He pressed to his feet and tugged Eric gently till they were facing one another, his glowing green eyes soft and sympathetic, his brows knit together.

Dread made Eric's stomach drop to the carpet, and he raised his hands to clutch at where Tony was still carefully gripping his shoulders. "What is it?"

"It's his Venator gene," Tony whispered, his voice husky, raspy, colored with an emotion Eric had never heard there before. Fear. Tony was afraid of what this meant. "It's activating."

"No." Eric shook his head, looking down at Chase's sleeping face again. The boy was paler than normal. A thin sheen of sweat glittered around his brow. And even in sleep, his forehead was creased with pain, his mouth pinched. "No. He's still a baby yet. Not much older than Lu. He didn't even test positive till a couple of years ago. If anyone's was going to activate, it would be Bert."

Bert. Goddess. Bert was going to freak the fuck out. They all were. If Chase's gene had activated and the vampire activity continued to increase like it was, it was only a matter of time before another of the kids was struck with the same changes. And if the Council of Creatures found out . . .

If they found out, there would be nothing Eric could do to protect the kids. The moment their genes activated, they became property of the council.

The only way he'd been able to protect them this long was by arguing that as their genes weren't active—without the heightened senses, the extra speed and strength, the quickened healing—they would do more harm than good out in the field. He'd spend his entire time trying to keep them from getting hurt instead of fighting vampires like he was supposed to be doing. But . . . But if their genes activated?

Fuck. Fuck. Fuck.

This couldn't be happening. They were still babies. None of them was even old enough to *drink* yet. They were children still. *Kids*. Goddess. They were just *kids*.

His kids.

He had to think of something. He needed to find some way to keep them out of the field. To protect them. To keep the rest from activating the way Chase had. To cover up Chase's sickness as something not related to his Venator gene at all. A lie. A story. Something believable. An outbreak of food poisoning at the cafeteria. Something.

Eric's chest heaved with each panted breath, his vision tunneling. But his mind worked a mile a minute.

Could he get Vanessa Cochburn to help with that? The Dean of Moondale U was in no way beholden to the Council of Creatures. The university was in and of itself a third party to both the government of Ironport and of Moondale. Cochburn didn't answer to either of them. She could do something to help Eric protect his kids. But would she? Or would she turn them over?

"Pretty boy." Tony's voice was muffled. Not nearly loud or clear enough to pull Eric from his rapid thoughts. They were a runaway train speeding toward a crash, and even Eric's awareness of it couldn't slow them down.

She was dating Ava, but what did that really mean? Did that mean she was on their side? He didn't know enough about their relationship. And so far, Vanessa hadn't done anything to help in their fight against the vampires other than providing his kids a safe harbor. Was that enough? Would she—

"Eric!" Tony shook Eric. Eric's gaze was ripped away from the middle distance to the worried squint of Tony's eyes. "Breathe, baby," Tony instructed, and Eric realized that he wasn't. Not really. He was taking in shallow sips of air. Not near enough to fill his lungs. "In."

Eric inhaled, following along with Tony. Listening to the way he took in air, held it, let it out through his nose. Again. In through his mouth. Hold. Out through his nose. The room came back into focus, and Eric could see Chase moving from the corners of his eyes. Shit. He'd probably scared the kid half to death.

"You good?" Tony asked.

"Yeah. Good." He wasn't, but he was better than he could have expected given the situation. "I'm just . . . trying to think of what to do."

"Well, the first thing we're gonna do is not panic. Yeah?"

"Yeah." Eric nodded, drawing in another long breath. *Don't panic. Easy.*

"The kid says we can't tell Hunter." Tony looked over at where Chase was sitting up on the bed, and Eric followed his eyes. He didn't like the idea of keeping something like this from Hunter. Chase was his kid brother. But not just that, they were all each other had. It had been that way for a couple of years now. But the fear on Chase's face told Eric all he needed to know.

"Okay. We don't tell Hunter." Eric slumped, putting his weight against Tony's hands, trusting in his boyfriend to hold him up. "And we'll need to come up with a cover story. Food poisoning. Something."

"A stomach bug?" Chase asked hopefully.

Eric frowned. "It'll look suspicious when none of the other kids get sick. Which . . ." Which they still might get sick. If his suspicions were true. But he'd cross that bridge when he got to it. "We can't trust them all to lie for us. Even if they'd want to."

"No." Chase shook his head, a wince of pain making his face crinkle. He breathed through it for a moment before continuing. "Bert is the worst liar."

Eric laughed softly. "He totally is." This was going to fucking suck. "We'll need to keep this from them too, for as long as possible."

Chase shifted around on the bed, the springs squeaking under his weight, looking as uncomfortable with the idea of hiding something from his classmates as Eric felt. It was only a matter of time before someone caught on, once Chase was up and about. But if they were careful, maybe . . .

The hyper focus was strong today with Hunter.

Which was good because there was a lot of shit to do. Paperwork to catch up on. Fangs to examine. And so long as he kept his hands busy with the mundane things, the things he could do by rote, his mind could wander. Turning the problem of tracking Dash around and around in his head. Looking at it from all angles.

He didn't have a solution. Yet.

But Rus said he could drop by over the weekend to chat about the Ghost Tracer and ways to modify it, and he was going to sit down with Tony and pick his brain later. Between the three of them, Hunter had little doubt they could come up with something. They all would come at the problem from a different angle, and it would find them the best solution. The one most likely to wind up with Dash meeting his death at the pointed end of a stake.

He was so focused on his tasks, on the problem in front of him, that the music Hunter always worked to faded into the background along with the ticking of the clock and any other noise from the building settling around him.

Including, apparently, the first few knocks to the door of his lab before it burst inward and two suited Huntsmen stood in the light from the hall looking aggravated.

"Hunter Delacroix," one of them said, and Hunter finally looked up from his work, his safety goggles magnifying his eyes to Kewpie doll proportions.

"Huh?" Hunter blinked at them, his nose wrinkling, his goggles shifting along with the movement. Flicking his gaze to the broken door, he huffed. "You're going to be responsible for fixing that."

"Hunter Delacroix," the woman repeated, her eyes narrowed, a piece of paper held in one hand as she stepped toward him. "The Council of Creatures has issued a subpoena requesting your records."

Hunter's heart lurched into his throat, and he only just managed to swallow the organ beating hard at the back of his mouth enough to croak, "What?"

"We are here to confiscate any and all records you have about the recent vampire activity," the man behind her said, his tone hard, a large bin in his hands.

"Any interference in this procedure will be seen as going against the council and might result in a charge of treason," she warned, and motioned for the man to head over to the file cabinet in the corner. It was small by comparison to all the data Hunter had collected over the years, but the older stuff was all moved to the Huntsmen's archives after a certain point. He still had access to the digital files, but the paper he didn't usually need after a time.

"Oh." Hunter's skin was too cold, his fingers going numb with panic. He needed to get the fuck out of here. He needed to stop them from taking those records. He needed—

The man was already loading them into the bin, not even waiting for Hunter to show him which were the most recent. He'd just grabbed a handful and stuffed them into the bin before going back for another.

And Hunter?

Hunter was fucking frozen in fear. His heart beat so hard against his rib cage, he could feel it in his fingertips. His eyes were fixed on the man loading the bin with paper. The woman stood in front of him, as if she would keep him from stopping them. Not that he was even *trying*. He was too scared. Goddess. He was such a fucking coward.

He didn't know how long it took them. But by the time the bin was full, his filing cabinet was leaning dangerously forward with the weight of the still pulled-out drawers, and bile had risen in his throat, and he still. Couldn't. Move. He didn't know if he'd ever be able to move again. Maybe he'd stay there, frozen, until the day he died.

"Hunter?" Tony asked, his voice carrying in the echoing silence.

When had Hunter's music turned off? Had the agents from the council done that? Or had the playlist run out? He didn't know.

"Hunter, what happened?"

"They know," was all Hunter could say in answer as he leaned heavily against Tony, trusting him to take his weight.

CHAPTER 7

TONY HAD NEVER SEEN Hunter like this before. Fear had suffused his every pore. He stank with it. Sour, and rank. A tremble made his steps stutter as Tony tried to help him across campus. And he didn't even know about Chase yet. He definitely couldn't know about Chase now. Not if they were going to keep Chase from being pushed out into the battle against the vampires.

"You're okay." Tony tried to sound soothing, but he wasn't sure it was working. He'd never been the nurturing type. Even with Lu, who he'd been taking care of for at least a few years at this point. And now he'd been forced to take care of both the Delacroix siblings in a single day.

"They know," Hunter repeated. It's all he seemed able to say since Tony had walked into his lab and found the place oddly hollowed out. Empty. A shell. Hunter, too, looked that way.

Tony's memories of Britt's funeral a few months ago were vague and indistinct, but he didn't remember Hunter looking this . . . *lost*. Like his world was caving in around him. Like he didn't know what to do next. Maybe because at least then there had still been the prevailing faith that Eric could protect them. *All* of them. Hunter included. What happened between Tony and Dash had thrown that all into the fucking blender.

Breaking it down to tiny pieces, turning it into slush. Even Hunter had been shaken by it. Although Tony hadn't realized that until this exact moment.

The realization left Tony wrong-footed, stumbling at Hunter's side as they both nearly went to the ground. He'd had no illusions about Eric's ability to keep them safe. Mainly because he'd never had anyone to do that for him before. And as powerful as Eric was, as capable, Tony couldn't shake how he'd been raised. Couldn't undo literal decades of trauma teaching him that the only person he could depend on was himself. Only *he* could protect himself. Only *he* could make sure Lu didn't have to suffer the way that he had. He hadn't known Eric long enough to feel he could depend on him by the time the illusion shattered for the rest of them.

"We'll figure it out," Tony promised. Although he wasn't sure how, at this point. Eric had made it clear that the Council of Creatures was going to do what they wanted. And even if they didn't pose a problem, there was still the Huntsmen organization to deal with. *If* they managed to convince the council to skirt the rules for them, there was no skirting the community that had birthed all of them.

"How?" Hunter asked. They'd stopped on the sidewalk leading to the dorm, and Hunter blinked at Tony, eyes wide and hopeful. Like he thought Tony would be able to give him a solution they hadn't thought of to that point.

It was silly, really. They both knew Tony wasn't the one in charge here. He wasn't the planner. Out of the three of them, the leader was Eric and the planner was Hunter. Tony was a grunt. Just good at slaying. And up until a few months ago, he hadn't cared about anything else. Now . . . Now things were *different*. Now he had Eric, and the kids, and—

And Hunter, he realized. He had Hunter.

And Hunter was looking at him like Tony could maybe fix this for all of them. Hope made his dark-brown eyes twinkle. Tony's breath caught in his throat. His heart slammed against his chest. It wasn't fair how pretty Hunter was. Wasn't fair of him to look at Tony like that. Not when he was with Eric.

Tony resisted the urge to shove him off, knock him into the grass. He swallowed, hoping Hunter was too preoccupied to notice how his face heated at the attention.

"I don't know yet," he admitted, and pointedly ignored the way warmth tingled from every place he and Hunter were touching. The press of their hips against each other. The clutch of Hunter's hand on his shoulder. The point at which Hunter's shirt had ridden up along his waist, and Tony's fingers brushed warm, smooth skin above his jeans. Goddess. Tony could get lost in it. It wasn't fair. It wasn't right. Hunter didn't want that from him, and Tony should— He should keep his attraction to *himself.*

"But I'm sure between the lot of us . . ." He swallowed— not even a year ago, he wouldn't be thinking this way, wouldn't be considering himself a part of a team, a family, and yet here he was—and continued. "We'll think of something. Eric will probably want to call a team meeting once he knows."

Hunter nodded, taking a deep breath and doing his best to straighten up, but he couldn't seem to shake the desire to make himself as small as possible. His shoulders hunched forward, almost bringing him to a height with Tony.

"We just need to tell him, and pretty boy will help us figure all of this out." Goddess, he hoped he wasn't lying when he said that. "The others too. I'm sure he'll want to pull the whole gang in on this."

"Probably." The thought seemed to bolster Hunter, and he took on more of his own weight. A relief. Tony didn't particu- larly want all the drama that would come with him half drag- ging Hunter into the house. And there *would* be drama. There always was with this crowd. It was fucking exhausting. "Sup- pose we better get it over with then, huh?"

"Seems so."

Tony started back up the sidewalk again, Hunter hobbling along at his side. The door opened before they even made it onto the porch, and the sun fell on a pale-faced Eric.

"They called a meeting," Eric said, not waiting for them to get inside the house before he dropped another bomb on them. "The Council of Creatures want me there at first dark."

"Just you?" Hunter asked. He pulled away from Tony, finally standing under his own power, but he still looked wobbly. Like at any second his knees could give out on him. So Tony didn't remove his hand from where it waited outstretched to catch him.

"Tony is technically no longer under their purview." Eric was still in the doorway, even as they approached close enough to push past him. Tony wondered if he realized that he was blocking them from entering the dorm. Likely not. He was distracted. His big honey-brown eyes—like the first of the fall's cooked caramel—never settled on one thing for long. Tony's face. Then Hunter's. Then over their shoulders. Then off to the side. Then back. Nervous. Twitchy.

"Like that's going to stop me," Tony muttered and watched as Eric's lips ticked into a small, indulgent smile. It made the warmth that had faded from his cheeks reignite.

"What about me?" Hunter pressed. He too was starting to twitch. His fingers tapped at his sides, rings clicking against each other with the movement.

When Eric's eyes jerked back to Hunter, the smile slipped from his face. He didn't look angry, but he didn't look happy either. Tony was sure that Eric knew this wasn't Hunter's fault, but even that knowledge couldn't keep a person from trying to cast blame where there was none. Emotions weren't rational like that. "They've gotten all they need from you."

"I'm going anyway." Hunter lifted his chin as if refusing to wilt under Eric's displeasure. Good for him.

"Of course you are." Eric nodded like he hadn't expected

anything less. "In the meantime, we've got dinner to get done. I want the kids fed before we head off. And I can't trust Janet to do it." He muttered that last part irritably to himself.

"I heard that!" Janet shouted from where she was flopped on the couch like she didn't have a single care in the world.

How long was Eric going to let her hang around the dorm and leech off the rest of them? He was such a soft-hearted fool sometimes. It was a shame Tony liked him so much. A real shame.

With Janet no longer at the helm, Eric had no idea who the Huntsmen had chosen to represent them on the Council of Creatures. He hadn't really had time to think about it.

But now, staring down a pair of light-brown eyes framed by thick dark brows so much like his own, Eric wished he'd devoted some time toward figuring it out. If only so he wouldn't have been completely blindsided when his brother approached the long table the council sat at while they held meetings.

Eric took a half step back, nearly knocking into Hunter where he flanked Eric on the right, but that was all the surprise he could afford to show. Anything more than that would be perceived as a sign of weakness, and the council would rip into him for it, use it as leverage against him. But that didn't mean Eric's heart hadn't started racing hard in his chest, a cold sweat running down his spine.

Oliver Marcelino, for all he was thirteen years younger than Eric, looked every inch the Marcelino heir to the throne. Carefully pressed slacks. Neatly buttoned dress shirt. Perfectly coifed dark-brown hair. A gold watch big enough to club someone with. And while he and Eric shared the same eyes, there was a cold distance to Oliver's that made Eric's gut twist.

How long had it been since he'd seen his brother? A year? Two? He couldn't remember anymore. After Nonna's funeral, his parents had promptly taken Oliver and split, leaving Eric behind *again*. They'd been back maybe a handful of times since. For meetings with the other Huntsmen families. Never for holidays. Never to see Eric.

The age-old ache that accompanied their abandonment settled into his chest, into his bones. The joints in his fingers throbbed like they did sometimes when it rained, signifying he needed to wear his braces to bed.

Fuck.

He hadn't been expecting this. And it completely put him on the back foot.

Hunter was rigid beside him, knowing perhaps better than even Eric himself how much the appearance of Oliver Marcelino was going to fuck over all of them, but he didn't say anything.

Tony's head was tilted to one side. Eric glanced at him from the corners of his eyes and caught the way Tony's eyes were narrowed in consideration. He was putting the pieces together. And whatever he thought he saw, Oliver's next word removed all doubt.

"Brother." Oliver smiled thinly, showing perfectly white, perfectly straight teeth. He'd been able to get braces when they were kids, unlike Eric, who had to wait until the college gave him insurance to get his. The differences between his and Oliver's upbringings were so staggering, it was like they'd had different parents. Like they were completely oppo-site down to a cellular level even when looking at Oliver gave Eric a weird sense of seeing himself at twenty.

Fuck. Oliver was only twenty. The same age as most of Eric's kids.

"Oliver," Eric pressed the name past a tongue heavy with too many emotions, some of which he couldn't even name.

"You look well." But Oliver didn't exactly sound happy about it.

He was baiting Eric, and they both knew it. Trying to draw Eric into a messy family confrontation that would make him look like an ignorant, immature child, incapable of making decisions for himself and his kids. Well, Eric wasn't going to fall for it. He was more professional than that.

"Thanks." Eric ran his hands through his hair and stepped up to the table, the lights bearing down on him, burning the back of his neck. "Well?" he asked once he was at a place where all the members could read his face easily, and where he could look them directly in the eye. "What's this all about?"

"We've had a chance to look over the records we received from Mister Delacroix," Oliver said, all business, but the thin smile stayed on his face. A snake ready to unhinge his jaw and devour a mouse.

"That was fast," Tony muttered.

Oliver's eyes flicked behind Eric, and Eric saw his jaw tick in irritation. Eric had been told to come alone, that they didn't need Hunter, and that Tony was no longer a part of this community. Ignoring orders was a good way to get his ass handed to him, but Eric needed them there. He needed them at his side as he faced all of this and did what he could to protect their kids.

"Be that as it may," Oliver said through his teeth. "Given the evidence, we think it best that the next generation of Venator be brought into the fight. It is clear you cannot keep up with the demand of your duties, and we cannot afford to have Ironport overrun with these vermin."

"They're not ready." Eric shook his head, his hands tightening into fists at his sides. "And none of their genes have activated. Until they do, they're—"

"You're telling us that you've been training some of these children for the last ten-odd years, and none of them are ready to head into the field?" Oliver raised a brow, his gaze sharpening. He had Eric over a barrel, and he knew it.

"That's not what I'm saying." Eric took a deep breath through his nose, his nails digging into his palms. "I'm saying that with their genes still dormant, they are at a—"

"Surely all those years of training will have made up for their lack of an active Venator gene. After all"—Oliver's smile grew wider, a cruel light coming to his eyes—"you were only thirteen and had no training at all, and you survived. Didn't you?"

"That's not the same."

"How is it not?"

Eric opened his mouth and faltered. He didn't have an explanation for that. No way to refute what his brother said. It was true. He'd been thirteen, untrained, impulsive, *stupid*, and somehow, he'd survived. And if he could, they should be able to too, if he'd done his job right. But this wasn't about the kids' capabilities, and he was sure that Oliver knew that. This was a punishment of a kind. Oliver lashing out at Eric. For what? He wasn't sure.

"I'll go back into the field," Tony volunteered, stepping up beside Eric. "I may not be a Venator, but I have the training, and my werewolf nature still puts me at an advantage against the leeches."

"The numbers are very clear. This threat is too great for even two Venator. It will require the entire force we have here in Ironport." Oliver was taking some twisted, vindictive pleasure in this, and Eric hated him for it more than he'd ever hated his brother before.

"Then call in reinforcements," Eric protested. "There are other Venator around the world who could be called to help. Drawn from places where the vampire population is lower, or less aggressive. They can spare—"

"Out of the question." Oliver's tone was cutting, angry, final. He would not see any more argument over this.

Eric swallowed, bile rising in his throat. He was going to be sick. He was going to throw up all over Oliver's fancy-ass leather shoes. They were probably Italian. Their mother had probably picked them out for him herself. Tears pricked at the backs of Eric's eyes. When was the last time their mother had even looked at Eric?

"We should turn our attention to finding Dashfield Chadwick," Hunter said. He moved to Eric's side, his hand brushing subtly against Eric's, trying to provide comfort where there was little to be found. Eric wished they could hold hands. Wished that too wouldn't be seen as a weakness. But he knew better.

Oliver's eyes flickered between the three of them, a note of realization twitching at his brow, but he didn't say anything. Whatever he'd noticed, he'd be holding on to for later. Eric's stomach rolled over.

"Dashfield Chadwick is no longer our concern. He disappeared after you faced off against him and has not been seen since. There is no proof that he's even still in the area."

"No proof?" Eric scoffed. "The uptick in fresh vamps isn't proof enough?"

"No. It's not." Oliver fixed his eyes on Eric, looking down his nose at his older brother. "We have made a decision. You will carry it out. If you do not take the young Venator into the field, they will be removed from your care. I'm sure there is another Huntsman in the area who would be more than happy to watch over them."

Eric's ears rang, his vision flickering with darkness. They would take his kids from him. They would demote him. They would disband his class. Ruin all his efforts, and everything he'd sacrificed all his life to keep them safe would go to waste. He couldn't have that.

"Have I made myself clear?" Oliver asked, seeming to need to drive the nail into the coffin.

"Yes, sir," Eric replied, relieved when the words didn't sound as faint as he felt.

"Dismissed."

CHAPTER 8

ERIC WAS PACING. His steps creaked under his weight as if the house itself were upset right along with him. Tony was starting to get a headache from following his progress from one side of the bedroom to the other, but he couldn't seem to stop.

They were in Hunter's room. It was the largest of their three bedrooms, with a big bed in the middle of the room covered in a black velvet comforter that, if it weren't for the big windows along one wall, would make the place look like it belonged to a vampire, not a witch. Tony didn't know how he'd ended up in here with them. He'd never actually been in Hunter's room before, just seen it from the door as he made his way down the hall to his own cramped space, more closet than bedroom. It was beside Eric's room, the one with the ensuite bathroom that he and Hunter had been sharing of late.

Eric had grabbed his wrist after they left the Council of Creatures and not let go, even as they climbed into the back of his car, Hunter taking the wheel. *That's* probably how he had ended up in here with them.

Eric.

Because Tony would follow Eric to the darkest depths of the After—where the demons dwelled—if Eric fixed him with that look. The one that said he needed Tony by his side. The one that said he was feeling lonely, and vulnerable. Tony didn't exactly feel like a safe person to be around when someone was in that mindset, but Eric didn't seem to care. It was a wonder, small and fragile, leaving Tony in awe of how he had become safety to Eric.

"Calm down, hon," Hunter said from where he sat on the bed beside Tony. There was a careful distance between them. Not enough space that it looked like Hunter didn't want to be anywhere near Tony, making him feel unwelcome, but enough that Tony knew Hunter didn't want to touch him.

Tony tried not to think about that, narrowing his focus to the way Eric's hands shook as they lifted to brush through his hair. He was on the verge. Had been since they left the Council of Creatures meeting. Clearly upset by having to come face-to-face with his brother. Tony didn't know the story there. Hadn't even known Eric had a brother—just two parents who fucked off the moment Eric had tested positive for a Venator gene. Hunter had never said anything to him about the Marcelinos deciding to have another kid to replace the failure that was Eric.

Something pinched in Tony's chest at that thought. It wasn't right. None of this was right. But there wasn't anything he could do about it either. His situation wasn't more or less fucked up than Eric's, it was just differently fucked up.

"I am calm," Eric said after too long a pause, his voice soft, scared. Tony hated it. It made the wolf in his chest claw at his ribs. A howl crawled up his throat that he had to swallow forcefully, which only made the wolf more disgruntled. It wanted to rage. It wanted to rampage. It wanted to . . . protect? Huh. That was a new one.

"No. You're not," Tony said, maybe the first words he'd bothered with since the decision had been handed down. He couldn't say he wasn't afraid, because he was. He wished he wasn't. But it wasn't just Eric's little class of gremlins on the line in this. It was Tony's sister too. The last remaining family he had. And she was freshly eighteen. Nowhere near old enough in his mind to be hunting vampires for all he'd been doing it since he was much younger.

Eric whipped around as if he were going to snarl at Tony, but instead he fixed him with a look akin to a scared rabbit. Mouth slightly agape. Brows drawn up so far, they practically disappeared into the hair that had fallen over his forehead. Skin slightly paler than usual, his moles standing out in even starker contrast.

"Come here." Tony lifted a hand before he could think better of it, his palm out, fingers curled slightly. An invitation, a call. This wasn't his bedroom. This wasn't his bed. He shouldn't be calling Eric to it. But Hunter didn't make any move to stop him.

When Tony glanced at Hunter out of the corner of his eye, Hunter was watching them, his head tilted curiously, a smile ticking at the corners of his lips, making his dimple pop.

Eric stood still, panting slightly. His breaths made his chest jump.

The wolf in Tony's chest rumbled, alert and watching. As if it would give chase. As if it would leap from his ribs and snap at Eric's heels as he ran through the house. Tony ignored it. Shoved it further into the corner of his mind. Forced himself to remain still, his hand outstretched. He couldn't let the wolf go after Eric for this moment of weakness. Not when Eric saw him as a safe harbor. Not when Eric trusted him with this. He wouldn't fuck this up. Not again.

"Come here," he repeated, voice gentle.

Eric made a soft, wounded sound in the back of his throat and lunged forward, latching on to Tony's hand like it was the last real thing in his world. And Tony tugged, reeling Eric in until they both fell back onto the bed behind him, Tony's arms curled tightly around Eric's shaking form.

"It's okay," Tony murmured into the top of Eric's head

where he buried his face against Tony's chest. "It's going to be okay."

He lifted his chin, hooking it into Eric's hair to look up at Hunter, mouth pinched as if daring Hunter to say anything, to kick Tony out when Eric clung to him like a lifeline. What he found there, though, was a soft look of awe. Hunter's lips were parted gently, his jaw slack, his dark eyes wide behind his wire-framed glasses that glinted in the low light of his room.

The expression made Tony uncomfortable and he had to look away, focusing his attention on the man in his arms who seemed to be trying to bury himself beneath Tony's rib cage. It wasn't fair that the great Eric Marcelino had to feel this way. Wasn't fair that someone had torn him down, ripped him up until he was shredded into tatters of what he had once been. Tony's fingers clawed into Eric's shirt, holding him closer.

"We should get some rest," Hunter said after what felt like too long a silence.

"We can't sleep," Eric protested through a mouthful of Tony's shirt. "We need to figure this out."

Hunter sighed, running a hand through his own long curly hair, frowning when it got wrapped around his many rings and snagged. His dark eyes met Tony's, pleading, as he mouthed the word *please*.

Tony sighed. Hunter was right, of course. None of them were in the right headspace to deal with this now. They were all too wound up, too emotional. Any solution they came up with would be formulated under desperation, and that would lead to more problems. But it didn't feel right to go to sleep when this hung over their heads. And honestly, Tony didn't know that Eric would even be able to sleep.

"I'm okay. I can talk," Eric protested but didn't bother pulling his face away from Tony. Instead, he seemed to push himself closer. "We need to figure this out."

"Hunter's right," Tony said, his tone gentle as he lifted a hand to stroke through Eric's hair. "Besides . . ." He met Hunter's eyes and gave a nod. They were a team in this. In protecting Eric from himself. In making sure Eric and the kids were okay, even as the world railed against them. It felt kind of good, honestly, to be part of something with Hunter. Tony shook the thought away. He needed to focus. "We'll want to talk to the rest of the adults about this, right? Ava and Kalla. They'll be able to help us think of a good solution for everyone."

"I guess." Eric sounded like he might be pouting, but neither Tony nor Hunter could see his face to know for sure.

"That's settled then," Hunter murmured softly, his fingers brushing down Eric's back, grazing Tony's when they passed. A tremor went up Tony's arm, lifting the hairs. Electricity. Attraction. Tony ignored that too. He didn't have time to parse it out and, even if he did, he couldn't act on it. Hunter was Eric's. "Come on, Eric, let's get you into some pajamas and into bed."

Hunter didn't wait for any further arguments. The springs groaned under him as he rose and went to the dresser pushed against one wall. Tony tried to extricate himself from Eric. If he and Hunter were going to bed, they weren't going to want Tony there. He'd slink back to his room and leave them to—

Eric's fingers tightened in his shirt, the seams protesting under the pressure, but Eric wouldn't let go. Tony was trapped. He lifted his eyes to look at Hunter, as if he could ask him to intervene, but Hunter had pulled three pairs of black sweatpants from his dresser along with three oversized T-shirts. One for each of them.

Heat crawled up Tony's neck, settling in his ears. "Thanks," he murmured, and Hunter merely nodded. "All right, doe-eyes, time to get dressed for bed."

Eric lifted his head finally, his big brown eyes soft and pleading, but he didn't say anything.

"I'm staying too," Tony agreed, and shoved any thoughts about what this could mean and how this might change things from his mind. Then he wiggled from under Eric and made a show of taking the clothes Hunter had pulled out for him so he could change.

He felt Eric's eyes on him the whole time, as if Eric expected him to bolt at any moment. But after a few minutes of them all working around each other, and some silent bickering over who was going to be where in bed, Tony settled under the heavy black comforter to Eric's right, his body between the other men and the door, with Hunter on the other side.

It didn't take Eric long at all to drop off, and when he did, Hunter tapped Tony's hand lightly where it held Eric to him.

"What is it?" Tony whispered into the dark.

"Thanks for staying," Hunter whispered back. "It means a lot to him."

"He didn't exactly give me any other choice." Tony pushed the words out through a throat gone tight so that they sounded gruffer than he'd intended.

Hunter chuckled gently, a warm, happy sound that made something hot curl up in Tony's belly. "You're just a big ol' softy, aren't you, sweetheart?"

Grateful for the dark that hid his rapidly darkened cheeks, Tony grunted in annoyance. "If you tell anyone . . ."

"Your secret's safe with me." But it sounded like Hunter was still laughing, and Tony could imagine the twinkle in his dark eyes as he said it. It made the warmth in his stomach twist hotter. His fingers twitched against where Hunter hadn't moved his hand after tapping him lightly to get his attention.

"Can you—" Tony swallowed, biting down hard on his tongue. He wasn't even sure what he'd been trying to ask Hunter for. It was a vague, amorphous thing. A longing he couldn't—and probably shouldn't—put into words. Because this? The three of them curled up in bed together? Eric sleeping between him and Hunter, letting them take care of him the way he never let anyone else look after him? Hunter and Tony whispering into the dark like they were maybe something more than friends? It couldn't last. It was a good thing. A beautiful thing. And if Tony had learned one thing from his shitty father, it was that good, beautiful things didn't last. He'd already pushed his luck in wiggling back into Eric's life. There was no sense in getting greedy.

"Yes?" Hunter asked, and Tony had to be imagining the note of invitation in his voice. He wasn't offering Tony an opening.

"Tell me about his brother?" Tony finally said, deciding to change tack. It was safer this way—keeping Hunter at a distance. It meant he couldn't get hurt doubly so when he was eventually cut out of Hunter's and Eric's lives. And he would be because good, beautiful things couldn't last. Not for him. And because Hunter and Eric were meant for each other in a way Tony would never be able to touch.

Hunter sighed, disappointed maybe, then started to speak.

Chapter 9

THE KITCHEN WAS QUIET, but Eric knew that couldn't last. Not with the bomb he was about to drop on the group he'd gathered—Kalla, Ava, and Janet all sat around the table. He could already feel their voices pressing at his eardrums, threatening a headache. He would have to lie down after this, the curtains pulled, a cold rag across his temples. Nothing else would get done today. But that was fine. At least they'd have figured out what to do with the kids.

Kalla stared down at her coffee, her hands spread to either side of the mug, fingers splayed as if she'd push from the table and leave at any moment. Alert. Weary.

Ava was blinking slow, heavy blinks, like she was struggling not to fall asleep as she took another sip from coffee that no doubt scalded her tongue. She didn't even wince, which was a testament to how tired she was.

Eric felt that all the way to his bones. Even with Tony and Hunter wrapped around him, he'd slept poorly and woken early, wiggling out of the bed as he did his best not to wake them. They both had looked so peaceful, so relaxed. It was a shame the world had to come crashing down on them again.

"What's this about?" Janet asked. She was leaning back in a chair scooted as far from the other two women as she could manage, slumped, relaxed, and insolent. Eric wasn't sure why she was there. He hadn't invited her. But she'd appeared in the kitchen before Ava and Kalla arrived like some kind of phantom. Fucking vampires, man. Eric didn't think he'd ever get used to living with one.

With a deep breath—and the press of Hunter's hand on the small of his back, while Tony shifted in closer, his shoulder warm against Eric's—Eric stuffed his hands deeper into his pockets and said, "The Council of Creatures has ordered that the kids have to begin going out in the field with me."

"*What?*" Kalla asked, the word hard, cutting, and furious at the same time Janet said, "When?" in a tone that was largely curiosity, at the same time Ava shouted, "You've got to be fucking kidding!"

"They can't just . . . they can't just *do* that," Ava continued, her fury rising with every word while Kalla sat there staring at her mug as if it had personally offended her. "They don't— The kids don't even— They can't!"

"They can, actually," Kalla pressed into the silence left by Ava running out of steam. "They can do whatever they damn well please. They're the ruling body in this city."

"But—" Ava's breath was still coming in hard pants, her chest heaving. Her blue eyes were wide and wild, searching Eric's face for any indication that there was something he could do. Something he could pull. He'd always been able to protect the kids. Always been able to find some workaround. It was what he was known for. No one thought he'd be able to get the council to agree when he proposed a class specifically to train Venator. No one thought he'd manage to get the University of Moondale to take them in. But he had. Because he was stubborn, and determined, and he got things done.

Not this time.

"Eric," she pleaded. "You have to be able to do something."

Guilt crawled along Eric's skin. His throat clogged with it. His fingers went cold with dread. He wished he could. "If

I could, I would," he said, his voice breaking over the words. Hunter's thumb rubbed a soothing circle into the small of his back, and Tony leaned in closer, offering his silent strength. They'd agreed to let Eric oversee this meeting, but now he kind of wished they hadn't. At least if they led, none of this would be his fault. "If the order came down from any of the other council heads"—Eric's throat clicked on a dry swallow—"I could appeal to the Huntsmen and possibly get it overturned. But this came direct from the Huntsmen head himself, and I can't go against a direct order."

Ava's face paled, her entire body going still. Kalla wasn't fairing much better at her side, her hands so tight around her mug now that Eric wasn't sure the ceramic could take much more of it.

"Who did take over my seat?" Janet asked conversationally, seeming to ignore the tension in the air. She could be such a bitch when she wanted to be. Eric forgot that about her sometimes. Once upon a time, it had been a trait he'd liked. One that he'd join in on, when they'd been friends as kids. But then she'd turned that on him, and he'd seen how much it could hurt.

Eric's breath caught in his throat, his vision narrowing to a point. Because he couldn't speak the name. He couldn't put it out there in the air. It would make it true—not that *not* saying Oliver's name would protect any of them from him. He wasn't fucking Beetlejuice. But Eric found himself unable to say it.

And when he continued to stumble, Hunter filled in for him. "Oliver Marcelino."

Ava sucked in a sharp breath, and her eyes flicked to meet Eric's, sympathy drawing her brows together. She knew. She knew better than any of them how Oliver could cut Eric to the bone. But she wouldn't say it out loud. Her gaze flicked from his to the library at the back of the kitchen, the double doors with their glass, an invitation to make an escape, to talk this out.

Eric shook his head. Not yet. He needed to get this dealt with first. Once that was done, then he could have an emotional breakdown with his best friend about the fact that his kid brother was back in town and apparently determined to get him and his kids killed.

Ava tilted her chin down, a silent acknowledgment coupled with a knowing look. She understood how much he appreciated the offer.

"All right then," Tony said, leaning over the table, his hands placed on the worn wood surface—discolored from years of dinners and homework—his smile feral. "We need ideas on how to keep the brat pack safe."

"I suppose you couldn't just . . . lie?" Ava offered, her focus back on the problem at hand.

"No." Janet shook her head, and for the first time since all of this started, Eric was glad to have her on their side. She knew the inner workings of the Council of Creatures. She'd be able to help them. Maybe not a lot, but that knowledge at least would come in handy. "If they suspect, they'll send someone to monitor Eric, and if they catch him ignoring an edict . . ."

She didn't have to say it. Most of them knew what would happen. It settled around them, an uncomfortable silence that threatened to drag them all to the ground under its weight. Treason was not something the Huntsmen took lightly. And without Eric and Tony there to protect the kids, there was no doubt at all that Dash would ensure they all died as quickly as possible. Even if they didn't have anything to do with the stupid fucking prophecy.

"Okay then." Ava let out a long, slow breath, reaching for her cup and gagging at what must now be lukewarm coffee. "Other options?"

"We proposed Tony go out into the field instead," Hunter

offered. "But they don't consider him a Venator anymore. So even if he does go, they don't see him as backup for Eric."

"Backup." Kalla scoffed, rolling her eyes and brushing a bright-blue loc back from her face. "If they knew anything at all about the fight against the vampires, they'd know that the kids will be more of a distraction than a help."

"They don't actually give a fuck," Janet said with a shrug. "This isn't about the vampires. This is about exerting power. And if it is about the vampires . . ." She frowned, her gaze flicking about the room, never landing on a single face. "You know they know exactly what they're doing. They know it'll put Eric in more danger if the kids are in the field. That's what they want. What Dash wants. He knows that if one of the kids gets into trouble, Eric will sacrifice himself to protect them."

"You think Dashfield has his fangs in Oliver?" Kalla asked, but she didn't sound surprised.

"Don't be naive, Regan." Janet rolled her eyes. "Even if the money wasn't as good as it is—and let me tell you, it's good. Dash has got deep pockets. There's still the prophecy to think of. If Eric lives, the Huntsmen as we know it dies. And if they lose power, that means people like the Marcelinos will be left flapping in the wind."

"Okay," Eric said, hoping to derail this conversation. It made something unsettled and slimy twist in his gut—the idea that he would be what disrupted his very species. The idea that he was meant to take over. "Tony isn't considered backup, but that doesn't mean he can't help out. It also doesn't mean you guys can't either. They never said that I couldn't bring more adults into the field, they just said the kids had to be there."

"What're you thinking?" Hunter asked, his head tilted, eyes shining. He looked like he already knew where Eric was going with this, and he approved. It was a relief.

"We take it in teams." Eric ran a hand through his hair. It

was still bed mussed and greasy, but it didn't matter because this could work. He knew it could.

"All of us?" Ava frowned.

"No. Not all of us." Eric sighed. "But Kalla is good in a combat situation. Between she, Tony, and I, we should be able to keep all the kids safe. And that way we don't all have to go out every night either. We can take shifts. Switch off." Not that Eric would be taking any nights off, and they all had to know that. He couldn't leave the safety of his city—his family—to anyone else.

"I want to take a team too," Hunter volunteered.

"Three would be enough." Eric shifted on his feet. Hunter had already given plenty to this fight. He'd lost his wife. And even if he hadn't, he wasn't the best fighter they had. He'd never been trained to be in that kind of situation. He tended to panic. Eric couldn't, in good conscience, send him out with the kids and expect him to be in charge. Not if they had other options. They'd all wind up dead. "That'd be two kids per adult."

"Then I'll take command center," Hunter pressed. "So the kids can take breaks too. It's the least I can do."

"I'll help with that." Ava smiled, seeming glad to have something she could help with.

"All right then." With a slow exhale, Eric let the stress of the situation out, his shoulders relaxing. "Hunter, you're in charge of figuring out a schedule and which teams will work best together. You know everyone best."

"Roger, roger." Hunter gave a playful salute.

"Tony, I need you in charge of weapons. Make sure we have enough to go around if we're going to send that many people out at a time."

"Yup." Tony nodded.

"Ava, you can figure out where we need to set up our patrols using the Ghost Tracer?"

"Sure." Ava shrugged.

"And Kalla, I want you to check in with your morgue and funeral home contacts. I want to know how Dash is getting his hands on these dead bodies so easily. He's lining someone's pocket, and I want to know whose."

Not that Eric would be able to do anything about it. He didn't have access to the Marcelino accounts anymore and couldn't throw his money around the way Oliver could. And threatening whoever was supplying Dashfield with the bodies wouldn't help him at all. It'd just get him in trouble with the Council of Creatures, who insisted he kept his head down. The normies didn't know about the vampires or the magical world at all, and if he went around shaking people down to keep them from working with someone still thought of as a respectable citizen of Ironport, it would draw unwanted attention.

"All right." Kalla pulled out her phone, clearly about to start on that task right away as she rose from the table, and like that everyone was moving. Chairs scraped against the linoleum as people went off to fulfill their tasks, and Janet slunk away to do whatever it was vampiric ex–Council of Creatures heads did.

Ava stood behind her chair, her nails tapping against the back of it, and nodded again toward the library, a clear indication that as much as Eric might want to escape the discussion of his brother, he wasn't going to. His feet scuffed against the floor as he followed her into the library, the door shutting behind them with a wave of Ava's hand. His ears popped as a sound dampener spell went up to keep people from overhearing—not that everyone else in the house didn't know what was going on with Eric's brother, but it was a nice thought.

"Are you okay?" Ava asked before he even had a chance to flop into one of the worn leather recliners.

He shrugged, his hands deep in his pockets. "I'm not going to lie and say it wasn't a shock. It was."

"Right. And I'm sure he was a bastard about it. He always was. Superior little shit."

"You could say that." Eric would be lying if he said it didn't make him feel better to have Ava on his side about this. She'd always been that way. She could be prickly and sarcastic. She could roast Eric better than anyone else in his life. But when it came down to it, she always had his back. Whether that was against an ex, or a brother. She was always in his corner.

"Are the rest of *them* here?"

Them. She didn't have to say who she meant. He knew. His mom. His dad.

"Dunno." He tried to sound nonchalant about that, but he knew Ava saw right through him. "They haven't called, and honestly, Oliver and I didn't sit down and have a chat after the meeting."

Ava snorted. "You know if you want me to go and hex him, all you've gotta do is say the word. Impotence would look good on him."

Eric bit the inside of his cheek to keep himself from laughing. "Nah. I think I'm good, Ava. I just need . . ." He took a breath, the humor fading away. "I just need to get the kids through this. Find Dash. Put a stake in him. And get on with things. Maybe then Tony, Hunter, and I can finally, you know, *focus* on our relationship."

Ava lifted a brow in question, and Eric realized he'd probably said too much, but it was too late now. She wasn't going to let that go.

"They're dancing around each other," he said by way of explanation.

"Tony and Hunter?" But it didn't sound like a question, it sounded like Ava just wanted confirmation for something she'd already noticed.

"Yeah." Eric curled his legs up into the chair with him, leaning on his knees as he settled in. "I can tell they're both into each other. But it feels like neither wants to make the first move."

"Have you tried . . . I don't know . . . *talking* to them?" Ava asked, her smile teasing. "You know, sit them both down like adults, and hash this whole poly thing out?"

"No." Eric huffed, his breath ruffling his flopping bangs. "There hasn't been time. And what would I even say?"

"I dunno." Ava shrugged. "Never been in a polycule before. But what about, *Hey idiots, I like you both, you both like me, you both like each other, why don't we all bang it out?*"

"If you ever say *bang it out* again, I will throw up," Eric warned. "And then jump off the clocktower on the quad."

"Dramatic."

"Honest."

"Fine. But the point stands. Maybe you should sit down and talk to the two idiots. Unless you think they'll work it out themselves?"

"No." Eric sighed, leaning his head back to look at the ceiling. "I know they won't."

"Then what the fuck are you waiting for?" Ava leaned forward over the arm of the chair she'd settled in so she could press into his space. Her eyes glittered with wicked amusement. Bitch.

"Let's just get through this first. Okay?"

Ava shrugged. "Whatever. It's your relationship. Just don't come crying to me when it causes a fight."

He blinked at her blandly.

"Fine. Do. But don't expect me to be sympathetic."

"Wouldn't dream of it."

CHAPTER 10

THE RIDE from Ironport to Moondale was tense, and Hunter didn't think it was only because of the pressure they were all under from the Council of Creatures. There was a strange crackling in the air between him and Tony now. Something left unresolved that he didn't think he could name, even if he tried, but it felt like those first few days after he and Eric had clicked.

Chemistry. Electricity.

Hunter wanted nothing more than to take a break from this whole fucking mess and explore it. Push the limits of what Tony thought he knew about their relationship and open a new door into something more. But they didn't have time for that. Not with Oliver Marcelino bearing down on them. Not with the threat of Dashfield B.M. Chadwick looming in the air. Not with Ava sitting in the passenger seat.

Maybe he shouldn't have brought her. If he hadn't, then it would just be him and Tony and a half hour drive to Moondale. Plenty of time to hash out whatever shit was between them. But no, Ava was there too. Her eyes flicked to him as if she knew exactly what he was thinking. She probably did. Ava was too perceptive by half. It had always been a bone of contention between them. That coupled with the way she and Eric seemed to communicate through glances alone bothered Hunter more than he'd ever admit when he first became friends with them. After all, how could he ever compete with that kind of bond?

Separated at birth. Platonic soulmates with a capital P. Whatever Eric and Ava wanted to call it, there was no competing with it. He'd never be that close to Eric, no matter how much he wanted to be.

Over the years, Hunter had learned that it was okay that he wouldn't. His bond with Eric was different, and if he'd tried for what Eric had with Ava, he wouldn't have everything else he got. He'd made peace with it. He wondered what Tony thought about that connection, if he thought about it at all. Tony had a sister, so maybe he didn't. Maybe he understood it better than Hunter ever could because he had a brother instead of a sister. A subtle difference, but a difference all the same.

He shook himself and focused on the road again, his fingers tapping against the steering wheel at ten and two, his truck trundling down the winding roads through the mountains toward the town sitting on a piece of land surrounded by water on three sides.

Tony let out a long-aggrieved sigh after a couple of minutes, probably tired of the quiet that had settled between them like a shroud. "This Icarus chick, what's she like?"

"Brilliant," Hunter replied. He couldn't help it. There was some kind of hero worship there he didn't want to examine too closely. He hadn't known Icarus Ashthorne long at all, but what he'd seen of her had left a lasting impression.

"She's a necromancer," Ava added, brushing her hair over her shoulder. "But she specializes in technomagic. No one else is doing the things she's doing to bring the two fields together."

Tony snorted, clearly unsettled with the way they were praising some witch. Hunter wondered if he was jealous. He wasn't going to call him out on it.

"It sounds like a bunch of bullshit," Ava agreed readily

with a shrug. "But it's true. I've never seen someone think outside of the box like she does. And you put Hunter and her in a room together working on the same project, and it's like . . ." She shook her head, her green hair falling into her face. "Well, it's like magic." She laughed.

"Then why were you two so against joining her coven in the first place?"

Hunter lifted his eyebrows, his gaze flicking to where Tony stared fixedly out the window. He hadn't known Tony had been paying attention to that whole drama. Honestly, he didn't think Tony paid attention to anything when it came to Hunter. But to know that he'd listened when Hunter had been telling Eric about the Coven of the Forgotten and how he and Ava had waffled about officially joining . . . it made something settle within him. Of course, Hunter hadn't been upfront with Eric about how they'd wavered because originally Rus thought they'd have to move to Moondale, and Hunter didn't want to leave the dorm house. He knew what reaction Eric would have to that.

Tony was different though. Greedier. Selfish. Not in a bad way, just . . . He'd understand. "At first, she thought the only way we could join was to move to Moondale and tie our magic to the land that way. Ava didn't want to have to make the drive every day to her shop."

"And you?" Tony turned his head so he could look at Hunter in the mirror.

There was a spark there, burning low and slow, that Hunter couldn't ignore. Tony had to feel it too, there was no way he didn't. But neither of them acknowledged it. Did they both want it to go away? Did they not know what to do with it? Hunter wasn't certain anymore. Things weren't the same as they'd been when he, Tony, and Eric laid in bed, Tony and Hunter whispering into the dark while Eric slept between them. The light of day made things . . . realer.

"I couldn't leave the house," Hunter murmured. It was a

vague statement, but Tony's brows lifted slightly as if he understood. Although if he understood that Hunter meant he couldn't leave Tony either, he didn't know. They really needed to sit down and have a chat about that, iron out what this all meant to them. Later. Once everything else was settled.

"Rus's kids will be in school," Ava continued as if she didn't notice what had passed between Hunter and Tony, but Hunter wasn't fooled. He caught her looking at him out of the corner of her eye again, her mouth pursed in thought. "So will Az probably."

"Az?"

"Rus's wifey," Hunter supplied easily.

"Her partner." Ava rolled her eyes with a soft scoff. "Az will be the elder for the Coven of the Forgotten on the Board of Magic once everything is finalized in a couple of weeks."

Hunter scoffed right back. "I've seen them together. It won't be long before Az is Rus's wifey."

Ava shrugged, seeming unconcerned with squabbling about it anymore. She knew he was right anyway. But the gentle bickering had eased them into something else. Chatter. Hunter was grateful for it, even if he noticed Tony sneaking glances at him in the mirror.

Icarus Ashthorne was waiting for them on the big wraparound porch of her house when they got there. Her hot-pink hair was tied back in a messy ponytail, a crow—probably her familiar, if Tony were to guess—perched on her shoulder as they chatted about something. The warmth of a fall that hadn't quite gotten its hold on the land yet had her in short sleeves and shorts, and Tony could see the scars that littered her arms glinting in the sunshine. Signs of all the times she'd used her blood to call the dead mixed in with freckles.

It sent a chill down Tony's spine. He'd never met a necromancer before, and honestly, he didn't think he'd ever wanted to. They fucked with things they weren't supposed to. Played with forces beyond the natural world. Pushed the limits of what was possible. And from what Tony knew of them, most were evil. But Hunter and Ava trusted her enough to join her coven, and Tony trusted them. Although he didn't know when that had happened. He shrugged the bemusement aside.

"You're early," Rus said by way of greeting, her head tilted to one side, gray eyes zeroed in on Tony, making another shiver race down his spine. Hunter had asked if Tony could come, but Tony hadn't given much thought to how Rus would feel about having a Venator on her turf. Most of the magical world seemed to have little use for Venator outside their position as exterminators, so why should this witch be any different? He was used to that, wasn't he?

Tony lifted his chin, his shoulders hunching slightly to make himself a smaller target for whatever vitriol Rus was about to spew about him and his kind.

The crow grumbled, flapping his wings as if he might take off at any moment, the movement making the hair falling from Rus's ponytail flitter around.

"Cool it, Darcy," Rus muttered, swatting him away until he hopped off her shoulder and went to perch on the rail to the porch, but she didn't take her eyes off Tony.

"Problem?" Ava asked and took a step closer to Tony as if in solidarity. There was a defensiveness to her tone that Tony kind of appreciated.

He'd never had that before—friends willing to put themselves in the line of fire when someone was being a dick about things. Sure, Eric would do it, but that was different. They were fucking. It was like . . . mandatory. Or, at least, Eric seemed to think it was. And there was Sage, but they were hardly ever around when shit like this went down. And Tony didn't expect the same treatment from any of Eric's friends. After all, they didn't know Tony from a hole in the ground. And yet . . . here Ava was, taking another step closer, her shoulder coming in front of him as if to block Rus's view of him. It was kind of— No, not kind of, if *was* nice.

"Werewolves make him nervous." Rus's gaze flickered between Tony, Hunter, and Ava, seeming to take in the way Hunter and Ava had closed ranks around Tony as if he was something fragile, something that needed their protection. He wasn't.

"Yeah, well," Tony grumbled, nudging them aside so he could take another step toward the porch, his hands stuffed into his pockets in forced nonchalance. "I'm not exactly a fan of big-ass birds either."

"Fair enough." Rus shrugged. "Come in. Az made muffins this morning and Nando left some iced tea in the fridge."

"That'd be great, thanks." Hunter smiled, but he let Ava go ahead of him, lingering at Tony's side so he could put himself physically between Tony and the crow when they passed it.

Rus led them through a big foyer with black painted stairs, down a narrow hall with black wallpaper, to a kitchen at the back of the house with black cabinetry, a black table, black appliances, and checkered black and gray tile. Tony wondered if she'd done the decor herself or if the house had come that way. It seemed cliché for a necromancer to live in a house that was legit just shades of black. But he wasn't going to say anything.

He settled into a chair between Hunter and Ava, his fingers drumming on the table as he waited for Rus to pull a pitcher of tea from the fridge. She set it on the table along with some glasses and a plate of the most delicious looking muffins he thought he'd ever smelt. They were warm and pumpkin-y, with an underlying sweetness of dark chocolate. Their scent was almost enough to block out the smell of rotted earth and petrichor that was folded around Rus like a shroud—likely a consequence of her necromancy.

"All right," Rus said once everyone had a small black plate with a muffin and some tea in front of them, "what can I do for you all?"

She asked as if she didn't know, but Tony was pretty sure Hunter had filled her in on what they needed. Still, it seemed she was nervous, like she didn't know how to start. She picked at the wrapper on her muffin, crumbs clinging to chipped black nail polish.

"We need a way to use the Ghost Tracer to track one creature specifically," Hunter said, taking the lead, and for once Tony was grateful for it.

He hadn't been anticipating how . . . intense being near Rus would be. He'd known from what Hunter and Ava said that she was a necromancer and a medium. Known that she was powerful, and clever. Known that Hunter had some weird kind of crush on her—in a totally not romantic sense, but still. But he hadn't been prepared for the smell of the dead lingering around her. Or the way he swore he caught whispered conversations floating from every corner of the kitchen. Like the veil between them and the After was thinner here. It was creepy. He didn't like it. The dead were meant to stay dead, not—

"I see." Rus hummed, tapping her fingers on her plate, her head tilted to one side as if she were listening to something beyond their hearing. "I can come up with a spell and coding combo so you could track someone, but I need something to tie it to. Something distinct to the creature you're trying to track."

"Like what?" Ava asked.

Rus shrugged. "For a Fae, a true name would work. For a

human, their social media presence is usually pretty good, depending on their age. But it has to be something that ties them to this world. Something that is . . . well, not necessarily physical, but—"

"What about blood?" Tony leaned forward, almost knocking over his glass of tea in his rush to insert himself into the conversation. He hadn't really considered how he'd contribute to this discussion. He didn't know fuck all about magic, after all, and the words spilled from his lips without much forethought.

Rus's brows lifted, her mouth twitching as if she were pleasantly surprised, then she nodded. "Blood would work. But how are you going to get it from him?"

"Especially when he can turn into *mist*," Hunter grumbled, stuffing half his muffin into his mouth.

"Right, and if we catch him to get blood, why not just stake him then and there?" Ava sighed. She pinched the bridge of her nose as if a headache was coming on.

Tony frowned, his chair creaking as he threw himself against the back of it again, nose wrinkling in thought. "Vampire blood doesn't last outside of the body like human blood does unless it's in a container."

"Right. And even if that weren't the case," Hunter added around a mouthful of muffin, "I'm not letting Eric go up against that bastard unprepared."

Tony thought Eric would probably have something to say about that, but he didn't push it. Hunter was right anyway. They couldn't let Eric face off against Dash right now. Not until they had a plan of attack. And especially not if they didn't have the element of surprise, which was why they wanted to track the bastard, to get the leg up on him.

"Have things gotten bad in Ironport?" Rus asked.

"There have been a lot of fresh turnings recently," Ava supplied. "Eric's been facing off with sometimes as many as fifteen a night."

Rus whistled, shaking her head. "And you think this is coming from one vampire? The one you lot faced down a couple months back?"

How much of what was going on had Hunter and Ava spilled? Tony frowned. But if they trusted Rus, and she was willing to help them, he supposed he shouldn't say anything. The more powerful creatures they had on their side, the better when it came to Dash.

"He's got it out for Eric." Hunter's rings tapped against his glass as he took a sip from his tea. "Some stupid fucking prophecy."

"Ah." Rus nodded as if she knew all about stupid fucking prophecies, but she didn't expand on that point. "So he's sending armies of the undead to take out your boy."

"Something like that." Hunter sighed.

Armies of the undead. The fresh turnings. The— "What if we captured a freshly turned vamp?" Tony asked, his lips pulling back into a snarling smile.

"Why would that help?" Ava turned to look at him, her nose wrinkled.

But Hunter was looking at him too, and Tony could see the same thought Tony had dawning on Hunter. "Because they have to drink Dashfield's blood to turn. And not a little bit either. Lots of it."

"Right. Some of it could still be in their system." Tony nodded eagerly. "We just have to trap one and cut it open."

"Would it even still be viable at that point?" Rus leaned forward, her gray eyes bright with an interest that freaked Tony out—a sharp, curious light there that belied the cleverness Hunter and Ava had told him she possessed.

"Maybe. Maybe not." But Hunter sounded more confident than he had this entire conversation, a smile pulling at the corners of his mouth. A smile Tony had put there. It made Tony's heart stutter, the wolf rumbling soft and low beneath his ribs. "But there's only one way to find out, right?"

"Right." Tony grinned back at him, feral and cutting.

"Then you just need to figure out how to trap one." Rus hummed, her brows pinched together in thought. "Some kind of talisman, or summoning circle maybe? I'm not sure that I have anything that'd—"

"Leave that to me and Tony," Hunter told her, but he didn't take his eyes off Tony, a sparkle in his gaze that lit up his entire face. "We've got enough experience with vampires to figure it out, don't we?"

"Yeah," Tony breathed, heat crawling up his neck. "Yeah, I think we do."

CHAPTER 11

ERIC WAS WAITING for them when they got back to the house, and Hunter knew it probably should have put him on edge, but it didn't. It was a relief to know Eric was taking this thing as seriously as the rest of them were. That he knew what was at stake—pun totally intended. He may not have any blood siblings in this thing, but Eric loved the kids like they were his own. He wasn't going to put Chase's life on the line, not if he could help it.

Not that Hunter had *actually* been worried about that, it was just a relief to see it.

"Did you have lunch?" Eric asked the moment they were through the door, pushing to his feet from the couch, his hands brushing down his T-shirt and jeans like he could will away any wrinkles that might be lingering. Unsettled. Nervous. Goddess, Hunter wanted to wrap him up in a blanket burrito and shuffle him off to his bed. Squeeze Eric between himself and Tony and pretend the world outside didn't exist until Eric stopped looking so fucking *tired*.

"I'll make something," Tony volunteered before Eric could beat him to it. "You should sit and listen."

It was a kindness, something that surprised Hunter. Tony tended to be gruff and brash, the opposite of this caring nature. Logically, Hunter knew Tony was the nurturing sort— he'd seen the way Tony took care of Lu, after all—but he'd never seen Tony be this way with anyone else. It was— Well, it was honestly kind of hot to see Tony with Eric when Eric was looking like one wrong move might send him over the edge. It made Hunter feel like they were on the same team.

"I can—"

"Nah." Tony shook his head, cutting Eric off. "There's left-overs in the fridge. I'll just heat them up. Go and sit. We've got shit to tell you."

Then he looked over at Hunter, met his gaze, and nodded once, and Hunter wanted to fucking melt with no real explanation why.

"Come on, hon," Hunter murmured, taking Eric's hand to lead him to the table in the kitchen so he could force him down into a chair, then grab him a cup of coffee from the cooling pot. With a murmured spell, it was heated back up and he slid it in front of Eric before sitting beside him.

"What happened with Ashthorne?" Eric asked as he took the mug. He didn't lift it to his lips, just wrapped his fingers around the ceramic as if he needed the warmth, like it wasn't unseasonably warm out, damn near seventy. The humidity made Hunter's hair curl in increasingly ridiculous ways.

"We need to get our hands on some biological matter," Tony supplied from where he was pushing the tray of half-finished ziti into the oven to re-heat.

"Biological matter?"

"To tie the magic to," Hunter added. "So we can track him."

"How the fuck are we supposed to get—"

"Blood." Tony threw a tea towel over his shoulder and leaned against the back of the chair beside Hunter's. "We've got an idea of what we're doing, princess. You don't need to worry your pretty little head about it. Right, killer?"

Hunter blinked at him a moment, not sure if Tony had been talking to him, then he laughed softly, shaking his head.

"Right," he said before he turned back to Eric and filled

him in on the conclusions he and Tony had come to while they were in Moondale. It wouldn't be a simple process, but this was more than they'd had before they drove out there to see Rus, and Hunter was going to take the win. Goddess knew they fucking needed one.

"Okay," Eric said when Hunter was done explaining, his voice faint, his knuckles turning white around the mug in his hands. He didn't look relieved at all by the idea of them having a plan finally, and Hunter didn't get why. If Ava were with them, she'd probably have known without even having to ask, but they'd dropped her off with Vanessa Cochburn—the dean of Moondale—for lunch before heading home.

"What's eating you, pretty boy?" Tony slid the tray of ziti onto the table between them as he sat on the other side of Eric and held a fork out to Hunter and Eric each. Hunter didn't bother to complain about the lack of a plate. He took his utensil and slid some noodles from the pan.

Eric took a deep breath. Whatever he was about to say, it looked like he thought it was going to piss one or both of them off. "I think before you go out on patrol with the kids, I need to run some sparring drills with you."

"What? Why?" Tony asked, a forkful of cheese and noodles halfway to his mouth. He didn't look pissed, not yet, but he was well on his way, if Hunter knew anything about him. "Is this because of the wolf? Because I have it—"

"I know." Eric held up a hand and turned to finally meet Tony's eyes, a pleading look pinching his brows together that made Hunter feel like he was watching something private. Something he shouldn't be privy to, even if they had all snuggled the night before. "I just want to be sure, okay? I promise it won't take long, and then you and Hunter can go out to the lab and start on your vampire trap prep. Okay?"

Tony swallowed, his jaw working as if he were chewing on his tongue. His green eyes were glowing, blazing, and if Hunter listened close enough, he thought he heard a growl rumbling in his chest. But Tony seemed to be holding it together well enough.

"This is just to make sure the kids don't get put in a tight spot. It's nothing personal, Tony, you know it's not," Eric said reasonably. To his credit, Tony deflated slightly. Hunter knew from experience that it was hard to argue with Eric when he got like this, when he was being protective and kind. It was hard to be mad at him, even if he hated what Eric was saying, when Eric was simply being the . . . the *hero* he'd always been.

Tony seemed to agree, because the growl petered off into something that could almost have been a whine, so low that Hunter wasn't sure anyone else heard it besides him. Which was weird, wasn't it? Eric should have been able to hear it with his enhanced senses from his active Venator gene. Unless he wasn't saying anything, to let Tony have his peace? To save him the embarrassment? Hunter shook himself.

"Fine." Tony rolled out his shoulders, stuffing the fork into his mouth as if completely unbothered. "But eat your fucking lunch first." Then his gaze flicked up to meet Hunter's, and he was swept away again by the way Tony took care of the people around him. By the way Tony was everything Hunter had thought he'd been at first—brash, harsh, brave—but he was also so much more than that. Kind. "You too, Gandalf. I'm not having either of you fuckers passing out on me when we've got shit to do."

Hunter scoffed, affronted, but didn't rise to the bait. He set to work demolishing what was left of the ziti from the night before right alongside Eric and Tony.

Tony didn't like this, which wasn't terribly surprising. Being challenged by anyone pissed him off, especially when that challenge came in the form of exposing one of his weaknesses. And like it or not, the wolf was a weakness.

It had saved him, sure. Cut the connection between himself and Dash caused by Dash's venom and blood, but it also wasn't in sync with Tony. It acted out. Made him more volatile than ever. And he knew that. He didn't need Eric to point it out to see what a danger he was not just to himself, not just to Eric or the vampires, but to the kids as well if he were out in the field with them and the wolf were to take over.

But they didn't have much choice. Tony wasn't going to sit back and watch as Eric faced this alone. Not if it meant he might lose Eric.

The wolf let out a soft whine, and Tony scoffed at it. At least they agreed on one thing. They needed to keep Eric from getting himself killed.

"All right," Tony said, tossing his shirt into the corner of the room. "How do you want to do this?"

"Hand-to-hand." Eric offered up a shrug, bending to tie his tennis shoes better. "Up close and personal seems to get the wolf going the most."

"So you're hoping to piss it off and see how well I can keep it locked down?" Tony rolled his eyes. "Brilliant idea, champ."

"You got a better one?"

"Not really." Tony rolled his head from one side to the other, his neck popping in the quiet of the small training room off to the side of the basement. He stepped forward to square off with Eric.

Eric was broader than Tony, his shoulders built for swimming or weightlifting as they moved beneath the T-shirt he had on. His feet were spread wide on the mat, shoes peeking out from under his sweatpants as he took a breath and centered himself.

"Well?" he asked after a moment of them staring at one

another, his head tilted to one side curiously, a dimple appearing in his cheek like he was trying not to laugh.

Tony waited a beat, a breath, then he launched himself at Eric, wrapping his arms around his waist to knock him from his feet. It didn't work. Eric was fluid as he side-stepped the attack like a matador to a raging bull, reaching out to pat Tony on the ass as he went.

"Too slow, baby," Eric teased.

Tony knew what he was doing. Knew he was trying to rile him up. Get him angry to prove that he couldn't control himself, couldn't control the wolf. Test him. The wolf rumbled in his chest, clearly annoyed at the taunt, and Tony thought he felt the points of his teeth dig into his cheek a little more, but he swallowed the emotion and went at Eric again.

Eric let him get a hand hold this time, not at his waist, but awkwardly over one shoulder. He grunted, annoyed. Eric brought his knee up and landed a solid blow to Tony's abdomen that left him wheezing, but he didn't let go. He dug in harder. His feet squeaked against the mat as they grappled, Eric trying to buck him, Tony hanging on for dear life.

Another annoyed grunt, and Eric scooped low, getting himself under Tony so he could throw him over his shoulder and onto his back.

"Stop using brute force." Eric panted with annoyance, holding a hand out to help Tony stand that Tony knocked away. "Show me that speed."

"What the fuck are you on about?" Tony rolled to his feet, his hands already clenched into fists. The wolf was pacing in his mind now. Chomping at the bit. Snapping and snarling. Wanting out. Out. Out. So it could get at Eric. Prove to him that Eric was nothing more than a trumped up human. But Tony had better sense than that. The moment he let the wolf out, the moment he lost control, he was fucked. Eric would bench him. He would not be fucking *benched*.

"You've got that wolf in you, right?" Eric asked, his eyes

narrow but sparking with something—a fire Tony had seen that first night they met. The night he'd called Tony *kid*, told him to go home and hide, stay out of the field. "You need to figure out how to fucking *use* it."

"So, it's not just about—"

Eric snorted.

"I thought you wanted to make sure I could keep it under lock?" Tony blinked, confused.

"You said that. Not me." Eric rolled out his shoulders again, a smile on his face that was sharp, jagged. "I don't actually think you'll let it turn on the kids. I want to see how you make it work for you." Eric lowered himself into a fighting stance, his hair falling into his eyes. "Again."

The beast in Tony's chest roared to life, thrilled at the idea, and Tony lunged. He let the power of the wolf propel him forward until he barreled into Eric with his shoulder, throwing him backward, off his feet, skidding across the mat on his back. It only took a second, and then Tony was on him, his legs straddling Eric's hips, his clawed hands fisted into Eric's shirt, leaving behind holes. His teeth were bared as he panted hard in Eric's face.

"This good enough for you, pretty boy?"

Instead of answering, Eric grabbed him by his long blond hair and smashed their mouths together, groaning when Tony's sharp teeth cut his lip, the taste of metal flooding their mouths. Tony gasped, his hips grinding down into Eric's, feeling Eric's hard cock rub roughly at the fabric of their pants, but unable to stop himself as he rutted against it. Eric let out a sharp, whining sound and Tony snapped, lost what little control he had left. His hips jerked harder, pressing himself so close to Eric that he might be able to crawl inside of him.

Eric didn't seem to mind. His hands slid from Tony's hair down his naked back to grab his ass through Tony's jeans, meeting him thrust for thrust.

It didn't take long. It was almost embarrassing, pathetic really, how long it *didn't* take. But fighting had always wound Tony up, and he had to admit, he'd needed this, maybe as much as Eric seemed to when he cried out, letting Tony swallow his sounds as he came a second after Tony did.

Eric let out a soft, almost wounded sound when his head flopped back onto the mat while Tony practically gnawed on his collarbone. It wasn't sexy, but Tony couldn't seem to make himself stop. The wolf was sharp and persistent in the back of his mind, possessive in a way Tony had to say he agreed with.

"Feeling better, sweetcheeks?" Tony rumbled against his skin.

"Yeah. I needed that." Eric breathed a soft laugh but didn't bother to move.

Tony hummed, pressing a biting kiss to Eric's Adam's apple before he rolled onto his back beside him, staring at the popcorn ceiling of the dorm house basement. It was terribly dated.

"I meant what I said," Eric murmured after a long moment.

Tony grunted a questioning sound.

"I'm not worried about you turning on the kids."

"Then what the fuck *are* you worried about, Big Ricky?"

Eric was quiet for long enough that Tony didn't think he'd answer, then he said, "I'm worried you'll get yourself hurt by being reckless, and the kids won't be able to save you."

"So what? You're not going to let me go out with them?"

"I didn't say that."

"Then what the fuck are you saying, princess?"

"I'm saying I think you need to learn to work with your wolf. You don't have your Venator abilities anymore, and without them you're more of a sitting duck than you ever were before. But the wolf can make up for that. Maybe you should . . ." He cleared his throat, clearly unsettled with what he was about to suggest, and Tony braced himself for something he knew was going to piss him off. "Maybe you should reach out to your sire. See about joining the—"

"Fuck you," Tony snarled, and pushed up to his feet without looking back at Eric. "Fuck you, Marcelino. You and the horse you rode in on. I don't need a fucking pack. I'm not a fucking animal."

"Right. Right. Okay." Eric sighed, and he sounded like he wanted to say more, but he didn't press it. Maybe he knew he'd already pushed too far for one day. "Well, Kalla and I are taking first patrol tonight. You've got some time to get your head on right."

"Fine," Tony snapped, then he went to grab his shirt and stomped back up the stairs. He couldn't fucking believe Eric was pulling this shit with him. Suggesting he fall in line with a pack. That he bow to his sire. Like he was some kind of beast. Some *animal*. Not . . . not a Venator. Not anymore.

Tears pricked Tony's eyes, but he sucked them down and kept right on stomping up the next set of stairs toward the second floor of the house. He thought he heard Eric mutter something about him going to the lab to see Hunter, but Tony wasn't in the fucking mood to play scientist with Eric's little boyfriend.

CHAPTER 12

"WHEN DO I get to use a sword on a hunt?" Lu asked. Her bright green eyes were fixed on the sword Eric had slung over his shoulder. He didn't know why he'd grabbed it. It wasn't his go-to, but he had a feeling he wanted to impress Lu and Fin on this hunt. There was something about teenage girls that always made him feel like he was under close scrutiny. Maybe because he knew from firsthand experience how fucking mean they could be.

"The moment you can lift one," Tony snorted into the com in Eric's ear, and Eric could imagine him rolling his eyes at his sister's antics. They were so very similar sometimes. Biting and sarcastic. Eric wondered if Tony saw it. He also wondered if Tony knew that it made him a bit envious of the way Tony and Hunter seemed to mesh with their siblings— even if Hunter and Chase weren't blood related. Meanwhile, Eric and his own brother were—

He shook himself. He wasn't going to think about that. He had no control over what Oliver did. And there was no changing the way his parents had set them up against each other. All he could do was move forward. Try to protect the people who did give a flying fuck about him. When he tuned back into his surroundings, Lu and Tony were bickering back and forth via the coms.

"Don't be such a prick, Tony," Lu bit out. "I'm perfectly—"

"Please, pipsqueak. You don't have the arm strength to so much as—"

"Enough, you two." Eric laughed softly, shaking his head. "If you want to learn to use a sword, we'll set up some training for you. But until then, stick to what you know." He held a stake out to Lu, who took it with far less grumbling than her brother likely would have. "You geared up, Fin?"

Fin nodded, giving her own stake a twirl before shoving it back into her pocket. "All set."

Eric cleared his throat around the swell of pride that threatened to choke off his airways. Fin and Lu were the newest kids in his class. They started a few months back when Lu and Tony moved to town, but they'd come a long way in that short amount of time. Made progress like he'd never seen before. It likely helped that Lu had been training with Tony since she was old enough to hold a stake, and that Fin came from a traditional Huntsmen family that believed in raising their kids to be hunters from day one, gene or no. But still, that didn't change how he felt.

"All right then." He bumped his door shut with his hip and turned to look at the sprawling graveyard. It was the largest in Ironport, spanning for blocks. And normally Eric wouldn't have wanted to start two hunters in training on this kind of territory, but he had to go where the threat was likely to be, and there had been five funerals happening at the same time here—victims of a car accident on one of the major highways.

Five chances for Dash to turn the freshly dead into something far more dangerous. And if what Eric knew of Dash's tactics lately held true, he wouldn't miss the opportunity to throw any bodies he could get at Eric. None of the recently turned had been particularly strong humans, they were just average Joes trumped up by vampire blood. By far, not the most strategic, but Eric saw it for what it was. Dash was trying to wear him down. Quantity over quality.

"How many do you think we'll see tonight?" Lu asked, her voice oddly hesitant. Eric had never heard her sound scared before, but it made sense. She was all bluster and showboating in class, but this was a real threat. He knew that feeling all too well.

"Hopefully max five." Eric shrugged and tried to sound much calmer than he felt. He couldn't let on how much he was worried about having the girls out with him. It would make them more nervous. They needed to believe he could protect them. He needed to step up and be the hero they always made him out to be.

"That's not too bad." Lu rolled her shoulders, her tennis shoes crunching on the gravel as she followed him through the small side gate one of the staff members had left unlocked for them. It paid, sometimes, to have connections.

"We can handle that many," Fin assured in her quiet, steady way. She was always like that. Calm. In control. Eric didn't know how she did it—she was fucking seventeen—but it made him feel more relaxed having her around.

"Definitely." He glanced over the hilly graveyard. There were no trees to block sight lines, but there were plenty of statues and monuments. Even a couple of mausoleums where a vampire could tuck themself away. He would have to be careful, aware. He stopped for a moment, taking a breath of the quickly cooling air. It was dusk, and despite how bustling other parts of Ironport still were this time of day, a heavy silence had settled here. Eric didn't like it. "Do we have any data on nests in the area?"

"Not that I've seen on the radar," Hunter reported.

"But that doesn't mean anything," Tony added.

"Shouldn't you be in bed?" Lu sniped. "You have patrol tomorrow, you should get some rest."

"Who's the parent here, Louisa?" Tony asked. "Pay attention to your surroundings, shithead."

"I am paying attention—"

"If all you two are going to do is bicker, I'm locking you out of the command center," Hunter hissed, and Eric thought he heard Hunter give Tony a shove. Tony grumbled something under his breath but ultimately fell silent. "Tony's right, though. There weren't many recently dead over the last couple of days. He's got to be running out of corpses."

"Which means he'll fall back on old tactics." Eric sighed, scrubbing at his face.

"Can't he turn living people too?" Lu asked. She wasn't looking at Eric as they walked over old graves covered in wire grass and weeds, toward the recently dug plots Hunter had showed him on the map.

"He could," Eric conceded. "But it'd be more difficult. For one, it'd draw more attention."

"And two, it takes longer," Hunter added. "He has to bring them to the brink of death by exsanguinating them, then fill them with his own blood."

"If he uses the recently dead, he can skip that step," Tony agreed. "He's been lucky so far. With Ironport being as large as it is, there's usually no shortage of car accidents or other deaths."

"Have you heard from Kalla yet about her contacts at the morgues and funeral homes?" It sounded like Hunter's fingers were clacking against the keyboard, likely flicking between the map of where Eric was, and where Kalla and her team had wound up, around the hospital.

"Nothing yet," Kalla reported, breaking into their conversation. "I had to leave messages since it was the middle of the workday. I expect calls back tomorrow morning. If not, I'll swing by their locations and get answers."

"How's the hospital looking?" Eric panted as he climbed onto one of the taller monuments to get a better lay of the land. He didn't like how quiet it was. Yes, it was still early, the sun still just above the horizon, but something felt wrong about this. Maybe he'd get lucky. Maybe he brought Fin and Lu out here and they wouldn't see any action. But then again . . . When had Eric *ever* been lucky?

"Quiet. Aside from Nik and Kate bickering like little shits." Kalla sighed.

"Of course they are." He probably should have put them in separate groups, but Bert would have been just as bad, and Chase was still out of commission—it had only been a couple of days since his gene activated. That just left Fin and Lu to group with either Nik or Kate. Lu couldn't go with Kalla, because Tony didn't trust her, and Fin didn't really know her. There was no good way to cut up the group. All he could hope was that Nik and Kate would— "Tell them to get their heads out of their asses or I'm giving them extra homework next week."

Kalla snorted softly but relayed the message, and her end of the line fell quiet.

The sun had dipped fully below the horizon, the last rays streaming up through the air, when Eric heard the first sound of unlife. A quiet moan. Overturned earth. He whipped around and caught sight of the young guy who'd caused the accident—a drunk driver—digging his way out of his grave.

"Lu. Fin," he murmured quietly, and they both ripped their gazes away from where they were watching in fascinated horror to look at him. "He's going to come for me, hard and fast, probably. I want you two to scoop around behind him and take him out."

A quick nod, and the two girls melted into the dark of the surrounding cemetery as Eric dropped from the monument and made himself an easy target. He tucked his hands into his back pockets and started whistling, taking an easy stroll toward where the guy was still struggling out of the compact earth.

"Hey there, buddy, need a hand?" Eric asked, a grin curling the corners of his lips. Cocky. Arrogant. *Foolish.*

"Eric! Look out!" Lu shouted, and Eric whipped around but not quick enough. Never quick enough.

Fuck. Why hadn't he felt them coming? Why hadn't Hunter seen them on the radar? What kind of game was Dash playing with all this?

The vampire behind him grabbed him by the arms. They were bigger than Eric by a lot, at least two heads taller, and built like a fucking wall. And they were faster, stronger, less frenzied than the feral, rabid vamps he'd been dealing with recently. Although there was still that blank light in their eyes, like they didn't quite have control over themself or their own body.

No matter. Eric knew what to do. He spun on his heel, breaking their hold, and dropped out of their reach. The sword on his back swung out easily from its sheath, and he swiped at the vampire's legs, cutting them off at the knees. Black blood coated the ground, thick and viscous, filling the air with the cloying scent of rot.

Another swing of his blade, and he'd beheaded the vampire still trying to struggle from his grave, leaving behind nothing but dust and fangs. Eric kept the momentum, spun again, and took the bigger vamp's head clean off. He'd meant for this to be a fight the girls could help with. Meant to let them try their hand at this. But he wasn't playing with their safety.

Especially not when two more vamps took the place of those he'd just killed. These weren't fresh vamps either, he could see it. Their movements were more fluid, as if they'd greased their joints past the point of rigor mortis.

The sword made things easier. It allowed him to keep moving even as he had to jump over a headstone to get some distance between himself and the coming attack. He heard a squeak from over his shoulder and looked back to see the girls dealing with their own threat. The remaining four victims of the accident had surrounded them, backing them into a corner.

"Nope. Not happening." Eric side-stepped another clumsy lunge from a long-haired vampire, slicing through her reaching arm and severing it so it landed on the ground with a loud thump before he flung himself away. The two vampires who had been trying to grab him followed, hot on his heels, but he didn't stop. Couldn't.

Between Lu and Fin, they'd managed to slam a stake into the stomach of one of the vampires, but it didn't do anything other than cause them to lose their only weapon.

Fuck. Fuck. Fuck.

They weren't prepared. They weren't ready for this. He'd told the council. He'd been very clear about this. His students were practiced in the theory of fighting vampires, but they had no real-world experience. And they certainly weren't ready to deal with these kinds of numbers.

"Eric," Tony hissed a warning into Eric's ear.

"I've got it." Eric threw himself at one of the vampires, dropping his sword in the scuffle as he grabbed the stake the girls had been using and jammed it upward into the vampire's heart. They burst into a shower of dust, and Eric rolled to his feet.

One down. Five to go.

He could do this.

CHAPTER 13

"ERIC?" Tony's voice came out strangled. Raw. His chest was lifting and falling in hard, short bursts. Panic was settling in; Hunter could see it on his face. "Eric. Answer me!"

Hunter hit a button on the keyboard in front of him, putting their mics on mute, and reached for Tony's hands, forcing his chair around away from the screen to look at him. It squeaked on the hard plastic wheels, but with Tony facing him Hunter could get a better gauge of how to handle this. Tony's green eyes were glowing with an unnatural light, his fingernails lengthening, going sharp. This was exactly what Hunter had been worried about when Eric said Tony was going to be in charge of a team of kids in the field. He hadn't said as much because he didn't want to start a fight, but Tony's lack of control set Hunter's teeth on edge.

"All right, sweetheart," Hunter said, giving Tony's hand a hard squeeze, forcing him to meet his gaze. They didn't have eyes on the kids and Eric aside from the radar. There was nothing they could do for them from there. Hunter had already sent a message to Kalla that Eric needed backup, and she needed to get there as soon as she could. What happened now was out of their hands. Still, Hunter understood Tony's panic. That was his kid sister out there in a graveyard surrounded by vampires with only Eric for protection.

"Fuck off." Tony's snarl curled his lip back from teeth

gone sharp. Alarm bells should probably be ringing in Hunter's head at the obvious threat the wolf posed, but all he felt was a sudden shiver of *want* go down his spine.

"Nope. Not happening." Hunter shook his head. A long piece of dark-brown hair fell into his face, but he refused to let go of Tony's hands to push it away. "You need to take a breath with me. You know the drill. In."

"Fuck. You." Tony's eyes glowed brighter, hair crawling across his neck, a growl rumbling from deep in his chest. It made Hunter want to slide into his lap and press his face into Tony's neck to feel his erratic heartbeat against his lips. To see how soft that fur was against his cheek. He wouldn't. He wasn't a complete fucking idiot. Didn't mean the urge wasn't there.

"Maybe later," he said flippantly.

That got him a grin. Tony's brows raised high on his face, the growl cutting off, his lips twitching at the corners. It wasn't much, but it was enough.

"You trust Eric, right?" Hunter pressed the advantage, his thumbs rubbing slow circles into the tops of Tony's hands.

Tony scoffed.

"Right?"

"Right." Tony rolled his eyes, but they weren't glowing as brightly as they had been a second ago. He was back to himself, the panic and anger simmering into something more manageable. Something that meant Hunter didn't have to be afraid for his pretty face.

"He's got the highest slay average in the entire Venator community," Hunter continued, not bothering to acknowledge the gruff annoyance he was getting from Tony now. Getting into a bickering match wasn't going to solve anything.

"Mine is second." But he didn't sound as pissy about that as he might have a couple of weeks ago. Instead, some pride seemed to lace the words. Like he was honored to be second to someone like Eric. As he should be.

"Exactly. Eric is the most capable Venator in several generations. He's lived the longest. He has the highest slay total. And he's not new hat at this. He's been doing this for decades." As he said it, Hunter felt better and better about it himself. He trusted Eric, sure he did. Even he would admit to being freaked out about the idea of his brother going out into the field with just Eric between him and five vamps. But he was right. Eric was the best the Huntsmen community had ever seen. He'd far outlived the average Venator lifespan. He'd proven himself time and time again that he was capable, driven, and terrifying in his own right. Just like Tony. "Lu and Fin are safe with him. Probably safer than they could be with anyone else."

Tony nodded, conceding this point in the small movement. His breaths had evened out and he held Hunter's hands back but didn't clutch hard at them anymore. "He's got this."

"He does," Hunter agreed. Warmth swelled in his chest at the way Tony reacted to his subtle comfort. They weren't friends, they weren't anything, but Tony trusted Hunter with this. To bring him back down. To see how vulnerable and scared he was about his sister. To tell him the truth about Eric's brother. There was something in that. Something that hadn't been there weeks ago. Something Hunter wasn't going to examine too closely lest he scare Tony off. "And I've sent word to Kalla to provide backup. She's already on her way."

"Okay. Yeah. Okay." Tony sighed, his shoulders dropping as he relaxed further. There was silence for a couple of seconds, Hunter and Tony holding hands, the clock ticking away. Hunter hadn't realized it before, but when he'd twisted Tony around, they'd moved so Hunter's knees were straddling Tony's. It was unbearably intimate. Hunter wouldn't do this with just anyone. Maybe he shouldn't even be doing it with Tony given the strange ground they stood on, but Tony needed comfort, and Hunter was helpless but to provide it.

"You good?" Hunter asked. He didn't want to break this moment between them, but they needed to get back to Eric and the kids. He could focus on this burgeoning . . . *thing* with Tony later.

"Yeah. I'm—" Tony took a deep breath, his hands tightening around Hunter's again as if perhaps he didn't want to let go. The feeling was mutual. Goddess, was it ever. "I'm good."

"Cool. Then let's get back to our boy?"

"Mm-hmm."

But neither of them seemed to want to let go of each other. Goddess, Hunter was fucked, wasn't he? How had he even gotten to this point? Unable to stop holding hands with someone. Unable to look away from his boyfriend's other boyfriend. He'd only just lost Britt, what? A few months ago? More? Less? He wasn't sure anymore. The time all blurred together. And now here he was, losing it over someone else. Someone who he hadn't even known more than a handful of months. Life was fucking wild, wasn't it?

"Okay." Hunter forced himself to let go of one of Tony's hands, the one on the far side, so he could spin back to look at the screens, clicking the button that would turn the sound back on. The other hand remained stubbornly twisted around Tony's.

Tony turned too, shifting, and for a moment Hunter feared he'd let go, that whatever small—near insignificant, honestly—intimacy they'd found together would be lost as they refocused. But instead, he threaded their fingers together, rubbing his thumb over the cold metal of Hunter's thumb ring, heating it slowly with his body heat.

Hunter wondered if they'd ever speak of this again. If they'd leave this room and pretend this never happened. The thought of it made something in his chest twist painfully. He didn't want that. He wanted . . . He wanted quiet truths spoken into the dark. He wanted fingers—too warm because of his werewolf nature—threaded with his own. He wanted something like what Eric and Tony had, but different. Their own.

"All right, Big Ricky," Hunter said, forcing his voice into a lightness he didn't really feel, "how's it looking?"

"It's looking like a bunch of dead vamps." Eric was panting, his voice strained, but he didn't sound hurt. "I've got some more teeth for you."

"Super." Hunter didn't let the relief show too much in his tone but he saw Tony relax out of the corner of his eye. "I'll call Kalla off then."

"Do that. We don't need her, do we, girls?"

"I killed my first vamp!" Lu piped up, her voice far too chipper for the situation they'd just been in. These fucking kids, adrenaline junkies the fucking lot of them, just like their teacher. "Do I get to keep the teeth?"

"No," Eric grunted. He sounded like he was trying to hold back laughter, probably shaking his head at the antics of his students. It was a nice sound. A relief.

"How much longer are we going to be out here?" Fin asked. She didn't sound as excited as Lu, but she never did really. From the little Hunter had learned about her over the last couple of months, she was a far more subdued child than the others. Quieter, calmer. More like his brother. Likely because of the homeschooling she'd gone through up until recently.

"Couple more hours. But it should be quiet now." Eric didn't sound like he believed it. He sounded like maybe he wanted to have Hunter come and get the kids, take them back to campus where they'd be safe away from the threat of sharp teeth and deadly speed.

"Don't speak too soon, pretty boy," Tony grumbled softly.

"Oh, sweetie, never." There was a cocky note to Eric's

voice that settled Hunter's rattled nerves. If he could sound like that, if he could be flippant and silly, then he was all right. At least for the time being.

"Ew. Gross. Please stop flirting with my teacher where I can hear you. You two are so nasty!" But it sounded like Lu was laughing, her tone light and happy.

They were okay, all three of them. Hunter hadn't let himself think the worst when Tony had been panicking, but now he considered it. The three of them could have been in some deep shit out there. Two untested Venator—without active genes—and one Eric against six vampires. It could have ended way worse.

"How does the radar look?" Eric's tone slipped back into all business, and although Hunter had never been on patrol with him, he could imagine Eric scanning the surrounding area, his hand tight around whatever weapon he was carrying.

"Nothing. But that doesn't mean anything." Hunter didn't like that they still had the cloaking magic to contend with. An antsy feeling crawled along his nerves. "I'm going to talk to Rus about that again, to see if we can circumvent it."

"Okay. Well, I'm going to go quiet for a bit. Me and the girls are heading to some of the other fresh graves to see if there is any evidence that we've got more risen. I'd like a better idea of the numbers we're looking at."

"Let us know what your total looks like. Gotta update your record so you stay on top, right Number One Venator?" Tony teased. He still hadn't let go of Hunter's hand, and Hunter felt his pulse skip at the gentle ribbing.

"Fuck off, man." But it sounded like Eric was laughing before he tapped the mute button on his end, and the mic went silent.

"While I've got you," Hunter said, carefully not looking at Tony. Part of him worried that if he did then Tony might notice that they were still holding hands, might pull away. He didn't want him to pull away. Not yet. Not ever, maybe. "Since you didn't come to the lab earlier."

"Yeah, sorry about that," Tony grumbled softly. He didn't turn either, didn't acknowledge the connection, like maybe he was afraid of losing it too. "Eric set me off, and I just didn't have the bandwidth to talk nerd after that shit."

"About what?" He probably shouldn't ask. Putting himself between Eric and Tony when they were clearly having some kind of fight was a stupid fucking idea. It was a quick and easy way to get them both pissed at him.

"This shit with my wolf," Tony responded, and Hunter tried not to let the surprise show on his face. He hadn't exactly expected a straightforward answer. He'd thought Tony would skirt the question or tell him it was none of his fucking business. That would be his right. "He thinks I should contact my sire. Get in touch with the pack. He thinks it would help me control it better. Use it."

"And you don't want to." Which was obvious by the way Tony was talking about it, but what Hunter didn't know was why.

"No. I don't want to. I'm not—" He sighed, his free hand lifting to run through his curly blond hair. "I'm not a fucking pack animal, okay? I'm a Venator, even if I've got Werewolf blood now."

"Well," Hunter licked his lips, half worried what he was about to say would set Tony off, but he had to say it now, didn't he? He'd already started. "Maybe he's onto something with needing to find a pack. Maybe—"

Tony snarled, his hand tightening around Hunter's.

"Hear me out, asshole," Hunter pressed, not backing down. "Maybe he's right that you need to find a pack to get a better handle on your wolf."

"But?"

"But maybe he's wrong about who it should be." Hunter lifted his chin toward the screen in front of him, the radar that showed the dots that were Eric and the girls at the graveyard, the one to the side with Kalla and the boys.

Tony grunted, perhaps surprised, then conceded, "Maybe."

"Give it some thought."

"Fine."

"Good. Now, can I get you to come down to the lab tomorrow morning so we can work on this thing to trap the vamps?"

"Fine fine. Just don't expect me too early."

Hunter shrugged. "So long as you come bearing coffee, I suppose that's fine."

"Deal."

Chapter 14

"AS PROMISED," Tony said, balancing two overfull reusable to-go cups and a bag of breakfast sandwiches that Eric had shoved into his hand on the way down the steps to Hunter's basement lab. They were still warm, the smell of melted cheese and bacon wafting through the air in a way that made Tony's stomach rumble. The temptation to wolf—*ha ha*—them down on the way had been strong. Maybe he shouldn't be making jokes about his werewolf nature yet, but if he couldn't make it go away, he might as well get a kick out of the wolf-associated puns, right? "I come bearing coffee and breakfast."

"You're a god!" Hunter crowed, dropping the tray of teeth he'd been examining onto the black counter pushed against the far wall of the basement. He held his hands out toward Tony. He opened and closed his fingers in a grabby-hands gesture that was impossible to resist, rings glinting in the harsh, bright lights. *Adorable.*

"Don't let your boyfriend hear you saying that. He might get jealous." And wasn't that a thought? Eric Marcelino jealous of the way his boyfriend talked to his other boyfriend. Fuck, this shit was complicated. Why had Tony agreed to this again?

"Eric isn't a jealous man." Hunter shrugged, taking a sip from the cup and hissing at the scalding temperature. It didn't slow him down though. He took another sip, this one ending in a moan that made Tony's stomach tighten. And yeah, sure, that was why Tony had agreed to this whole thing. Because he was thinking with his dick, and his dick wouldn't let him say no to Eric nor Hunter.

Tony shook himself and sipped from his own drink to swallow the feelings bubbling up in his chest. It was getting harder and harder to ignore the attraction he felt toward Hunter. Even worse still, Tony was beginning to realize it wasn't just attraction. There was more there too. Especially after the way Hunter had talked him out of his panic the previous night, bringing Tony back to himself in a way few others had ever been able to do.

"What're we looking at?" Tony asked as he slid onto one of the high stools beside Hunter. He hoped that if he could keep Hunter talking about science, then maybe he wouldn't think to bring up the odd intimacy they'd shared in the control room the night prior. Or the way Tony had been unable to let his hand go until well after they knew Eric and the girls were on their way back. Tony had always been a tactile person, but that was pushing it for someone who was essentially a stranger.

"Teeth." Hunter slid his coffee onto the table, the bag of sandwiches crinkling under his fingers before he pulled one out and took a big bite.

"Obviously." With a roll of his eyes, Tony leaned closer. The fangs on the tray didn't look any different than all the others he'd ever encountered. But he knew from previous conversations with Hunter that he could tell much more about the vampire the fangs had belonged to than anyone else. Age. How long since it had been turned. Even where it had grown up. Something about the mineral build up and the amount of fluoride or some shit. It made sense when Hunter said it, but fuck off if you thought Tony would be able to pin down how he did it.

"Obviously," Hunter repeated around a mouthful of food.

"Is that all you're gonna give me, big guy?" The pet name slipped off Tony's tongue a little too easily, coming naturally to him as they always had with Eric. He should probably give that some thought, but he could examine his idiocy later. Right now, they had bigger vampires to dust, so to speak.

"I was wondering if there would be enough DNA leftover to give us something to go off of to find Dash." The words were followed by a shrug, like the idea wasn't something genius in and of itself, something most people wouldn't think of, that most people wouldn't have been able to utilize probably.

"Was there?" Could it be that simple? Could they find Dash without having to trap a vampire and draw its blood? Tony's throat was tight at the thought. It would certainly simplify things. Be a fuckload safer than what they were planning to do too.

"There was some there, but it's not viable." Hunter frowned, rubbing at his nose in a way that made his glasses shift around on his face. He looked tired. Tony wondered if he'd even gone to bed last night after Eric and the kids had gotten back. It had been a rough night for all of them. It always was when Eric was out in the field. But after Lu was home safe and sound, Tony had slunk away to his room and curled up under the covers, pretending not to think about what Hunter and Eric could be doing in the bedroom a couple doors down.

"Not fresh enough?"

"Exactly." Hunter's head lifted, his eyes wide, brows drawn up in surprise, like he hadn't been expecting Tony to hit the nail on the head right off. That was fine. Most people didn't seem to know how clever Tony was. He enjoyed that fact. It allowed him to be underestimated in some instances. And in others, it got him out of having to do shit like Hunter did in the lab when he didn't want to. That was kind of the thing though . . . Hunter made him want to. "It degrades so fast after the vampire is slain. Almost like it goes up in dust with the rest of them."

"So why do the teeth remain?" He'd always wondered that. It didn't make sense. It wasn't all the teeth either. Just the fangs. The rest of the vamp became a pile of ashes, but the fangs were always left.

Hunter grinned, shaking his head in obvious amusement. "You know, I was never able to figure that out." The paper crinkled under his hands again as he finished off his sandwich, chewing thoughtfully while they both stared at the fangs in the little tray. They were innocuous looking when they weren't attached to a vampire. They could almost have belonged to something else. A snake. A house cat. Maybe even a pygmy shark. Something smaller and less terrifying than the creatures Tony had been fighting all his life.

"Just seems weird is all," Tony grumbled around a big bite of his own sandwich.

"Oh, it totally is. But maybe it's less science and more magic?" Hunter scratched his temple. "Kind of like how Crosses work. There is no science behind why an object of great belief and faith would fend off a vampire, and yet Eric has his pendant from his Nonna, and you have your paperback. Two items as unlike as they can get. But you both infused them with enough of your will that they keep vampires from going for the jugular—so to speak—when your back is against the wall."

Tony tilted his head, narrowing his eyes on the teeth.

"That's my theory, anyhow. Not sure what the magic *does*, exactly? Maybe it's the will of a creature scared to die, clinging to life in the only way it knows how, by leaving something behind? I mean, that's what we all want, isn't it? To leave something behind. Something to prove we were here. Maybe it's like that."

"Maybe." Tony didn't think that was it, but he also didn't think it mattered.

"Anyway, because I can't use the DNA on the teeth, we're still going to have to fall back on your blood idea." The lid clacked overtop the tray as Hunter closed it and slid it into a drawer.

"Right. Which means we need a way to trap a vampire. Eric did it before. You made him some cuffs for that, right?"

"I did, but with the numbers we're facing now . . ." Hunter frowned, shaking his head. He seemed unsettled, which was understandable. The threat they faced was more than any of them had dealt with before. "I don't think it's safe to send him in with something like that."

"You used stunner magic when you two worked together in the warehouse district that one time." Tony tapped his thumb against the side of his half-empty plastic cup as he considered this. There was a lot he didn't know about magic, but he'd seen the way that spell worked. "Couldn't we use that?"

Hunter hummed thoughtfully. "We could. But my concern is that Dash has done something to this new round of vamps. He's made them . . . rabid, to an extent. I don't know if my magic will be able to tap into the same things it did before to hold them."

"We don't know till we try." And so far, it was the best thing they had. It made Tony nervous not to have all the facts. Not to know what Dash was doing to these vampires to change them to the point of making them almost mindless. Not to have a way to track the threat coming for them. And he could see by the way Hunter fidgeted in his seat that it was bothering him just the same. They both had people to protect. Tony understood that better now that he'd helped Chase through his gene activating. He and Hunter weren't so different.

"That's true. I'd still like to have something else. Something with more certainty of working."

"I don't suppose you can make a great big cage out of the stuff you used for the cuffs?" And even if he could, how the fuck would Eric cart it around? Tony snorted to himself. That wouldn't do.

"I used iron." Hunter grunted, seeming to think the same thing as Tony, but he was too polite to call Tony out on being an idiot.

"Could he use iron the way witches use salt? The filings? Make a circle?" It would still require some doing. Probably too much for the ever-changing circumstances of the field.

"I mean yes, but a circle is easily broken. And it takes time to—" Hunter stopped himself, his head lifting to look at Tony with wide bright eyes. "Now there's an idea."

"Where's an idea?" Tony looked over his shoulder as if he might see what had set Hunter off.

Hunter didn't answer. He pulled a pad of paper from another drawer in the big table, along with a handful of pens. Then he was furiously jotting something down that Tony couldn't make out from where he was sitting.

Tony moved, pressing his chest into Hunter's back so he could look over his shoulder and see what the fuck he was doing.

In messy chicken-scratch scrawl that Tony could hardly make out, Hunter was writing what looked like runes, calculations, and periodic elements? He had started muttering to himself, so low even Tony's werewolf hearing couldn't make it out.

"You gonna tell me what's going on, killer?" Tony mumbled, trying to ignore how his gut churned at the way Hunter looked. His eyes were wide and sparkling. His hand moved so quick it was hard to track the movement, page after page being pushed aside as he tried to work out the problem in his head. Color appeared high on his cheeks. The flush of genius was . . . Well. It was really fucking sexy.

Tony's mouth was suddenly dry. He swallowed with an audible click, his eyes flicking around the next page of paper. He'd never seen Hunter work before. Not really, and shit, it was something else. The clock on the walk ticked away seconds turning to minutes turning to a half hour as Hunter kept working. He'd gone into some kind of hyper-fixated state, blocking out Tony entirely as he worked until finally he sucked in a sharp gasp. "That's it."

"What's it?" Tony asked, his fingers tight around his coffee that had long since gone cold.

"A cage." Hunter tapped something on the page that looked like a combination of an equation, some Nordic runes Tony didn't understand, and a couple metals—if he was remembering his periodic table correctly, which was entirely debatable. It'd been a long time since high school chem. "Well. Sort of."

"Sort of a cage?" Goddess, Tony forgot sometimes how much he both hated and loved talking to people who were smarter than him.

"A metaphysical cage. Using an array infused with iron filings and a little bit of magic."

"Wouldn't an array cause the same problem as my idea about the filings?"

"It would if we expected him to lay out pieces of it before luring the vampire into a trap." Hunter nodded. "That would present all the same problems."

"Okay, you lost me." Tony laughed softly. "If that's the case, how are we gonna use this?"

"Talismans."

"Wouldn't those be even more flimsy than a line of iron filings?" Tony was sure Hunter had thought of this, he just hadn't finished articulating his idea yet. He wondered if

Hunter ever really had to do this before, or if he had that freaky nonverbal communication thing that Eric and Ava seemed to have between them. Well, even if he did, he was going to have to say whatever he was thinking out loud for Tony to get it.

"Yes, if they were made of paper." Hunter grinned more broadly, as if he was delighted at the possibility of a new invention, a new weapon, a new tool. He probably was. It was a good look on him.

"If we aren't going to make them out of paper, what are we going to make them out of?"

"Metal!" Hunter crowed. "Azure Elwood has done some work with using pendants to create talismans. If we can create a sort of . . . a net? Almost? That Eric could throw down in a rush, where the talismans tie the iron to each other via the fabric itself . . ."

Oh. Okay. Tony was picking up what he was laying down. "It creates a constant circle."

"Exactly!"

Tony snorted. "Kind of like filling a hula-hoop full of salt and throwing it around a ghost."

Hunter threw his head back and laughed at the imagery, his throat bobbing with the sound in a way that made Tony want to bite it like a fucking apple. Shit. He needed to get out of here before he did something stupid.

"Looks like you don't need me anymore." Tony shifted on the stool, the metal creaking under his weight. He didn't want to go. He wanted to move in closer, feel more of Hunter's warmth seep in through his clothes, absorb more of his delighted genius.

"You got somewhere better to be?" Hunter raised a brow, his lips quirked as if he already knew the answer.

"Not really." Tony shrugged.

"Then why don't you help me build this thing, huh? You'll

get to see the forge they've got on campus. It's pretty *hot*." Hunter's eyes twinkled with the dad joke, and Tony found himself enraptured, already nodding along.

"Yeah. All right."

Chapter 15

THE FORGE WAS SO WARM, it made the loose hair that had slid free from Hunter's messy ponytail stick to the back of his neck. The humidity was going to be hell on his curls, but it was worth it to see the way Tony lit up, his eyes glowing with something other than anger for perhaps the first time since Hunter had met him a few months back.

"Cool, huh?" Hunter asked, nudging Tony with his shoulder.

"Cool." Tony laughed. He shook his head, nudging back in a way that could almost be mistaken as companionable. "Who even uses that word anymore?"

"Hey now," Hunter rumbled teasingly, "respect your elders, youngin'."

Tony snorted another laugh but didn't bite back. He seemed too distracted by the ringing of metal on metal deeper in the forge. The glow of fire heating metal rivalled even the sunshine outside. Hunter had to admit, he saw the appeal, which was why he'd wanted to bring Tony with him. There was something about all the humid air and the loud music of tools working that settled him. If he hadn't gone the way of the lab rat, he'd probably have wound up there with the other forge witches. Making athames, pendants, wands, and anything else the witches of the area needed for their craft. But alas, science was a louder mistress.

"You ever worked in one of these places before?" Hunter asked, tilting his head toward where a young witch dunked a long dagger into water to cool it.

"Is that a thing a lot of people do? Work in a forge?" Tony fired back. His green eyes glowed in what Hunter could only describe as pleasure. He was beautiful and bright in a way Hunter hadn't seen him for a long while. All sharp teeth and sharper edges.

"No. But you seemed the type to enjoy beating something into submission." Hunter's cheeks flushed hotly. It had nothing at all to do with the fires around them, and everything to do with how much his stomach curled with want. He was pushing his luck getting near Tony like this. But Hunter had always liked to play with fire. It's what first drew him to Eric.

Britt had been his safe place. The port in the storm. And he'd loved her so desperately, he still felt her loss like a phantom limb every single day. He woke up wanting to roll over and smile at her. He went home after working in the lab until late into the night wishing she were there to talk to about his work.

What Hunter felt for Eric—what he was starting to feel for Tony—was as different from how Britt had left him feeling as night was to day, and that was good. Less confusing. It didn't mean that Eric wasn't all consuming in the fire he lit in Hunter's chest, but having that love present itself differently left Hunter feeling less guilty. He wasn't replacing Britt. He was moving on. Like she'd wanted. That didn't make it any easier, but it made it simpler to understand.

"I mean yeah, maybe," Tony said, drawing Hunter out of his head. "I could see where you'd think that. But we don't exactly have a smithy on every corner in Miami." He shrugged, his arm brushing against Hunter's with how close they'd gotten while they were talking. Drawn together like the moon and the earth, only Hunter couldn't tell which of them was in the other's orbit. Not that it mattered much. Then Tony turned to him and caught Hunter in his gaze. "Is it common for people up here to learn to work with metal?"

"Not super common." Hunter scrubbed at the back of his neck, both wishing and not wishing he could look away from Tony. "But probably more common than most places. They have a course here for it. Bert's taken it. That's where he made Eric's sword."

Tony nodded and turned to watch the student work again. The fires of the forge danced in his eyes along with something else. Something like . . . interest.

"You could audit it, you know?"

"I'm not enrolled."

"Easy enough to fix." Hunter's lips twitched at the corners. This was something he could give Tony, even if the other man wouldn't let him any closer than this. "Eric can sign you up using his teacher account. And I'm sure Dean Cochburn wouldn't have too much heartburn about adding you at the start of the semester come fall."

"I bet it's expensive—"

"It could fall under the Venator program."

"I don't really need—"

"Dude, I know." Hunter shrugged again, unable to look away from the way Tony was watching the heated metal as it was twisted and turned into something different. "But if you sign up for it that way, the Huntsmen pay for it."

Tony's head jerked again so he could blink at Hunter, his mouth agape, his brows drawn together in surprise. Like he hadn't expected anyone, least of all Hunter, to want to do something nice for him. Hunter wondered how long Tony would have to be with them before he stopped being shocked any time one of their family unit reached out. He hoped Tony wouldn't continue to shy away from it. He prayed to the Goddess that people wouldn't stop reaching even when he did.

"So, you wanna come check out how I'd make these talismans or what?" Hunter tilted his head toward a free workstation, his brows raised in question. He knew he could acknowledge that expression on Tony's face. He could try to make this about feelings. But he'd learned more about him over the last few weeks, and Tony wasn't a feelings kind of guy. Better to ignore them and move on. Tony would come to him when he was ready.

"Fuck yeah." Tony laughed and followed Hunter over to the row of leather aprons hanging on the wall.

"We'll need to make a mold," Hunter murmured thoughtfully, his fingers tapping on the piece of iron he'd pulled from the cubbies. "Grab a bit of that wire, that'll be easier to manipulate."

"Why not just engrave it?"

"They're more likely to come out close to identical this way, and I want them as alike as possible. It'll make the magic I need to imbue in them easier to work with. But . . . Hmm . . ." There was some point to be made about engraving. It would give him better control over what the runes looked like. More like tattoo work than sculpture, which he was more comfortable with. "We'll try a couple of different methods and see what works best."

They worked in relative silence for hours on end. Sweat slowly trickled down Hunter's back. A bright flush settled into Tony's cheeks that made him look impossibly young. And Hunter thought—however stupid the thought might be —that he could get used to this. He could find peace and even happiness with how things were. The only thing that would be better would be getting closer to Tony. Maybe not lovers.

Maybe not how he was with Eric. But he'd at least like to be friends.

Steam hissed loudly in the silence of the late afternoon forge. They were alone, all the other students having left while Hunter and Tony tried a couple of methods of creating the mold.

Hunter brushed sweat from his brow with the back of his wrist.

"Will it work?" Tony asked. He was so fucking close, his skin was practically sticking to Hunter's. With the fire at his front and the werewolf at his back, Hunter was sweltering. Burning up. In the best way possible. His gut twisted with the proximity.

"There's only one way to know for sure." Hunter set the small medallion alongside the others they'd made. They gleamed in the warm glow of the fire. A beacon of hope for their mission of ridding Ironport of one of its biggest threats. Hunter held no illusions that once Dash was gone, another villain wouldn't fill the void he left. Ironport was a breeding ground for the power hungry—the Council of Creatures made it easy. But it would be nice to know that at least the person who'd taken advantage of Tony, nearly killed Eric, and caused Britt's death would be gone. It would feel like revenge in some small way.

"So we won't know until Eric tries them." Tony wrinkled his nose, and Hunter was pretty sure he knew what he was thinking. The next time Eric went out into the field, it might be with one of their siblings. Eric would be testing this with the kids as his only backup. Failure would put them all at risk.

Hunter swallowed, running a hand over the frizzing curls that haloed his head. "Unfortunately. I mean, I can feel the magic in it, but that doesn't tell us if it'll work against vampires like it should."

Tony let out a long breath, his hands shaking where he

brushed them down the front of his leather apron. "Okay. Well . . ."

"Yeah." Hunter didn't like it either, but there was no way around it. Even if Eric didn't take the kids into the field when he tested the array, it would still put him in danger. Any way they sliced it, someone Hunter and Tony loved would be in the line of fire. All they could do was pray to the Goddess that they'd done enough. Clearing his throat, Hunter straightened. "What do you think would work best to form the net?"

"Flexible wire cording would likely be too unwieldy for this kind of thing." Tony wrinkled his nose, his face clearing as he turned his mind to a new problem. He was a clever man, more so than Hunter had originally given him credit for, and that spark of intelligence made him impossibly more attractive. Hunter wanted to eat him up.

"Something more malleable would be better. Rope, or leather even?"

"You do leatherwork too, big guy?" Tony's lips quirked into a teasing, flirty smirk.

Hunter's collar was unbearably hot suddenly. Goddess, did Tony even know what he was doing? He had to. There was no way he could be oblivious to the way he affected people. "I dabble," Hunter said, taking a step closer, pulled by Tony's gravity.

"You know," Tony said, licking his lips, "Eric didn't tell me you were so talented. If he had, maybe—" He laughed, shaking his head, but he didn't look away.

"Maybe what?" Hunter pressed with his words, and his body. Suddenly so close to Tony he could look down into his impossibly green eyes and see the flecks of gold that surrounded the irises. Beautiful. Enchanting. Dangerous. But then, Hunter had always been the type who liked things that could be potentially bad for him.

"Maybe I'd have fought him more for you."

Hunter thought to tell Tony that he wouldn't have had to

fight. That Hunter would have gone willingly. That they could have formed a comfortable little triangle. But Tony grabbed him by his collar and pulled Hunter down until their lips crashed together hard. None of the gentle, restrained passion Eric usually exposed. This kiss was more like a battle of wills. A fight to see who would come out on top.

Grabbing Tony's hips, Hunter pulled him in until their bodies were flush together, swallowing a groan from Tony's throat. He gasped as Tony licked into his mouth, his tongue flicking against the piercing on Hunter's lip teasingly, his hands so tight in the neck of Hunter's shirt that Hunter could feel the seams digging into his skin. It didn't matter. Nothing mattered apart from the feeling of Tony against him.

Fuck. They could have been doing this the whole time? Why were they dancing around each other when they could have been doing *this*? It was so stupid.

The door to the forge swung open, letting in the cool evening air.

"The fuck are you two doing?" Bert asked, his voice shrill.

"Nosey fuckin' kids," Tony muttered as he pulled away, turning his head to glare at Bert. Hunter agreed whole-heartedly.

"Working on a super-secret new weapon for Eric. What do you want, kid?" Hunter asked, trying not to sound as annoyed as he felt.

"Eric's going out tonight. Wasn't he supposed to take a night off?" Bert replied, either having not seen the way Tony and Hunter were holding each other close in the darkness of the forge, or ignoring it in favor of what he'd come to tell them.

"The fuck he is!" Tony snarled. He untied the apron from around his neck and threw it onto one of the worktables on his way to the door, Hunter hot on his heels.

"YOU CAN'T TELL me how to—"

"Are you fucking kidding me?"

"It's my team, I'll run it however—"

"The fuck you will! You need—"

"Oh, for crying out loud, will you both just chill out!" Hunter shouted, putting himself physically between Tony and Eric, as if he thought it might come to blows. Eric wouldn't have pushed it that far. He was annoyed, sure, but he'd never take a swing at anyone in anger. He wasn't an asshole. Well, he wasn't *that* much of an asshole . . . *anymore.* Didn't mean there wouldn't have been a fight if Tony swung first.

"He's being an idiot." Tony poked hard at Eric's chest, the bone of his finger digging in enough to bruise. Eric did his level best not to wince or shift away from him. Showing weakness had never been an option with Tony, and that was doubly true now that he'd gone and gotten himself turned into a werewolf.

Eric wasn't stupid—however much the kids might give him shit about not wanting to do research and assigning them papers so he didn't have to. He knew exactly what was at the core of Tony's worsened moods. But if Tony wasn't going to seek help, Eric couldn't make him. He also wasn't going to bring it up again. Rehashing the same argument over and over wasn't going to get them anywhere. But that didn't mean he had to back down and cave to Tony just because he was puffing up his chest either. Eric was the senior Venator here, he was in charge. Period.

"I'm perfectly fine for another patrol." It wasn't like Eric hadn't been doing this every night since he turned thirteen. Grabbing a couple of stakes and following his nose to the nearest threat of vampires was as ordinary to him as making breakfast in the morning. Now wasn't any different, and why should it be? Just because he had help, didn't mean he had to sit out a hunt when he was more than capable of—

"You haven't taken a proper break in *weeks*," Tony snarled, his lip curling back to show off his teeth. They hadn't lengthened and sharpened to the points they did when the werewolf was on the edge of his consciousness. Good. Maybe he was finally learning a bit of control. But Eric wasn't going to get his hopes up.

"I don't need a—"

"I have to go with Tony on this one, Big Ricky," Hunter said, forcing himself between them again. He brushed Tony's hand away from Eric's chest, giving it a squeeze that Eric didn't miss, before turning back to face him. "I know you're used to going out every night," he offered placatingly. "But that was when you weren't facing upward of fifteen vamps a night. The threat level from Dash is too high for you to run yourself into the ground. What will you do when we finally catch up with him? Will you sit out then?"

"No. I'll—"

"Right, and you expect to be able to go up against him if you're strung out from a month of no sleep?" Tony continued. They were ganging up on him, and he didn't even have the liberty to find it adorable because it would make the fact that he couldn't back down harder. He was the most capable of the lot of them. There was no reason he shouldn't go on patrol. Especially since it would be Chase's first night out after his gene had activated. Someone needed to be there for him to make sure he didn't expose himself.

"I'll be fine," Eric groused. He wasn't going to win this, he knew that. Not with Hunter and Tony in agreement. That didn't mean he had to like it. "I've gone out on my own before when I was more tired. Hung over. *Sick*. I'll be fine."

"Don't care." Tony shook his head.

"He's right. If you can't be trusted to get some proper rest between patrol nights, I'll have to force you." Hunter's eyes narrowed, his gaze hardening. A threat. One that Eric knew for a fact he would make good on.

He didn't want to find out what ways Hunter planned on *making* him get some sleep. So, he swallowed, his gaze flicking from Hunter to Tony and back, never seeming to settle. Hunter was standing right in front of Eric, with Tony looming over his shoulder like an attack dog. "You know things were a lot easier before you two jackasses decided to bond."

"Tough shit." Tony smirked, triumphant.

"Yeah, sorry, hon. I really have no sympathy for you on this one. You get what you get." Hunter shrugged, a grin crawling up the corners of his lips.

"You're the one who wanted to date both of us." Tony brushed past him into the kitchen. He reached for the coffee pot to pour himself a cup of the mostly cooled sludge leftover from earlier that afternoon when Eric had needed a pick-me-up after classes.

"Don't remind me." Most days, dating both Tony and Hunter seemed a blessing, a dream Eric hadn't imagined. But then they got like this. All protective and demanding, Eric wanted to rail against their care because he wasn't used to having that. People didn't look after him. The only person who ever had was his Nonna, and she'd been gone for years now. Even when he'd had her, it was never like this. She knew what he was. Knew what was expected of him. It was what had killed his grandfather after all. "If I'm not going, then does that mean you *are*?"

"Don't see anyone else that can take them, do you?" Tony took a deep drink from his mug, his face contorting into an expression of disgust, but he went back for another gulp.

"Babe, just let me make you a fresh pot." Eric rolled his eyes and took the mug without further prompting, dumping it in the sink on his way to the coffee maker to start the process over again.

"I'll go with them," Hunter volunteered. "We probably should have two parties out again. That seemed to work last night, so we have backup in case someone gets into trouble."

"I'm not going to get in trouble." Tony scoffed.

"No, he's right," Eric said, parroting their tactics a few minutes ago. "We said we'd do two units. Hunter can take the safest area—the hospital again—and you can head for the clubbing district. It's a Friday. There will be enough normies out to act as an all-you-can-eat buffet. Better that you run a check."

"Are the brats even old enough to get into the clubs?"

"Bert and Chase are, they just can't drink," Hunter volunteered. "You can take them and I'll take Nik and Kate, since they didn't see any action last night."

"That works." Eric nodded, slipping the pot back into the coffee maker. "I was wondering how I was going to work that, since I've only got six kids, and we're doing teams of two."

"I thought Hunter was going to work up a more solid rotation." Tony's fingers tapped impatiently on the counter, his gaze fixed on the slowly filling coffee pot. He was strategically avoiding Hunter now that they weren't teaming up against Eric, like he was embarrassed by something. Eric didn't have time to sort out what that all was about. He'd have to ask Hunter later.

"I can do that tonight while I sit in the control room." It

left him unsettled knowing Tony and Hunter would be going out without him as backup. Hunter wasn't supposed to be on patrol at all. They'd decided he'd sit tight in the makeshift control room they'd set up in the attic of the dorm, trading off with Ava while Eric, Tony, and Kalla took shifts. But Eric could see how he should've realized that wouldn't work. He'd made the plan counting on the fact that one of the two teams every night would be run by him, but if Hunter and Tony were going to insist he got some rest, they would have to actively trade off. They needed another adult with combat skills.

"Sit in the control room?" Hunter raised an eyebrow, clearly annoyed. "I thought we just had this discussion about you getting some rest."

"Running the control panel isn't resting?" Eric blinked innocently at him. He was being purposefully obtuse, and they all knew it, but he wondered if either of them would call him on it.

Tony scoffed, but instead of arguing further, he grabbed the coffee pot and poured himself a cup before taking a swig of the still steaming liquid. It had to scald his mouth and throat, but he just scowled. "Fine, but Ava is on babysitting duty."

"I don't need a babysitter!" Eric squawked.

"Sure you don't, hon." Hunter shook his head. "I'll shoot her a text. She should bring over some yarn for you. Keep your hands moving so you don't crawl out of your skin."

"Do you think we can bribe her to slip a sleeping potion into his drink?" Tony smirked over at Hunter as he downed at least half of what was left in his mug.

"Probably."

"I hate both of you, you know that?" Eric groaned, tilting his head back to stare at the ceiling. Goddess, maybe they were right. Maybe he did need a break. He was tired. And he couldn't remember the last time he'd gone to bed without at least the niggling of a headache. It would be nice to be the one sitting at home biting their nails, waiting to see when their partner came home for once.

Scratch that.

Waiting around to see if Hunter and Tony would get into trouble out on patrol was *not* nice. It was fucking nerve wracking. Eric had never been so stressed in all his life. It was much worse than being out there and facing the vampires himself.

How the fuck does Hunter do this semi-regularly?

Well, it probably helped that Hunter was much less of a control freak than Eric. He'd always been far more relaxed, which was why they got on so well, even when they weren't dating.

"If you don't sit still, I am going to take Tony up on his suggestion and knock you out," Ava grumbled. But she wasn't much better. She was sitting behind the wall of monitors in the wheely chair, her leg bouncing up and down so the chair made a loud creaking noise. It was teeth-grindingly high pitched. Eric was going to have to toss that chair when no one was looking. He knew it was all the kids' favorite, but it was annoying as fuck, and he couldn't spend another night in this room with someone fidgeting nervously and the chair squeaking at every tiny movement. He'd lose his fucking mind.

"Bite me," Eric sniped. He clutched his crochet hook so tightly his hand was starting to cramp, and forget about the tension, it was way off from his usual. He was going to have to frog at least five rows on this fucking thing. Probably more like twenty. But Hunter had been on to something about keeping his hands busy. It kept Eric mostly calm until he saw the dots that were his boyfriends and his kids appearing in their respective patrol areas.

"We're set up at the hospital," Hunter reported, his tone relaxed, calm. Eric wondered how much of that was honest, and how much was for his benefit. It was always hard to tell with Hunter when he wasn't right in front of Eric. He was too good at modulating his voice.

"Okay." Eric breathed out, a little relieved. They'd made it there without incident, which was one hurdle covered. "It should be a quiet night there. So far it seems like Dash is getting his blood other ways. But without me in the area, I don't know how the newly turned will react."

"You think they'll go for the nearest source of blood?" Ava tilted her head up at the wall of screens. Eric couldn't see her face, but he knew what she was looking at because it was the same thing he was looking at. All the neutral normie dots that surrounded the living supernatural dots. He knew she was remembering what they'd learned recently—that humans were more appetizing than magical creatures. Freshly turned vamps would go for the highest populated areas. That's why Eric had sent Tony to the clubbing district.

"Yeah. Either they'll sniff out the blood bank shipment, or they'll head for the clubs. It depends on where they dig themselves out." His gaze flicked to the graveyards dotting Ironport. There were as many near the hospital as near the clubbing district. Eric didn't like that this was a coin toss. It was purely chance where the vamps went. A *heads, I win; tails, you lose* situation. "How's it looking where you're at, Tony?"

"Remind me when we get home that I fucking hate drunk people," Tony grunted. "What the fuck are you looking at? Turn around!" he snarled at someone who was either walking past him or standing in front of him in line. "I'm not talking about you. Mind your business."

Eric bit back a laugh, coughing into his fist. "Okay, sunset was about ten minutes ago. We'll know where they're headed in another ten minutes. Ava and I will keep an eye on things from here and let you know where they spawn at. That should give you a few minutes to get ready."

"Roger, roger," Hunter chirped at the same time Tony mumbled an annoyed "Fine."

CHAPTER 17

HUNTER WISHED he had joined a coven years ago, for perhaps the first time in his entire life. It would have given him the extra magic he needed to make this whole thing less nerve wracking. He wouldn't be entirely without concerns for his and the kids' safety, but he might feel more confident in his ability to protect them all.

The air around the hospital was too still. No sound of insects or raccoons in the dumpsters. Just the consistent creak of Kate's tennis shoes as she paced back and forth, and Nik's slow, steady breathing. It was making Hunter jittery. Nervous.

All he could hope was that the recently risen would head Tony's way, but even that felt like a terrible thing to want. That way led to his little brother. The one who had been sick the last few days. Hunter trusted Tony to protect the kids. To look after Chase when Hunter couldn't, but it didn't make him feel any more relaxed. He wished he could have been the one with Chase, but he wasn't in charge of the teams.

"Kate, I'm going to need you to sit still for about half a second," Hunter said softly. He was trying to keep his tone and his face from being confrontational, because he wasn't a fucking idiot. One didn't snap at either of the Regan sisters. Kalla and Kate were both well known for biting people's heads off with little to no provocation. Kalla had mostly grown out of the habit, but Kate was still young that she could go off at the drop of a hat. Goddess, he didn't fucking miss that about Kalla when they were younger. Especially when she used to go after Eric.

Kate's head whipped around, her dark-brown eyes—so much like her older sister's—narrowed in aggravation. "I'm just—"

"Don't care," Hunter cut her off with a shake of his head. He knew pulling rank here might make her even pissier, but honestly, they all needed to calm down for a bit. They weren't in danger. Yet. They might not be at all, if the vamps went the other direction. And besides, "We need to save our energy. If they come this way, you're not going to want to have wasted it pacing around."

"Fine." She huffed, crossing her arms over her chest as she stopped by Nik, leaning against the wall in the shadow of the overhang next to the loading dock at the back of the hospital. The bulb was out—either broken or dead—giving them plenty of cover without having staff call the police on them. Not that Kalla would let any units be deployed, but it was better if they went unnoticed.

"Do you think they'll come this way?" Nik asked. He didn't sound nervous, which was unusual for him. Hunter wondered if his fear had pushed him beyond that point. He wasn't even fidgeting with the front of his shirt like Hunter had seen him do in stressful situations.

"We've got a fifty-fifty shot," Kate said, answering for him. "There are about as many graves in this area as in the other side of town where the other team is."

"Do I want to know how you know how many graves are in each cemetery?" Hunter frowned. He supposed these kids had to think about shit like that. It was a part of their job after all. But he didn't have to like it. They'd all been forced to grow up too fast despite Eric's best efforts to keep that from happening. Kate shouldn't be counting graves, she should be worried about how she was going to sneak into one of the clubs downtown with a fake ID. She should be partying and getting into typical young adult trouble. But here she and Nik were, standing outside of a hospital, waiting for a blood delivery, talking about how many graves surrounded them.

Kate shrugged, pulling her phone out and opening what looked to be the Notes app based on the yellow background. "Some people build furniture."

"Counting graves isn't a hobby!" Hunter squawked.

"Is it an average or an exact count?" Nik leaned over her shoulder to get a better look at the numbers.

"Pretty close to exact. I try to update it at the start of every week." Kate scrubbed at her nose as if embarrassed by Nik's nearness, but she didn't push him away.

If Hunter wasn't so focused on the fact that she kept a fucking tally of how many graves were in any given cemetery, he might have more bandwidth to examine that. As far as he knew, none of Eric's kids were in relationships, but just because he didn't know it, didn't mean it wasn't happening. It would probably be weird for them to keep the "adults" in their lives up to date on who was dating who. Didn't mean Hunter wasn't curious. He wondered if Eric had noticed anything . . . Maybe he'd ask once they got back to the house.

"Where do you even *find* that information?" Surely it wasn't public record, right? Hunter wouldn't know, he'd never gone looking for something like that. It wasn't exactly something he needed to know on the regular. But someone whose very life could hinge on how many fresh dead bodies there were to turn into undead threats? Someone like Eric? Like Kate? Like Hunter's little brother? They all needed to know that. Hunter's stomach twisted at the reminder.

Kate shrugged again. "Kalla gave me access to the records for the area."

"All right folks," Eric said, his voice a gentle rumble into the com device in Hunter's ear. A reminder. He was barely holding it together, Hunter could hear it in his voice, but he doubted the kids noticed. Eric was too good for that. "Sun's been down for a bit now, they should be rising. Stay on alert."

Tony fucking hated this shit. It wasn't even so much the whole hunting thing. He was good at that, always had been. Nor was it the fact that he now had two young charges to look after—even if one of them was Bert, who seemed to despise him on some principle that Tony was unaware of. No, it was the club thing.

He hadn't been hunting in this kind of situation since he'd turned, and the music was too loud, pounding at his ears even from where they stood outside, leaning against a brick wall in an alley off the main road. Waiting. The smell of alcohol mixed with body odor, perfume, and too much Axe body spray—seriously, why the fuck did guys think that shit smelled good?—turned his stomach. If he didn't have to face off against a vamp soon, he was going to lose it.

"They don't even realize the danger they're in," Bert scoffed, a superior tone to his words that made Tony grind his teeth.

Of course, the normies didn't know the danger that lurked around them. They couldn't see the forest for the trees when they were surrounded by the paranormal and the supernatural. Most normies didn't even believe in ghosts, and that was the easiest of them to imagine was real from Tony's perspective. After all, ghosts were just lingering energy. The leftovers from a person who couldn't let go. But even those seemed outside of most normies' realm of imagining.

"They see what they want to," Chase murmured softly. He was a calming presence at Tony's side. Not relaxed, but not actively winding himself up the way Bert seemed to be. Tony didn't see how Eric put up with the kid day in and day out for years on end. It was untenable.

Bert snorted, rolling his eyes. "They don't even acknowledge the ones who go missing."

"Would you if you were in their shoes?" Chase pressed. It was exactly the question Tony wanted to ask, but he wasn't going to. Because he didn't need a fight with Eric's favorite in the middle of a hunt. It would only get someone hurt.

"What's the radar look like?" Tony asked Eric instead, tuning out the conversation between Bert and Chase and turning his senses to the street around them. He smelled normies, of course. But there were a couple werewolves, and one or two fae lingering around coupled with the electric smell of magic that tended to cling to witches. The supernatural mixed in with the humans, as normal as breathing. And all the while the humans didn't even see it. Wouldn't even recognize a vampire if it bit them in the neck.

"It's weird," Eric said, a note of unrest more prevalent in his voice than it had been earlier. He hadn't exactly been settled all night, but this was worse. Like he was sitting on the edge of his seat.

Tony heard Ava mumble something, but she must have had her mic off because he couldn't make out the words.

"What's weird?" Bert asked, suddenly all business, like he had detected the same thing in Eric's voice that Tony had. It should be reassuring to know that someone other than Tony could read Eric so easily, but it made Tony jealous instead. A green monster writhed in his chest at the reminder that he hadn't known Eric as long as some of the others.

"There haven't been any spawnings yet," Ava answered when Eric seemed unable because he'd started muttering to himself. Someone was tapping away on the keyboard, likely Ava given Eric's aversion to technology. "Stop touching that," Ava hissed, followed by what sounded like a slap.

"I'm just trying to get a better view of the area."

"You're going to fuck with Hunter's settings."

"Please don't fuck with Hunter's settings," Hunter piped up, and Tony had to bite back a fond smile at the antics of this weird group. This strange little family. He liked them, even though he wasn't one of them. Would risk his life to protect them. Already had.

Something thumped low and soft in his chest like he was on the precipice of some new understanding. Like he had all the pieces to a puzzle, he just needed to put them together. But he couldn't put his finger on how. He couldn't—

"They're here," Hunter's hurried whisper broke through whatever thoughts Tony might have had, freezing his blood and setting his heart racing.

A few hours ago, he'd been kissing Hunter in the forge. Pulling him in so close, Tony could feel Hunter's heartbeat against his chest. A short while after, he'd been avoiding Hunter's gaze in the kitchen, trying to sort out his mixed-up feelings before Eric noticed something between them had shifted. It didn't feel like cheating but . . .

And now, Hunter was in trouble. Vampires heading his way.

Fear crawled up Tony's spine.

No. *No.* Hunter was supposed to be safe. Eric had sent him to the hospital where he wouldn't see any action.

"Fuck!" Nik hissed into his own mic, and from where Tony stood on the other side of town, his heart in his throat, he could hear the sounds of a scuffle.

"How many are there?" Eric asked, his words calm but quick, leaving absolutely no room for argument.

"Five," Kate responded, but Tony was hardly listening by that point. He was trying to figure out how long it would take him to run across town to get to Hunter and the others. If he could make it before the vampires tore through their tiny group.

They shouldn't have split up like this. It was too fucking dangerous. It left them vulnerable. Open to being more easily outnumbered. It was taking too much of a risk, especially with the kids as untested as they were, and with Hunter not being a combat-ready witch.

Could Tony even make it there before the vampires sucked all three of them dry? No. No. It'd be fine. Hunter was an adult. He had spells and magic on his side. And Nik and Kate weren't amateurs. They'd trained with Eric the longest outside of Bert. They knew what to do. They wouldn't panic. They had this in the bag.

Just breathe, Tony. It'll be okay. They've got this.

"Eric, should we head that way?" Bert was asking when Tony was finally able to hear past his own shallow breaths again.

Fuck. He didn't have time to panic like that. Not when it was someone's neck on the line. And just as he gasped in another deep breath, the hairs at the base of his skull stood on end.

"We can't," he told Bert before Eric answered.

Bert turned to fix him with a hard, annoyed look. His brows pulled together, his lips pursed. He opened his mouth, and Tony could already hear the grating way that Bert would try to cut him down.

They didn't have time for a fight, and Tony wasn't going to give in to the urge to argue. "We've got our own blood-suckers coming this way, kid."

"How many?" Chase pushed away from the wall, his dark eyes so wide in his pale face, they practically swallowed up all his features.

He had no doubt felt the same signs Tony had. Curious how even as a werewolf he was able to sense vampires the way he had as a Venator. He wondered if that was a hold over, or if all werewolves could. Maybe he'd figure that out later. Or maybe it would fade with time.

"Can't tell. What's the radar look like on your end, pretty boy?"

"I still don't see anything," Eric said, an edge of panic creeping into his voice. "He's found a way to block their signature again."

"Welp, we'll just have to meet them halfway." Tony pushed off from the wall as well, rolling out his neck and shoulders as he turned in the direction of the hair-raising feeling at the other end of the alley. Away from the normies, thank the Goddess.

"Act as a barrier between them and the normies." Bert nodded and settled at Tony's side as if he'd always been there.

Something hummed along Tony's nerves when both boys fell in a step behind him as they started toward the approaching threat, but there was no time to examine that either. Not when there were bloodsuckers coming their way.

"Head them off at the pass," Chase said in agreement.

"Exactly." Tony's lips peeled back from his teeth in a snarl. Then his long strides were eating up the pavement, his vision sharpening to peer through the shadows at the small horde of vampires approaching them from the warehouse district.

CHAPTER 18

THE VAMPIRES DESCENDED upon them in a way only vultures who'd found fresh roadkill could. All sharp fangs and taloned hands. And Tony didn't have a single moment to overthink what was happening. He was immediately inundated with too many swiping hands. Snapping jaws.

It was easy to fall into it. To lose himself in the constant movement of fighting.

A sloppy fist to his jaw that would no doubt leave behind a bruise.

Stake to the heart.

Dust.

Clawed fingers around his throat, pressing at his windpipe, digging nails into his skin.

A kick to the vampire's stomach. His paperback warm in his hand, protecting his neck.

Stake to the heart.

Dust.

His back slammed to the brick wall, knocking the wind out of him, making his ears ring.

A vampire's fangs at his neck, using the distraction, digging in. The venom going right to his blood stream. His vision swam for a moment, then nothing. No dizzy high. No happy daze. Just the cold of the brick on Tony's back. The ache of the fangs in his neck.

"Huh. That's new," Tony muttered to himself, getting a better grip on his stake and slamming it through the brittle bones of the vampire's shoulder blade, right into its heart. Dust.

It was brutal. Methodical. Nowhere near as fluid and efficient as Eric's movements, but it got the job done.

Another leech replaced the last, drawn to the scent of Tony's blood on the air. Then another, and another. Ignoring the two young Venator in favor of the werewolf. Crowding in so close, Tony felt like he was looking at a Hydra instead of a vampire. Fangs dripped with venom. Eyes red with bloodlust.

Tony snarled, snapping his jaws in return, showing off his own fangs, but the vampires were all too far gone. Pushing, pressing, shoving forward until his arms were pinned to his chest. If he wasn't careful, they'd squash him before they even got a bite out of him.

"Hey, kids," Tony called to Bert and Chase. He couldn't see them over the heads of the vampires, some of which were far taller than him, but he knew they were there. Eric had trained them too well to leave a man behind when his back was against the wall like this.

"We got you," Bert answered right before a vamp at the back burst into a cloud of dust, followed by another.

A smile ticked up the corners of Tony's lips. He was warmed by the way Bert and Chase had his back. Before coming to Ironport, that wasn't a thing he got to have. He was always on his own. Just Tony McMahon against the world. Now he had Eric. He had Hunter. He had the kids. That meant something, but there was no time to think about that. They had to get through this horde of vampires.

Another got close enough to sink their fangs into Tony's neck, scraping at his skin, but that also put them at perfect staking range. If he could just get his fucking arms up from where they were trapped against his chest by the press of bodies around him. He lifted a knee, jamming it into the vampire's stomach, but it didn't do anything. They just kept drinking. His head was starting to spin from blood loss. His vision darkened around the edges.

Another puff of dust. Another. Tony lost track of them as his vision swam and then Bert and Chase were before him.

"Hey, Tony, you okay?" Bert asked, real concern in his voice as he and Chase reached for Tony to keep him from sliding down the wall.

"Yeah." Tony sucked in a deep breath, hoping it would stop him from feeling like he was going to puke.

It didn't. That was never a good sign.

Usually, his Venator gene would help him recover rapidly from blood loss, a fun side effect of that nature, but he wasn't Venator anymore. He was a werewolf, and it appeared wolves didn't regenerate their blood stores as quickly, even if he could feel the puncture marks on his neck already closing.

"Sit him down," he heard Chase say as he and Bert helped lower Tony to the ground slowly. "Do you have anything on you? Something with sugar."

"I've got like . . . some 3 Musketeers minis." The sound of shuffling followed Bert's words, then one of the kids stuffed a candy bar into Tony's mouth, and he chewed automatically even if he hated fucking nougat.

The sugar hit his stomach a moment later, and the buzzing in his ears dried up, making it so he could hear what was going on around him. That included the panicked sound of Eric asking over and over what happened. "Talk to me! Is everyone okay?!"

"Tony just got a little woozy from blood loss," Chase reported as kindly as he could manage. It didn't make Tony feel any less foolish. He shouldn't have let the vamps that close. Not when he didn't know what the venom would do to him anymore. For all he knew, it could have made him sick. Could have killed him. And he'd taken the chance. He was sure Eric would have something to say about that once they got back to the dorm. Tony was not looking forward to the lecture. Damn it.

"Tony?" Eric sounded scared, worried.

"I'm good, princess. Just a little dizzy. Looks like we're in the clear here," Tony said around a tongue that felt too big. Unwieldy. Dry. Sticking to the roof of his mouth. Well, served him right, he'd remember that the next time he decided to let a vampire snack on him.

"Okay," Eric responded, relief coloring his tone. "You should stay where you're at, make sure that part of town doesn't see any more action."

"Yes, sir." Bert's words were so crisp and formal, Tony half expected them to be accompanied by a salute.

Eric let out a soft, relieved sigh, then he asked, "Hunter? How is it looking on your end?"

"We're in the clear . . ." Kate responded almost immediately, but her words drifted off like that wasn't all. Like there was something else. She made a noise in the back of her throat, slightly panicked.

"Kate. What is it?" Eric pressed.

"Hunter is hurt," Nik answered, his tone forced into something calm and collected.

Tony's heart kicked in his chest, rising in his throat. Terror gripped his lungs. Hunter was hurt.

"*How* hurt?" Eric's voice shook, almost as much as Tony's hands.

When Tony looked up from where he'd dropped his stake near his feet, he met Chase's wide, dark eyes. They were so round, they swallowed up his face. Scared of what might have happened to his brother. And Tony? Tony lost it. What little control he had over himself was gone in an instant.

The wolf leapt forward from his chest, his bones snapping, rearranging. A pained howl ripped through the air.

"What was that?" Eric whispered into the mic on his end, and even without the device still in the wolf's ear, Tony could hear it. He could hear *everything*. The passing of cars. The soft shush of leaves. The skittering of creatures in the night.

He lifted his nose to the air and drank in the scent of piss and trash and death. The smell of the city—of Ironport. And above all of it, a scent he'd recognize anywhere.

Chase and Bert stood in his way, crowding in too close where they'd been looking after him a moment ago, their mouths open, eyes wide and terrified.

"What's going on?" Eric's voice sounded panicked again, but the wolf was beyond listening. He'd found the scent of the witch.

Ink and petrichor. Hunter Delacroix was easy to pick out among all the other scents. It had lingered on the wolf's clothes, in his nose, and he couldn't forget it even if he wanted to.

"He shifted," Chase whispered.

"Calm him down. You need to calm him down!" Eric's words shook with fear, but the wolf didn't care. He was going to find the witch and protect him.

"Hey there, big guy," Bert said, holding up his hands and moving closer to the wolf as if he meant to grab onto him. The wolf wasn't having any of that.

He snapped his jaws at Bert, a warning, and let out a short, sharp bark. When Bert faltered, he and Chase both taking a step back, the wolf brushed passed them and took off at a run. Following the smell of the witch through the city. Ignoring shouts and beeps as he wound his way through the streets.

"He's headed your way," Eric's voice still sounded muzzy when Hunter finally managed to sit up against the wall, his head throbbing.

"Who is headed our way?" Kate asked. She was standing in front of Hunter like a barrier, a stake held so tight in her hand that her knuckles were turning pale.

"Tony."

Nik patted Hunter's shoulder lightly, his hands gentle as if he was afraid he might further injure him. "Oh, well it'll take him a bit—"

"He shifted." There was a tightness to Eric's words that made Hunter's stomach turn. He was going to be sick. Either from the concussion or from how scared everyone around him was acting. It was just a matter of which would get to him first.

"Get me up," Hunter ordered Nik and Kate.

"What are you talking about?" Kate hissed. "You can't take on a wolf."

Hunter shook his head and started pushing to his feet without her assistance. He didn't think he'd *have* to take on Tony. If he was coming this way, it was because he was worried about Hunter. All Hunter had to do was prove he was safe.

"Hunter," Eric said, a warning.

"I've got this, hon." Even as his hands were trembling and his knees felt weak, Hunter got to his feet and pressed forward. "How far is he?"

"A mile. He's moving fast." Eric was nervous. Likely pacing the control room. "Don't set him off, Hunter. If you've got to stun him, do it. He'll get the fuck over it."

"I'm not going to need to do that." But he wasn't sure

about that. Something in his gut told him he'd be fine. A memory of the warmth that passed between him and Tony in the forge. The way Tony had leaned in, seeking his touch how he did with Eric sometimes. Needy. Soft. He just wanted to be taken care of. But he seemed unable to let himself show it.

"Hunter. I'm not fucking kidding. He's dangerous when he gets like this. Don't let him—"

"Eric," Hunter cut him off, his words sharp and crisp. "Shut the fuck up and let me focus."

Eric grunted but said nothing else and Hunter turned his attention to the tree line to the east, at the other side of town. He could hear Nik and Kate holding their breath behind him, but he kept his own slow, relaxed, willing his heart not to beat hard in his chest. Tony just needed to see he was okay.

A giant blond wolf charged through the trees, his coat glossy and shining under the yellow streetlights, looking golden. Tony was breathtaking like this, as much as he was when he was fighting, when he was angry and feral. Hunter held up his hands in a sign of surrender as the wolf wheeled to a stop in front of him.

A low growl rumbled from Tony's chest. A warning.

"I know, sweetheart," Hunter murmured gently. He held himself very, very still. Not reaching for Tony, hoping the kids behind him would follow his lead. "I know I scared you. I'm sorry."

Tony barked at him, baring his teeth. They glistened with saliva in the moonlight.

"Right, of course not." Hunter had no idea what Tony was saying, but he could guess. "But either way, I'm okay. See? Upright and all."

Pushing his golden head into Hunter's stomach, Tony whined lightly, the sound only more determined when Hunter hissed as he wobbled on his feet. He let out a slow breath, his hands falling to brush through the fur on the back of Tony's head, gentle and soothing.

The whine shifted to a pleased rumble, slowing and going higher and higher as Tony shifted back until Hunter's hands were brushing through Tony's curls instead of his fur. "I know, baby. Shh. Shhh." Hunter murmured, brushing the strands back from Tony's face until he could look down at him, clasp his jaw lightly, and force him to meet his gaze. "I'm okay. Really. Just hit my head."

"Okay," Tony whispered, voice rough.

"But you left the kids behind without protection," Hunter said, a gentle warning in his tone. It was unacceptable, and Tony knew it.

"I'm sorry." The words were muffled by the way Tony had buried his face into Hunter's shirt.

"You really need to speak to your sire. We can't have this happen again."

Tony sighed, his shoulders sagging as his arms wrapped tight around Hunter's waist, unwilling or unable to let him go yet. "Okay."

"Good." Hunter leaned down to brush a kiss to Tony's curls, then wiggled out of his flannel and draped it over Tony's naked shoulders.

"Kalla is picking up Bert and Chase. I want everyone home ASAP," Eric ordered.

"Yes, sir," Tony mumbled grumpily.

Hunter huffed a laugh, relief washing over him as he pulled Tony to his feet. His fingers smoothed over the bruises already appearing on Tony's neck and jaw. "Let's get to the car."

"What about mine?"

"We'll pick it up tomorrow morning. You need rest. And you can't drive naked. What if you get pulled over?"

Tony grunted but let Hunter lead him back to where he'd parked and shuffle him into the passenger seat as the kids climbed into the back.

Chapter 19

"YOU NEED TO SIT DOWN, you're giving me a headache," Ava said, but there was no bite to her words, just something quiet and resigned. Like she understood better than any what Eric was going through. Which was true in a sense. She'd never been through this situation before, but she was his closest friend, his Platonic soulmate (with a capital P). She seemed to always be able to feel what he was feeling.

"I shouldn't have let them go out without me. I shouldn't have let Hunter go out. I knew better." He did know better. He knew Hunter wasn't trained for this. And Tony wasn't good at team sports. The wolf simmered under the surface at all times, waiting for a chance to take over. This all could have gone so fucking wrong in so many ways. It was only by sheer luck that it hadn't. They might not get so lucky next time. He couldn't take this chance again.

"I know what you're thinking, and you need to stop it right now." Ava had risen from her chair and grabbed him by the shoulders, but he wasn't sure when. She met his gaze with narrowed, accusing blue eyes, her brows drawn down, her lips pursed into a disapproving frown.

"You couldn't possibly—"

"You can't take this on all by yourself. You know better than that now. You've grown, remember? You can't fall back on old habits." She gave him a little shake.

She was right of course. But it would be so easy to slip back into how things had been for most of his life. He didn't have to be alone, and Eric knew that now. The people around him had proven time and again that they'd have his back, that they'd be by his side, that this fight wasn't just his. But it would be easier if that weren't true. At least then he'd know they were safe.

"Eric." Ava's nails dug into his shoulders. "Don't make me hurt you."

"I'm not going to run off on my own again," he grumbled, but even to him it sounded hollow. He couldn't promise that, and they both knew it. Because it was in his nature to try to do things by himself. It was how he'd been raised. Even if he knew he had people now that he could count on, people who loved him, the urge would always be there to take matters into his own hands. And one day that urge might be too much for even him to fight against. Not today. But he couldn't make any promises about tomorrow or next week.

She squinted at him, her mouth downturned further like she didn't quite believe him. "They'll be back soon. Everyone is mostly unharmed. That's the best we can ask for."

Eric nodded. It *wasn't* the best they could ask for. Not really. The best they could ask for was that Hunter and Ava took up Icarus Ashthorne's offer to move to Moondale, that Tony and Lu stayed in Miami, that none of Eric's kids ever tested positive for the Venator gene. The best they could ask for was that he was alone in this fight in more ways than one.

He wouldn't say that out loud, but he thought maybe Ava knew what he was thinking anyway because she smacked him upside the head. "Stop that."

"I didn't say anything."

"You didn't have to." She shook her head and headed for the door so they could go down and meet the teams when they got back. He scuffed his slippered feet against the old wooden boards of the attic as he followed behind her. "I know you, dingus."

"Yeah, I guess you do." And it was terrifying, even for all Eric and Ava had been this way for years. It still struck him every time how scary it was to have someone know him inside and out that way. She saw all there was of him to see, the good and the bad. She saw his fears and his insecurities, and she loved him anyway. Ava was really the only reason he'd gotten through his disastrous breakup with Kalla Regan. Because as much of a fuckup as Kalla made him feel, Ava loved him anyway. She wanted to be around him, to talk to him, to know him, no matter what. Sometimes a best friend made all the difference.

"Oh buddy." Ava stopped on the steps from the second floor down to the first and let out a low whistle. "That answers one question."

"What question?" Eric peeked around her and sighed at the sight of Tony standing mostly naked in the hall next to the shoe rack, Hunter's flannel tied around his waist. The light shimmered off his top surgery scars, and Eric trod on Ava's foot to force her to look away. She didn't mean anything by it. But she was the curious sort, and she forgot sometimes what her face was doing.

Ava cleared her throat and shifted her attention to the kids instead.

"Only fairies get to keep their fucking clothes when they shift," Tony grumbled, heat in his cheeks as he ducked behind Hunter a little more.

"Do I even want to know how you know that?" Hunter chuckled. He nudged Tony closer to Eric, his brows raised high on his face. He'd lost his glasses at some point during the fight, probably broken beyond repair. Good thing he had a backup set.

"You aren't the only one who knows shit, Glinda." Tony bumped Hunter with his shoulder but refused to look at him.

Whatever had happened out there, it hadn't solved the way they danced around each other.

"Wow, an Oz reference? Really? Do you know *any* other famous witches?" Hunter chuckled lightly.

"Sabrina. Tabitha. Piper. Prue. Paige. Phoebe. Willow." Tony tilted his chin back to grin victoriously at Hunter, and Hunter's soft chuckles turned into all out laughter, transforming his face into something happier.

"Have a thing about *Charmed*, do you?"

Tony colored further.

"Or do you just have a thing for witches in general?" Hunter waggled his eyebrows, leaning into Tony's space.

"All right, that's enough," Ava cut in with a loud clap, and Eric was brought harshly back to the reality in which they had an audience for their antics. Goddess, he could watch these two idiots banter back and forth for hours. "No flirting in front of the children."

Tony scoffed, rolling his eyes. "We weren't—"

"She's right. The kids have school in the morning, and we should get you and Hunter cleaned up before bed." Eric shook his head and did his best not to be disappointed when Hunter nodded and Tony mumbled his agreement before following him up the steps.

Tony wasn't entirely certain how he'd gotten where he was— cleaned up and tucked into bed between Eric and Hunter. Both of whom were snoring lightly, their legs and arms tangled where they splayed over his middle. He had to admit he liked it. It was nice to be this close to them. Nice to feel snuggled safely and warmly between two other people.

People who could not only take care of themselves but him as well.

It made him feel . . . settled. Which wasn't something he was used to.

It also made him uncomfortable. Being close to them like this, knowing they cared about what happened to him, and he in turn cared about what happened to them . . . It meant he couldn't shake off the reminder that he'd agreed to reach out to his sire. That he'd put their lives in danger tonight because he'd been neglecting the beast in his chest. Ignoring it and hoping it would go away.

The trouble with that was . . . he didn't exactly have her number. Nor did he remember how to get back to the Night Market. Those days that he'd been afraid and doped up on vamp venom were a terrifying blur that he was doing his best to keep from his mind. They were so colored with what Dash had *done* to him—how the vamp venom had made Tony go willingly, made him *beg* for it—that he couldn't focus on much else.

That left one option. Sage. Who probably wouldn't even answer anyway, because they were a bitch like that. But Tony had to try. At least if he left a message, Sage could get back to him via text.

He rolled carefully over Eric, grabbing his phone from the nightstand on the way.

"Where're ya goin'?" Eric mumbled, half asleep, as he reached for Tony. His hands opened and closed in a grabbing motion. He was unbearably cute like this. Soft. Vulnerable. That's why Tony had to do this. Because Eric and Hunter and the rest of Eric's little Scooby gang trusted him with their lives. He couldn't fuck this up like he'd fucked up so much else.

"Bathroom," he lied. He wasn't an idiot. He knew the moment Eric realized where he was off to, he'd sit up and try to help, or at least comfort Tony while he made the call. Tony didn't need that. This was something he had to do on his own.

He waited until he was alone in the hallway before he unlocked his phone screen and only stopped when the hair on the back of his neck stood on end. A warning that there was a vampire near—

Janet gave him a wave from the other end of the hall. Her fanged smile glinted in the nightlights Eric insisted on so the kids wouldn't trip and fall on the way to the bathroom.

"Shouldn't you be sleeping?" he hissed, annoyed that the vampire-ex-mayor-turned-ally was lurking about the halls at all hours of the night.

Janet shrugged and was suddenly beside him, her vampire speed making her seem to appear at his side in a blink. "Shouldn't you?"

"I'm making a phone call."

"Yes. I see that. To your sire, I'm assuming?" She tilted her head knowingly, blond hair falling over her shoulder. He couldn't believe he'd missed all the signs of her other nature before. It was plain as day now that he knew it was there. Too-perfect skin. Too-bright eyes. The sharp teeth. The long nails. And the ease with which she moved, fluid like gravity couldn't touch her.

"Something like that. You didn't answer my question."

"Vampires don't sleep." She scoffed and rolled her eyes.

"So you're prowling the halls in the middle of the night like a totally sane person?" Tony sniped. He didn't want to deal with Janet. She was fucking weird, and he didn't have the energy after tonight's fiasco of a patrol. He needed to call Sage and get back into bed before Hunter and Eric knew he was gone.

"Someone's got to take the night shift." She gave another dainty shrug, then breezed past him as if that had been her plan all along. Over her shoulder she called, "Plus, the house gets lonely" before disappearing down the steps.

"Whatever the fuck that means." Tony shook his head and turned back to his dormant phone, unlocking it again and pulling up the contacts to hit Sage's number in the recent calls list.

Only to stall out when Sage answered with a "Tony, what's wrong?" after the second ring.

Why was Sage answering the phone? It wasn't even that it was too late for them to be up, it was just . . . they never answered the phone. Getting them to talk on the phone a few months ago when Tony needed advice about the vamp venom flowing through his bloodstream had been like pulling teeth. What changed?

"Tony?" Sage asked again, their voice sharp, worried.

"I uh . . . I wasn't expecting you to pick up."

Sage snorted, and Tony could imagine them rolling their glowing green eyes, brushing rainbow-dyed hair back from their face. "Yeah, well. I've got to wait for the ovens to go off anyway. Might as well have some company while Corey's out."

"Huh?"

"At the bakery . . ." They paused, seeming to realize that Tony had no idea what they were talking about, and let out a short laugh. "I've got a lot to tell you. But first, what were you calling about?"

Tony shook himself, leaning more heavily against the wall. "I need to get in touch with my sire. I can't—" He bit his tongue until he tasted metal, hating himself for this weakness. "I can't control it. And I can't afford that while I'm out fighting vampires."

Sage made a soft, thoughtful sound in the back of their throat, which was usually accompanied by a curious head tilt. "I'll text you her number. But I'm not sure how much she can do for you if you don't want to hitch your wagon to her pack."

"I don't."

"Figured as much." Sage chuckled, their clothes shifting as they probably shook their head in fond exasperation. "But wolves are pack animals. So even if you don't join up with Lowell, you're going to have to find your own. A team. A family. It's in your nature now, even if it wasn't before."

"That's stupid as fuck, you know that, right? Turning doesn't just—"

"Change a person's biology? Come on, Tony, you're smarter than that. And you're smarter than to sit here and tell me that shifting someone's biology doesn't change them. You transitioned, you know how it works."

"I'm still the same person I was before," Tony grunted.

"I know you are, but you have to admit, some things are different for you. You're more confident, more sure of yourself and your instincts. I know part of that is getting out from under your asshole father's thumb, but it's also about how you feel about yourself. Isn't it?" Sage was being too calm, too understanding.

Tony grumbled but didn't respond otherwise.

"Anyway, point being, you've been changed on a cellular level. That's going to have some side effects." It sounded so much like what Eric and Hunter had already said to him, but Tony still didn't like it. Maybe Lowell would have a different answer for him tomorrow when he called her.

"I'm not an animal."

"No. But a pack doesn't always mean other wolves, either. Lowell and her group might not be for you, but maybe someone else is." Sage sounded like they were trying to allude to a point, but Tony was too fucking tired to be bothered with the mind games.

"What the fuck are you trying to say?"

"Gee, I don't know, Tony." Sage scoffed. "Why don't you use that head of yours as something other than a place for your luscious locks?"

"They are pretty great, aren't they?"

"Fuck off." Sage chuckled, and there was more noise on the other end like they were shaking their head. "Can I tell you what I've been up to yet? Or is this call going to be all about you?"

"Fine. Go ahead." Tony sank down the wall until he was sitting against it.

"I moved to Eventide."

"What the fuck? Why?! I thought you liked it in Miami?"

"I did, but there was . . ." They hummed, displeased with something they had been about to say. "I was worried about you. I'm about a half hour away now. If you need me, I'm here."

Tony's breath caught in his throat, his hand trembling around the phone he held to his ear.

"But also," Sage moved on, knowing full well Tony wasn't good with emotions and it was best to coast on by them, "there was family shit to deal with here. So I moved home. I'm living with this girl I knew from when we were kids."

"Got yourself a girlfriend, huh?"

"Ew. No. Corey is . . . Well, I barely like her. And she'd sooner see me dead. But let's just say we have a common enemy. Anyway, she owns a bakery, so I'm helping out."

"That sounds nice." It also didn't sound anything like what Sage was doing in Miami. Hiding away in their room behind a wall of monitors, paranoid constantly. Tony had never asked who was after them, but he figured it had something to do with coming home to deal with "family shit."

"It's not terrible."

CHAPTER 20

"WILL IT WORK?" Eric asked, fingering the net carefully. There was a slight throbbing behind his eyes, exhaustion clinging to him, unwilling to let go. He forced it aside and focused on the net.

It was heavier than he'd thought it would be, likely because of the material they'd had to make it from. Some kind of braided metal filament that was far more flexible than Eric thought possible. He was continually amazed by Hunter's ingenuity, but this wasn't just Hunter. This was Tony too. They'd both sat down and dedicated their minds to the problem of Dash. To coming up with a way to protect not just themselves, but the kids, and Eric.

"It *better* fucking work," Tony grumbled, his chair creaking under his weight. "I haven't spent that many hours braiding since Lu went through her Rapunzel phase a few years back."

"We agreed we'd never speak of that!" Lu shouted from the kitchen where the kids were working on lunch. They'd shoved Eric out when he offered to help, saying they'd get it, but he didn't think he trusted them to use the stove by themselves. Yeah, they were all technically adults, but he didn't know if any of them even knew how to turn on the burners. He'd left the door between the library and the kitchen cracked on the off chance someone started a fire.

It gave Hunter and Tony time to give Eric the rundown on the net sprawled across the four-person table in the library. It was a work of art. A combination of science and magic unlike anything Eric had seen before. Maybe the most impressive thing Hunter had ever made. Eric wanted to tell him that. Wanted to praise Hunter and Tony for the work they put in, for the effort, but he knew they'd both shy away from it. Shrug it off. They'd have to work on that later. Now, they had bigger issues to deal with.

"No," Tony returned, his head turned so he could glare through the crack in the double doors from the library into the kitchen. "You *asked* me never to mention it again. I never agreed."

"I hate you." Lu hissed, but there was little real venom in her tone, just the disgusted fondness of a younger sister being teased by her older brother. It made something in Eric's chest ache. He'd never had that. Never would. He had the kids, true, but it wasn't the same. It never could be the same as having a sibling who loved him. And now that Oliver was back, so was the reminder that Eric wasn't an only child.

"Right back at you, brat!"

"Aww you had a Rapunzel phase?" Nik teased, and Eric didn't have to see him and Lu to imagine the way he'd tug at the ends of her hair, and she would lash out. "OW!"

"Don't pull my hair, you dick," Lu snarled.

"You didn't have to smack me, jeez, Lu." Nik huffed, but he didn't sound hurt, and the group moved back into their quiet, companionable chatter. Gentle bickering was broken up by the sounds of pots and pans. Eric didn't need to get involved. They had it covered. It was . . . comfortable.

Eric chuckled, shaking his head, and returned to the net on the table. "All right, tell me how it works then? How do I activate it?"

"You don't need to do anything special." Hunter shrugged, tapping at the metal pieces on each point of the net

—twelve in total. They glimmered in the yellowed lights of the library, warm and solid, and Eric could just make out the markings scrawled on them. Some rune, or emblem. Something he didn't recognize, but Hunter was putting his faith and their safety in it. Eric had no doubt it would work. "These will do all the heavy lifting. I've already imbued them with the magic they'll need to do their thing. Combined with the iron, they should act as a cage to help us hold a vampire until you can put some restraints on them and get them back to the house."

"Not the lab?" Eric frowned, brushing hair back from his face.

"We decided it'd be better if the council didn't know what we're doing," Tony supplied, his eyes flicking back to the crack in the door. The noise from the kitchen was still pouring through, covering most of their lowered voices. But if someone walked into the house, they'd know something was going on, and Janet was always lurking around. Eric wasn't sure how much they could trust her.

"We can't be sure they aren't still on Dash's payroll. Just because Janet left, doesn't mean he hasn't turned your brother to his side." Hunter didn't look at Eric when he said it. He was staring off over Eric's shoulder like he was afraid to see the hurt in Eric's eyes at what that could mean.

His own brother—his own blood—working with the enemy. It didn't hurt as much as Hunter probably thought it ought to. In fact, there was . . . *nothing*. No ache. No stabbing pain. No sense of betrayal. Not even any anger. Just a hole where the brotherhood that should have been between Eric and Oliver would have resided, and that emptiness was what actually hurt. The knowledge that Eric had never been given the chance to know his brother, and now he'd likely never get it. Maybe that was worse. Maybe it meant Eric was broken. Maybe he should feel something for the man he hardly knew, but he didn't. He didn't miss him. He wasn't betrayed by him working with the enemy. He was just . . . empty.

He shook himself. He could worry about that later. "Okay, that makes sense." Eric reached for the net, pulling it closer so it scraped against the table. It was warm under his fingers, the iron itching at his senses. Another thing perhaps he and vampires had in common. "So I just throw it over the vamp and—"

"Not over them." Hunter frowned, his dark eyes finally meeting Eric's, and Eric thought he saw a flash of pity, of understanding there. Like Hunter had been witness to all the terrible things that had gone through Eric's head at the thought that Oliver might be working with Dashfield B.M. Chadwick. But that wasn't possible. Mind reading wasn't Hunter's gift.

"Just throw it on the ground," Tony supplied. His own tone was careful, and Eric hated them both a bit in that moment. The feeling was vile and sharp in his chest. He hated how they *saw* him. How they thought they understood. They couldn't possibly. They had their siblings. A family bond unlike anything Eric would ever get to experience. They had no idea what he was feeling. He just—he wanted to be left the fuck alone, was that too much to ask?

Eric bit the inside of his cheek to keep from saying something he knew he'd regret. He didn't want to fight his boyfriends. They were trying to help. All they were doing was giving a shit about him, and he shouldn't rail against it so much. But this subject was far touchier than anything else, and his overall exhaustion only added to it.

"And maneuver the vampire onto it?" That would be easier than trying to throw it over a vampire and hoping they didn't wiggle out from underneath.

"Exactly." Hunter nodded.

"So when will we test this?"

"Tonight." Tony rubbed at his face. "I've got a shift at the mechanics', but I'll be in the area. If you need backup, call."

"We're assuming you don't want to take the kids out when you do this," Hunter added.

"You'd be right." Eric leaned back, his face tilted to the ceiling. The kids were going to lose their shit when they saw him walk out without anyone. All he could hope was that he'd manage to catch a vampire on the first try, and they could find Dash before this shit got any worse.

"We'll get this sorted, hon." Hunter's grip was warm and firm on his shoulder, a comfort. "Just catch the vampire and let the science twins do the rest. Right?" He held up his fist for Tony to fist bump.

"We're not calling ourselves that. Stop it." Tony rolled his eyes and headed for the door, leaving Hunter with his hand raised, unbumped. "I'll give you a lift into town, pretty boy. Be ready by five," he called over his shoulder before exiting to the kitchen. "What the fuck have you gremlins done to this place? It's a mess!"

"We're just making—" Bert started at the same time Lu snapped, "It's lunchtime, we—" at the same time Kate said, "We live here. We can do what—"

"Don't care. Clean this shit up. Eric isn't your maid, and he's got enough shit to do without cleaning up after you little shits." Tony clomped across the tiles, not giving a backward glance to the chaos he left in his wake.

"Do you think he's okay?" Eric asked Hunter after a moment.

"No. I don't think he is." Hunter sighed, his rings glinting as he ran his fingers through his hair. "But . . . none of us are. Are we?"

"No. Guess not."

"I didn't realize this was where you worked," an unfamiliar voice called from above where Tony was currently underneath an old Dodge Charger that everyone else in the shop refused to touch for the entire month Tony had been out sick. Not that he could blame them—the owner was a complete asshole. Picky and unwilling to compromise on the work they needed done to the car.

Tony sighed, thunking his head against the dolly he'd used to slide under the engine block. He didn't have to be familiar with that rasping, scratchy voice to know who it belonged to. "How the fuck did you find it then, Lowell?"

"Sage." Lowell leaned over the top of the car, peering down at him through the space between metal to meet his gaze with a pair of sharp brown eyes.

"Of fucking course." Why would Tony have expected anything else from his best and pretty much only friend? Especially after what Sage had said about flying from Miami to be closer in case he needed them. They had always been the mother hen sort, only made worse by the amount they knew about Tony's history.

"Are you going to come out here and talk to me, or are we going to keep chatting around spark plugs and grease pans?"

"You say that like you know shit about cars," Tony grumbled, pushing out from under the car and sitting up to lean against the front grill. Lowell had moved to sit on the bench across from his workspace, making it easy to meet her eyes.

"Are you assuming I don't know anything about cars because I'm a woman? Because I've got to say, McMahon, I didn't take you for the misogynistic—"

"Give it a rest." With an eye roll, Tony pulled the rag from his back pocket and wiped grease from his hands. "My little sister could change oil and spark plugs before she was old enough to drive. It's got nothing to do with gender and everything to do with the fact that you look like you just came down off a mountain with nothing but a backpack and a canteen."

Lowell tilted her head, steel-gray hair falling into her eyes for a moment before she brushed it away. "Fine. You're right." She shrugged. "Why learn to fix my own car when I can pay triple A?"

"Fair point." Everybody had their thing. For Tony, it was cars. For Hunter, it seemed to be science. Eric . . . Tony wasn't sure about Eric. They'd been messing around for a few weeks now solid, and he still wasn't sure what Eric was like outside of work mode. He never seemed to turn it off. Not fully anyway. He was always worrying about the kids, or about the increase in vamp activity, or thinking up lesson plans, or . . .

Well, come to think of it the only time Eric really let himself relax was after they'd fucked, but who was counting? Tony wondered if Eric turned his brain off more with Hunter. Maybe he did. Maybe that's why he hadn't been enough for—

"Wherever your brain just went, we're not talking about it," Lowell snapped. "I'm not your psychiatrist, I'm your sire."

"Please"—Tony rolled his eyes again—"I'm not coming to you for relationship advice."

"See, that's already more than I needed to know about you." Lowell flapped her wrist through the air as if waving away a gnat. "Sage said you're having trouble controlling your wolf."

Scrubbing at the back of his neck to hide the flush, Tony pushed to his feet and made his way over to his tool cabinet to look for what he needed to continue his work. "Yeah. I'm struggling to keep it under wraps during high stress situations. The other night, I wolfed out and went running through the streets."

Lowell snorted a laugh, and when Tony turned to glare at her, she didn't flinch. "Thought that might have been you. Got reports of some giant wild yellow dog and was like, *bet that's McMahon.* You're lucky it was so late at night, and you were mostly in the party district, or you could have gotten us all in trouble."

"Well tell me how to fucking control it, and it won't happen again!" Tony slammed the wrench he'd been holding back into its place in the drawer.

Lowell tilted her head, her gaze following him as he dug around needlessly in the drawer of tools. He could feel those sharp eyes on the back of his neck, watching, waiting, picking him apart piece by piece. He didn't like it. But he didn't have any other choice. Who else was he going to ask about being a werewolf? It wasn't like people wrote books about this shit. There weren't self-help groups, or Werewolves Anonymous. There was just this. Just Lowell.

"See, that's where you fucked up," she said in a tone that was soft, reasonable.

Tony gritted his teeth. "Where *I* fucked up? It's not like this shit came with an instruction manual."

"Yes, where *you* fucked up." Lowell flapped her wrist again, crossing one leg over the other. "You're so busy seeing the wolf as something other, you're not listening to him at all, are you?"

"Of course I'm not! He's fucking angry! I don't have time for this shit. If you don't have any real advice, fuck off. I'm waiting on a call from—"

"He's angry because you're angry, you moron." Lowell clicked her tongue in annoyance. "He's not separate *from* you, he's a part *of* you. The reason he keeps leaping forward without your say so is that you haven't made peace with that yet. Instead, you're trying to control him, rein him in. Goddess, I swear, people these days are so dense. It's like they don't even—"

"Then what do you suggest?" Tony forced himself to sound calm, his fists so tight his nails dug into his palms. He had a feeling he wasn't going to like nor want to take whatever advice Lowell was about to dish out. But he'd agreed to hear her out at least. He could bitch about this shit to Sage later.

"Meditation," Lowell said easy as breathing as she stood and passed Tony on the way to the door, patting his shoulder. "I recommend trying out one of those apps on your phone. They're great for beginners."

Then she left, and Tony was still standing there, his hands tightened into fists, his eyes wide. Stunned. *Meditation.* What the fuck did that have to do with anything?!

"That was fucking useless," he grumbled, and finished grabbing the tools he needed to get back to work.

CHAPTER 21

ALL IN ALL, it should have been an easy enough plan to put into motion. The vampires were absolutely feral for Eric's blood. He just had to lure one of them onto the array formed by the net and wrangle them into a pair of cuffs long enough to call Tony and have him come pick them up.

The trouble was that luring one vampire into the trap presupposed that there wasn't an entire *flock* of vampires after him.

Which there was.

"Fuck," Eric gasped, looking over his shoulder at the group chasing him. He'd meant to lead them around the corner and get at least one of them hung up on the net, but he didn't know what having more than one of them in the cage would do. Would it weaken the effects of the magic? Was it built to hold only one? Would it work at all? They hadn't been able to test it, so there was no guarantee.

Which was why the kids were sitting this mission out. Which was why he'd decided to go it alone.

"How many?" he asked into the earpiece, brushing sweat from his forehead with his wrist. Hunter was on the other end, watching Eric's back, ready to call in Tony if things got too extreme.

"Ten total." Hunter's voice was brisk, businesslike, matter of fact. He was worried. Really worried. He'd probably been on edge the entire time they'd been discussing this plan just hours ago, and hiding it. Eric wished Tony and Hunter wouldn't do that. That they wouldn't bury what they were feeling to make him feel better. He could take it.

But then— Well, he knew himself. Knew if he could do anything to mitigate their concerns, he would. He'd lay down his life to make sure they were happy. To protect them. Which he was sure at least Hunter understood, hence the holding back. Fuck. This was a fucking mess. This whole fucking thing. His relationships. His city. His job. He was—

"Then I've just got to take down nine, and lure one into the net. Easy peasy." Eric forced himself to sound more arrogant than he felt. He slipped on the persona of Eric Marcelino, most lauded Venator in several generations. The only one to live this long—despite Dash's current efforts. The man. The myth. The legend. He hated the feeling of that mantle. It was heavy and suffocating. It wasn't who he was anymore. But it was who he needed to be, at least for tonight.

"Eric," Hunter breathed, hesitant. Funny how all it took was a single bold line from Eric to knock him off his game. To bring the ever-flirting, ever-clever Hunter Delacroix up short. Eric would revel in his power if he weren't so fucking scared.

"Seriously, man, I've got this." Eric rolled out his shoulders, his fingers tightening around the stake in his hand.

The vampires were still coming. They weren't moving quickly, shuffling instead like zombies as they followed him at a steady pace. He wondered about that for a moment. That wasn't how they'd been moving before. Maybe because these were older corpses that had been turned, suffering from rigor mortis. He hadn't known that was a thing a vampire could do —turn a completely cold corpse. But it seemed Dash was running out of fresh bodies. How long before he started turning the normies en masse? Eric would have to catch him before that.

Eric didn't wait for Hunter to agree that he had this all

under control. It wouldn't do anything really for him to say it. Hunter would still worry. There were too many things up to chance and fate right now. And maybe Eric had a prophecy on his side, but he didn't know the statistics on how many prophecies hadn't come true because the person they were about died. So. Better he not know probably. It would make him nervous.

With a deep breath, he stepped back toward the fray. They were moving sluggishly enough that he could bottleneck them down the next alley. Pick them off one by one until there was only one left. Should be easy enough.

He skidded on the pavement. He hadn't worn the best shoes for this. Usually he was better about that, putting on tennis shoes with good tread in case he needed to be able to grip a smooth surface. But everything had been thrown into the fucking blender lately. His routine. His kit to come out. His best practices. Patrol after patrol with too many vampires to even keep count of was fucking him up in the head.

He couldn't keep doing this.

The corner of the building slammed into his hip when he lost his grip on the ground for a second thanks to some food wrappers. Bone and muscle throbbed as he staggered to get himself into a good spot in the darkened alley. Ready. Waiting.

And then they followed. A pushing, snarling, throbbing mass of teeth and venom. Hands thrusting forward to reach for him as they got stuck in the mouth of the alley. Shoulder to shoulder. Unable to coordinate with each other past their hunger that kicked into a frenzy at the scent of blood on the air as the wound on Eric's hip dribbled down his jeans.

It wasn't even deep. Just a scratch. But these vamps had his scent.

Dash had been sure of that—a realization Eric had come to the night Hunter and Tony had taken patrol. Those vamps hadn't gone after any of the civilians. They hadn't headed toward easier targets. They'd homed in on Hunter and Tony, likely because Hunter and Tony were so close to Eric. Likely because they carried his scent, and they were the only thing in the area that did. Eric being up the mountain hadn't saved anyone. It had put them in more danger.

He couldn't have that again.

He wouldn't.

Hunter and Tony meant too much to him.

Another deep breath, and Eric stepped toward the writhing mass of vampires trying to wiggle past each other to be the first to get to him. They only grew more frenzied the closer he got. It would make them sloppy. It would make them dangerous.

One broke through a moment later, and with them came a second. Eric moved quick, positioning himself to plunge the stake into the first then the second in rapid succession. Then they fell like dominoes. Wiggling through into the alley past one another. Lunging for him in jerky movements that made them easier targets. Evaporating into dust.

One. Two. Five. Nine.

Until there was only one left.

They ran for him. Limbs stiff from rigor mortis. Uncoordinated. But fast. Faster than all the others. It was a wonder they'd been at the back of the pack. And there was something . . . different about this one. They moved more cautiously. Almost as if they knew what they were doing. Almost as if they were conscious, but their eyes were still blank.

A quick step back, and another. He needed to get to the other end of the alley without turning his back on the approaching vampire, then he could circle around and lead them to the net. Easy. Just stay two steps ahead of the vampire. Don't trip. Don't fall. Don't turn his back. He could—

His back hit a wall.

The brick sent a shiver down his spine.

"Shit." He glanced over his shoulder. He'd gotten himself mixed up somehow, the map he always kept in his brain of Ironport blurring in his exhaustion. That was the only explanation for how he'd wound up cornered.

"That doesn't sound good." Hunter's voice was tight in his ear again.

"It'll be fine." Not a lie. Eric had dealt with circumstances like this before. He could make this work to his advantage. He just had to work his footwork right, dance the dance that would get the vamp turned around. It would be simple enough.

"Do I need to send Tony?"

"No." Eric shook his head, his gaze jumping around the alley, looking for a clean and easy break. It wasn't wide enough for two people, not really. There was a large dumpster to one side blocking the best exit, and above it, a fire escape. That might work. "I got it."

"Eric."

"Sh. Don't distract me." He had only a second to think through how much power he needed to put behind his jumps, and all the things that could go wrong before the vampire reached him. And in the end, he decided to chance it. He took a running leap at the dumpster with a silent prayer to the Goddess that the lid wouldn't give out under his weight.

It did give slightly. The plastic flexed in a decidedly worrisome way, but it bounced back enough to add to the height he needed to swing himself over the railing of the fire escape. His heel slipped and he almost lost his footing, but he managed somehow to haul himself over with just his arms and throw himself onto the metal grating.

"All right, out of arm's reach for the moment." The metal dug into his hands as he pushed up from his stomach onto his feet and took off at a run along the narrow walkway that led from one window to the next. He heard the vampire below him, rustling around, trying to figure out how to get at him.

"I'm sending Tony your way."

"Not till I've got the vamp in the net. I don't want to chance it getting free and attacking," Eric hissed through his teeth. They'd talked about this. He knew Hunter was worried about his safety, but they couldn't risk shit going sideways with Tony again. Not until Tony had better control over himself.

"The net will work." Hunter scoffed, clearly offended.

"We don't know that." Eric clambered over the rail of the fire escape at the mouth of the alley, his shoes slick on the rounded bar. He was going to have to make sure he came out in the proper attire next time. This shit was dangerous. He waited one breath, then launched himself to the ground, landing hard on his right ankle and causing a sharp pain to race from the top of his foot along his shin, nearly paralyzing him in the moment. He gritted his teeth and started running, trusting it to shake itself out. "Don't you *dare* put him in danger, Hunter. I'm serious."

"Fine." Hunter's rings tapped against the arm of his chair as he held himself back. Eric could picture him sitting there, annoyed but following directions. Because he knew, like Eric did, how imperative it was that Tony not come in too early. That he not put his neck on the line. It was bad enough that Dash was gunning for Eric like he was. If something happened to Eric, Tony would be their next line of defense. "I kissed him."

"When?" Eric didn't let his steps falter. He couldn't. He wondered if Hunter was telling him this now because he knew Eric would be too distracted to freak the fuck out about it. Probably.

"The other day in the forge." Hunter made a noise, a soft mumbled hum in the back of his throat. Like maybe he felt he needed to clear it but didn't want to seem too obvious. "He just looked so . . ."

"Okay." Sweat trickled down Eric's back as he rounded another corner, slamming his shoulder against it to maintain his balance. Fuck, he was getting tired.

"Okay?"

Eric laughed, breathless and too high. "Hunter, I'm not fucking blind. I know you're into each other too."

"Oh. Right." Hunter sounded sheepish, like maybe he forgot somehow that one of Eric's only real skills was situational awareness. He noticed things. About his surroundings. About people. And Hunter and Tony were so easy for him to read—much more so than books. "So . . ." Hunter dragged the word out nervously.

"I'm not pissed. But I will be if you don't shut the fuck up and let me focus on getting this fucker into your trap," Eric hissed, glancing over his shoulder to make sure the vampire was still following. "And I'm okay with it," he said when he turned back. The net was in sight. He just had to get the vampire across it. "I just don't know how you're going to get his head out of his ass enough for him to realize what's going on around him."

"Fair point." Hunter sighed.

"I'll help you work on him." Eric rolled his eyes. The toe of his shoe caught in the edge of the net and he stumbled forward, the vampire right behind him. The iron dragged at his senses, making him sluggish, like it wanted to keep him. If he didn't have the added forward momentum of tripping, he'd probably have been trapped right alongside the vampire. He whipped around to find them snapping their jaws at him, fingers clawing at the air like some horror movie version of a mime.

"You will?" There was a breathlessness to Hunter's voice, an uncertainty.

"Of course I will, you idiot. I want us all to work as much

as you do. It'll be way less stressful if he's not always feeling jealous and left out. Which he is, no matter what he likes to pretend." Brushing his hands through his hair, Eric did a quick circuit around the net. It was several feet wide, providing a good area for him and the vampire to fight in once Tony brought him the restraints, and it seemed to be holding up well enough.

"I noticed that." A small laugh escaped Hunter, and Eric imagined him shaking his head, his hair falling into his face. "So. Did it work?"

"Yeah, it worked. Send Tony my way. We'll be home in an hour or so."

"All right. See you soon, hon."

"Wait up for us?"

"Always."

CHAPTER 22

"DID you have to pick the biggest motherfucker who was following you?" Tony grunted as he helped Eric lift the struggling vampire into the trunk of his car. They'd taped warding sigils and containment characters to the inside so it couldn't pop out halfway up the road, but Tony wasn't sure this vampire was going to fit.

"They didn't exactly give me a whole lot of choice." Eric huffed beside him. He was whole, Tony was relieved to find. Not even bleeding apart from a scrape on his hip. Which was more than Tony could say for some of his previous nights out on patrol. But exhaustion still hung heavy around Eric's neck, making his posture slump even more than usual. "This was the one at the back of the pack."

"Yeah well, next time we should bring Hunter's truck." Tony hoped there wouldn't be a next time, but he didn't say so out loud. He'd become superstitious over the years, believing wholeheartedly that by saying something out loud he was somehow cosmically disqualified for the thing. He knew it was silly, but there were only so many times a person saw it happen before they started to see causation when there was only coincidence.

Eric snorted and rolled his eyes but didn't say anything. He helped Tony move the vampire's kicking legs until they were within Hunter's stunning array. They fell still, and he slammed the trunk. The sound echoed in the late-night hush of Ironport. "All right, let's go home," he said, brushing whatever imaginary dirt he might have gotten on his hands onto his jeans.

Home. Tony didn't think he'd ever get used to calling the dorm that, but it felt more and more true every day. That was where his sister was. Where all their shit was. Where he had a bed he liked, and someone kept restocking his favorite snacks in the pantry. But it was also where all of Eric's rugrats were. Crammed in so tight these days, it was like they were sardines. It was also where Hunter and Eric were. He was still having mixed feelings about that last one.

"Yeah. The sooner Hunter can figure out how to track that fucker, the better." Although Tony wasn't sure what any of them would do with the peace that might come after defeating Dash finally. Would they have to take up new hobbies? And what would happen with Eric and the prophecy? He was meant to tear down all the Huntsmen had built in the name of rebuilding it into something else, something better. Tony didn't envy him that position. He didn't think he'd want to be the leader of such an organization. But it was like Eric didn't even think about it at all. Like he'd pushed it from his mind. Maybe because he spent all his time running. What would happen when they finally slowed down?

"Definitely," Eric agreed, but there was something in the inflection of that single word that Tony had a hard time pinning down. Maybe Eric was thinking along the same lines as Tony.

They loaded into Tony's old red Mustang, and the engine rumbled beneath the hood as Tony started them up the mountain toward Moondale U campus. Toward home. A silence settled between them that was wholly uncomfortable. It itched at Tony's skin, making his spine bunch up as he tried to make himself as small as possible. He knew Eric was tired, but something lingered in the air between them. Something they needed to talk about. Tony just didn't know what it was. And *that* more than anything made him uneasy.

"I saw Lowell tonight," he said into the quiet, hoping it would alleviate the pressure to speak. And it did for a moment, the tension releasing almost so viscerally he swore his ears popped.

"Lowell?" Eric asked. He didn't turn to look at Tony. He leaned back in his seat, staring at the ceiling as if unseeing. He looked so fucking tired. Stretched thin like a rubber band that'd been used one too many times. This couldn't last. This constant running, fighting, fearing for the lives of the people he loved—it couldn't last. Eric would break under the strain of it eventually.

Tony wished there was something he could say, something he could do, that would take the load off Eric. But all he could think to do was take at least one thing off Eric's plate: the worry that Tony wasn't in control of his wolf. "My sire."

"Oh yeah? How'd that go?" Eric turned his head, squishing his cheek against the headrest. He looked impossibly soft like this. The moonlight washed him out. The adrenaline was wearing off to leave behind a man who was just fucking tired. Exhausted from so many years of fighting against a tide that never stopped fucking coming.

Tony wanted to stop the car, pull off on the side of the road, and drag Eric into his lap. Wrap his arms around his body, curl himself so tightly around Eric that nothing and no one could get to him without having to go through Tony first. He wanted to stay like that until Eric finally got some proper rest. The feeling was foreign. Tony had never wanted to do that for anyone before. He'd never been close enough to someone to feel like he ought to. But . . . Eric Marcelino was a world of firsts for Tony. Some of them less soft.

"I'm going to start meditation tomorrow," Tony reported. He hadn't actually thought he'd try what Lowell suggested. It seemed fucking stupid. Pointless. But he needed to do something. He needed to take at least one thing off Eric's plate. And what was a little meditation if it helped Eric sleep at night? Goddess, he'd gone soft.

"She thinks that'll help?" A delighted smile pulled at one corner of Eric's mouth. Not quite teasing, but adjacent to that.

"She says I need to find out what it wants." Tony shrugged, trying to shake off the way Eric's gaze warmed his skin. It wasn't sexual. But it wasn't not that either. "Meditation is supposed to put me in touch with it so I can do that."

Eric nodded, his stubble scraping against the leather of the headrest. "Okay. Well, whatever you need from us, let us know."

"Yeah." Tony swallowed past a lump in his throat. "I will."

"Good." Eric smiled, wide and lazy, and fuck it. The vampire could chill for a bit. Tony needed his hands on Eric *yesterday*. There was no one around them on the road for miles, and this late at night there wasn't likely to be. They just needed ten minutes, fifteen tops, for Tony to quell this feeling in his chest.

He didn't even bother with his blinker, just veered over to the shoulder and threw the car in park.

Eric didn't say anything, but he raised his dark brows in question, an amused glint in his eyes like even if he was asking what Tony was doing, he somehow already knew.

"Get your ass over here, Bambi, we've got time." They didn't really. He didn't know how long Hunter's magic would hold the vampire in the trunk, and he didn't care either. Nothing else mattered outside of getting Eric close to him, reminding Eric that he was alive even when he felt dead on his feet.

To his credit, Eric clambered over the center console without a word while Tony lifted the lever on his seat and it slammed back as far as it would go to make room for him.

Eric kicked Tony's car door with a grunt, but eventually settled in Tony's lap, warm and solid. Tony curled his arms around Eric's waist and pushed his face into his shoulder. He breathed in the smell of him clinging to his T-shirt. All deodorant—spicy and musky—and sweat. Tony loved that smell. He wished he could turn it into a car deodorizer so he could take it with him wherever he went.

"I'm all right," Eric assured, his arms curling around Tony and giving him a mirroring squeeze. It was soft, comforting. Tender in a way Tony didn't usually allow himself. "I'm all right."

"I know." He did know. It was just a matter of *how long*? If this didn't work, how much longer could Eric hold out? Even with help. Dash would get his way eventually—he usually did. Fear crawled along Tony's nerves, a reminder of what it had been like to be under Dash's control. Disgust churned in his belly. He'd wanted it. He'd wanted Dash to touch him, to tease him, to bite him. He'd practically rolled over and begged for everything Dash had done to him.

"You're all right too," Eric murmured, his fingers carding slowly through Tony's hair, his bitten nails scraping his scalp. Tony hadn't even realized he was shaking until he felt Eric holding the pieces of him together. "I won't let him hurt you again."

"It's not me I'm worried about, pretty boy." Tony scoffed, all false bravado. He *was* worried about himself, as selfish as that sounded, but he was worried about Eric too. And Hunter. And the kids. He didn't want to have to watch as any of them suffered the way he had.

"Still." Eric pressed a kiss to Tony's temple, his lips warm and chapped.

Tony knew it was an empty promise. Eric would do everything in his power to protect the people he cared about, but there was only so much he could do. He wasn't all powerful. He couldn't even keep the Council of Creatures from putting the kids into the field. In the end, they were two mostly human men railing against a world that would sooner tear them down than lift them up. If Tony's life had taught him anything, it had been his own fallibility. And unfortunately, even if Eric was the most kickass Venator in existence, he was just as powerless. His blood came just as easily.

"Shut the fuck up," Tony grumbled, pushing such depressing thoughts from his mind in favor of grabbing Eric by his hair and twisting his head until their lips crashed together.

The kiss started hard and rough. Both fighting for dominance. Teeth clacking together. Tongues warring. But then someone yielded, Tony wasn't sure who, and it slowed into a tender, soft thing. A slow, easy brush of lips that left Tony impossibly more winded. Because he didn't deserve this softness. It wasn't meant for him. But he'd take it just the same so long as Eric was giving it to him.

"I want you inside me," Eric murmured against his lips, dragging the kiss from there down to the sparse hair that lined Tony's jaw.

"Get your pants down." Tony shifted, reaching across the center console, even as Eric continued to nuzzle behind his ear, to fling the glovebox open and grab a packet of lube from inside. "Pretty boy, pants," Tony grumbled exasperatedly as he fumbled with the packet, struggling to focus with Eric's teeth on his earlobe, tugging gently.

"Yeah, I hear you," Eric muttered, pressing one more gentle kiss to the hinge of Tony's jaw before he leaned back against the steering wheel and started to wiggle his pants down his thighs.

It was a struggle, Tony could tell by the panted breaths, for Eric to get them down enough that Tony could reach where he wanted. He couldn't help but chuckle. Eric was adorably frustrated and flush faced, and he couldn't be blamed.

"Dick." Eric grunted once he'd gotten himself into a position that still looked pretty uncomfortable. "This would have been easier if we did it on the side of the road."

"And risk your pretty ass getting road rash? I don't think so." Tony smirked, sharp and mean, and brushed the pad of his finger over Eric's hole, cutting off any further arguments. His other arm looped around Eric's waist, holding him close so Tony could drag kisses down the side of Eric's face from temple to jaw. "I've got you, baby."

Eric pulled back for a moment, his eyes glassy, his lips kiss bitten, color high on his cheeks. He looked wrecked beyond belief, and they'd only just gotten started. He met Tony's eyes, something liquid and warm in his gaze that settled like soup on a cold day into Tony's gut. Tony gulped, his mouth suddenly dry when Eric said, "I know you do" like it was the most natural thing in the world. Like he trusted Tony not just with his pleasure, but with his life, with his . . . with his *everything.*

"Fuck," Tony gasped. The sound was pained and sharp like he was choking on air, cutting through the thickness between them, making Tony's eyes prick with tears. It had to be the inhale, it couldn't be the warmth in his chest. It couldn't be that Tony felt . . . "Eric, baby . . ."

"Shh. I know." Eric leaned forward again, brushing his lips to Tony's, pushing everything else from Tony's mind as Eric sank back onto his finger with little resistance. His hips moved slowly and languidly as he kissed Tony to match. Tender. Gentle.

Tony let out a soft, wounded sound, his thighs clenching as heat pooled low in his belly. He couldn't explain it, couldn't put it into words. And he didn't want to. There was something comforting about Eric taking his pleasure like this. Something soothing about the rhythm he set between them, reaching back to tap Tony's hand, a silent plea for another finger, more pressure, as he moved in Tony's lap. It was . . .

"That's it, sweetheart," Eric practically purred, and the words went straight to Tony's groin. "Let me ride you."

Tony nodded, unable to get words past the emotion welling in his throat. It was easy after that to lose himself in the gentle motion of Eric's body. In the way Eric slowly ramped himself up, showing Tony what he liked if he was to set the pace. Easy to sit back and watch, glassy eyed and panting hard, as Eric rode him, taking himself apart bit by bit until he came across both their stomachs with a shudder. Easy to lose track of the times his own legs clenched tight, his jeans getting wetter and wetter.

By the time Eric was done, they were both slumped against the driver's seat, their breaths fogging up the glass.

"I—" Eric started, his eyes soft, his face pressed into Tony's chest. "I feel—"

A thump came from the trunk.

"Hold that thought, princess," Tony chuckled, his voice strangled. "We've got to get the vamp home before it tries to crawl out of the trunk."

Eric chewed on the inside of his cheek, his eyes flicking around the car, not meeting Tony's, before he nodded. "All right."

Chapter 23

THE CLANKING of metal bounced off the cement walls of the basement Eric had suggested Hunter turn into a lab. The place was one half lab, one half training room for the Venator. The sound grated at Hunter's ears, making his shoulders scooch closer to them in the hopes of possibly muffling the racket. He knew it wouldn't help. He knew that no matter what he did—put in headphones, grab earplugs, cover his ears—he'd still hear the rattling of iron on the metal table the kids had managed somehow to get down the stairs of the basement with only minimal denting. There was no escaping the sound.

Just like there was no escaping the sight of the vampire Eric and Tony had delivered a few short hours ago to test.

Hunter's blood rushed in his ears, not loud enough to drown out the noise, but hard enough to give him a headache, the throbbing pain mounting so quickly he was almost dizzy with it. His stomach lurched at the smell of rot and congealed blood.

Hunter had never seen a vampire this badly decomposed. In fact, he didn't even know a person *could* be turned this long after death. It didn't make sense at all. It shouldn't have been possible. The blood was no longer circulating. It had been left so long in the body that it had started to blacken, to rot. He'd always thought there was no coming back from that. Clearly, he'd been wrong.

"Still, just because a person *can* do something, doesn't mean they *should*," Hunter mumbled to himself, grabbing the vampire's wrist so he could place another stunning spell on them, hold them still long enough to get what he needed from them.

Tony fidgeted in his periphery, the creak of an old wooden stool adding to the ruckus the vampire caused. Hunter cringed further but didn't let go of the vampire's wrist.

"If you're going to make a nuisance of yourself, go back upstairs." It wasn't that Hunter minded the company. It was nice to know he wasn't stuck in this fucking pit of a basement with just the house—who had proven itself to be a real bitch at times—for protection. But Tony's presence was distracting. Add to that the way he seemed to be on the edge of saying something they might both regret, and Hunter was struggling to focus.

Tony grunted what sounded like an apology, but it was hard to tell through the warbling sound of Hunter's blood in his ears. Whatever Tony was swallowing, Hunter wished he'd say it already.

It wasn't like Hunter didn't know that Tony and Eric had fucked on the way back to the dorm after they captured the vampire. It was all over Eric—his hair a mess, a slight limp to his steps. Likewise, it wasn't like Hunter cared. That was how this whole thing was supposed to work, after all. They were sharing Eric. Hunter had agreed to that, and he'd never been the jealous type. Which was why he'd known this thing between them would work, if only Tony would let it.

Hunter didn't think that was it, though. Tony hadn't shown any kind of discomfort with what they were doing before, at least not when it was his turn with Eric. He obviously didn't like it much when it was Hunter giving Eric what he needed. But Hunter knew they'd fix that right up if

Tony would get this heteronormative idea of monogamy out of his head.

Either way, it couldn't be that. It had to be something else.

The kiss Hunter and Tony had shared, perhaps.

Hunter shook himself, huffing at his inability to stay on task. He was tired, that was half of it. Tired, and easily distracted by the warm body behind him versus the cold one in front of him. But that didn't change things.

Squeezing the vampire's wrist tighter, Hunter forced himself to focus on the feeling of the magic burning along his skin like a tattoo needle. The tiny pinpricks of power had gotten slightly more intense since he'd agreed to join the Coven of the Forgotten. They'd only get more so once he fed his blood to the stone at the heart of Moondale and got the tattoo he and Icarus had planned to help tie him and Ava to the land there. But with it would come power unlike any he'd ever seen before. With it would come the ability to protect his family, the men he cared about.

The spell settled over the vampire like a net. Black and sparkling, it wrapped around their skin, stilling them until all they could do was blink at him, drool dripping from the corner of their mouth onto the table. Hunter's stomach twisted again, and he let out a sigh.

"I'm sorry about this," he murmured gently to the vampire.

Tony scoffed.

Hunter whipped around to glare at him. "If you've got something to fucking say, say it."

"You and Eric are such a soft touch," Tony grumbled, his tone not nearly as annoyed as he likely thought he was making it. He was trying to be tough and untouched by what he felt, but Hunter could see right through him. Just like he'd been able to see right through Eric once upon a time. To the scared young man beneath who wanted the people around him to give a shit about him but was too afraid to express not just need but want. There was a joke in there somewhere about toxic masculinity and how it made men weaker, how it was even worse for men like Tony, but Hunter disregarded it.

"Just because they eat blood, doesn't mean they don't deserve our respect as human beings." Hunter turned back to his work, the metal tray at his right rattling when he pulled a long, thin needle from it. He wondered—like a mad scientist completely at odds with what he'd just said—if a creature who'd been dead this long could even feel pain. It'd be interesting to find out, for science purposes, but the thought alone made him feel less humane. So he murmured a soft numbing spell, waiting a moment as the ink on his arms shifted, a single petal falling from a black-eyed Susan to land on the vampire's bare stomach. It settled there, just the black outline of a flower petal, letting Hunter know the magic had worked.

A long, slow breath, to settle his rattled nerves, and Hunter crouched over the prone form of the vampire, the needle pressing deep into their stomach. It took time to find the right place, to draw from it what he needed. He wasn't sure if drawing blood from the stomach would be their best bet, but he hoped it would be the freshest sample of Dash's DNA they could find. The bile might tamper with it, but it shouldn't be enough to ruin the sample given the fact that this vampire had been dead for such a long time.

By the time Hunter had removed the needle, Tony was at his side, leaning over his shoulder. "Did it work?"

"No way to know yet." Hunter frowned when a bit of decomposed skin flaked off the vampire's torso onto the floor. It would be a mercy to dust them before they could completely fall apart. But they needed to wait, at least until he'd tested this sample. He wasn't willing to risk Eric's safety again.

"Well come on then, what are you waiting for?" Tony bounced on his toes, his excitement more irritating than infectious.

Hunter rolled his eyes. "You're an impatient little shit, has anyone ever told you that?"

"Once or twice."

"Obnoxious," Hunter muttered, but it was half fond as he brushed past Tony on the way to the counter along the wall where he'd set up his microscopes and petri dishes. He had to be quick about this. Enough so that his theory about the blood turning to dust as it oxidized didn't have time to take effect. He'd have time to test that one later. After he'd gotten them the answers they needed. Priorities.

The petri dish was waiting for him, and it took only a second to squirt half the blood from the needle into it before clacking the lid down on top, sealing it as best he could. It wouldn't be as good as if he'd been able to suck all the air out of the dish, but it was something.

Setting the needle in the tiny fridge on the counter, he lifted the petri dish to the light to look at it. He'd never seen vampire blood outside of the body before. For some reason, Hunter had thought that it would . . . *do* something.

Wriggle. Hiss. Throw itself against the glass in an attempt to get at the living matter outside the dish. But it just sat there, innocuous and still. Dead. Like the creature he'd pulled it from.

"I wonder if it has something to do with how long the vampire has been deceased." He tapped thoughtfully at the glass with the fingernail of his index finger.

"What did you expect it to do? Act like when someone got a piece of Venom and it threw itself around, taking on a life of its own?" Tony sounded like he was laughing, and when Hunter turned to him, he found Tony's eyes crinkled at the corners, his lips curved upward. It was a good look on him. Hunter's breath lodged in his throat, and he had to cough to get it to move.

"Yeah, kind of," he murmured, turning his attention back

to the dish. "I mean, vampire blood is alive in a sense, isn't it?"

"Not outside of the body." Tony clicked his tongue. "It's parasitic, but not like that. It needs a host to work."

"How do you know?" Hunter blinked at him, mouth agape. He knew Tony was clever, but he thought he'd been the only one to do experiments on vampires. Although, he'd never had a live one on his hands before that he could take samples from. It was always just teeth. Just dust. Remains. Not the entire being. Not until Tony helped him come up with the means to trap one easily. Goddess, Hunter kind of wanted to jump his bones right then.

Tony shrugged, scrubbing at the back of his neck in a way that almost seemed bashful. "Just seems like common sense, right? I mean, how many times have we gotten blood on our clothes and skin, and not had it attack us even while the vampire was still alive? If the blood could act on its own, we'd be in a fuckload more trouble."

Hunter nodded slowly. That made sense. He hadn't even thought about it that way. Why would he? He didn't spend enough time in the field to interact with vampire blood straight from the host. Having Tony in the lab with him was definitely an asset.

"Okay then." Hunter set the dish down on the counter. "Let's see if I can pull Dash's DNA from it and use it to track him."

"Is it cool if I sit in for that?" Tony fidgeted with the hem of his shirt, his weight shifting on his feet as if at any moment he'd bolt back up the stairs.

"Don't see why not." Hunter shrugged. "Just keep quiet." Then he turned back to his work, settling onto a stool at the counter and sliding the dish under a microscope. He wasn't sure what he was looking for or how he'd find it, but he had to try.

It took longer than he'd like to admit to pick apart the strands of DNA wrapped in the blood he'd extracted from the vampire's stomach. But it wasn't really his fault. While the blood seemed still and calm on the surface, it was anything but on a cellular level.

It was cannibalizing itself over and over again until the strands were so mutated, so altered, they didn't resemble anything Hunter had ever seen before, human or otherwise. And it moved so quickly, he wasn't able to get ahead of it. He had to take a second sample, then a third, before he was finally able to identify a strand that was probably Dash.

"Why would it do that?" Tony asked, as they both watched the latest sample devour itself endlessly like an Ouroboros. There was a bit of fear in his voice when his next words left him. "Does it *always* do that?"

Hunter was reminded, sharply, that Tony had had vampire blood in his body before. That there had been a vampire feasting on him, using him, at one point. Of course this would be terrifying to witness, to think that this possibly had been inside of him. Hunter took his hand and gave it a squeeze, heedless of the sweaty palm and shaking fingers. "I don't think so. I've never examined the blood on its own before, but I think this might have something to do with the rabid nature of this fresh crop of vampires."

"So Dash has, what? Altered his own DNA to do this?"

"I don't know." He wished he did. Hunter wished more than anything that there were answers he could give Tony, if just to calm him down. But there were none. He didn't have enough evidence yet. "Either way . . ." Hunter took a breath, tapping on the computer screen he'd been looking at before Tony drew his attention again toward the projection of what was happening on the petri dish. His stomach soured at the red error message the DNA had kicked back. "The blood isn't working. The Ghost Tracer can't find anyone with that code in the area. Which means it's too mutated from whatever Dash did to this vampire."

"What should we do?" Tony whispered. He hadn't let go of Hunter's hand yet, squeezing it so hard that Hunter's rings ground into his bones. It didn't matter. Hunter wasn't going to let go either. He'd seep every ounce of comfort he could from their connection.

"We'll have to try something else. Bone marrow, maybe? Skin cells? Or maybe it's this vampire in particular because they're so decomposed?" He swallowed the bile that crawled up his throat. "I think we need a fresher sample."

"Eric isn't going to like this."

"None of us like this." Hunter lifted one shoulder in a halfhearted shrug.

Tony sighed and squeezed tighter before letting go of Hunter's hand. "Do ya want me to dust 'em?"

"Yeah. I think that'd be the most humane thing at this point." Hunter chewed on his bottom lip, teeth clacking against his piercing as they both turned to look at the still-stunned vampire. "I'll tell Eric, if you handle that?"

"Deal." Tony reached for a stake that he'd apparently stuffed into his back pocket at some point, and in one fluid motion, he jammed it through the vampire's heart. They burst into a shower of dust a second later, the stake tapping against the metal table where it landed. Then Tony turned back to Hunter. "Your job is gonna suck way more."

"No shit." Hunter snorted. "Come on, you've got meditating or some shit to do, don't you?"

Tony wrinkled his nose, but he led the way up the steps, back into the main part of the house where the kids were getting up for breakfast and Eric was piddling about the kitchen.

"Anything?" Eric spun around from the pan he'd been cooking eggs in, his brows lifted, his honey-brown eyes hopeful. All it took was a shake of Hunter's head, and his shoulders sank. "Right. Back to the drawing board."

"Yeah." Hunter breathed, ignoring the way his gut twisted at seeing Eric so beaten only long enough to slip across the kitchen, curl over Eric's back at the stove, and rest his chin on his shoulder. "We'll figure this out."

"Fuck yeah we will," Tony agreed wholeheartedly, startling a laugh out of both Hunter and Eric. The tension in Eric's body eased, his heart slowing, the panic fading.

When Hunter turned to look at Tony over his shoulder, his eyes glittered like he knew exactly what he'd just done. Hunter nodded his thanks, and Tony winked as if to say *no problem*. Hunter's stomach unknotted at the knowledge that no matter how complicated this relationship was, he and Tony were on the same page when it came to protecting Eric. That wasn't much. But it was something to build from.

Hunter could work with that.

# CHAPTER 24

THEY WERE JUST PULLING into Ironport on their way to the morgue, when Eric's phone buzzed in his pocket, the long repeated vibration of a call versus the short sharp burst of a text. He frowned, wiggling his hips, his foot on the break where they sat at a light, to get the device out of his too-tight jeans.

"What is it?" Hunter asked worriedly from the passenger seat. The car shifted under Tony's weight as he leaned forward as well to check in. They were all on edge with this whole thing, and Eric couldn't say he blamed them. The shit had already hit the proverbial fan. It was just a matter of time before another load followed.

"Someone's calling me." More wiggling, his fingers scraping too hard against the edge of his phone. Eric managed to get it out of his pocket in enough time to read the caller ID before it rolled over to voicemail. His stomach dropped at the name on the screen. OLIVER MARCELINO.

"Who is it?" Tony's fingers pulled a little on Eric's hair where he'd gripped the seat tight enough to make the leather creak.

"My brother." The words felt strange in his mouth. Logically, Eric knew that he had a little brother. Oliver was about fourteen years younger than him or so—Eric wasn't even sure anymore, it was hard to keep track of the exact moment his parents decided he was a lost cause and they needed to try again. He could probably have looked at the records of when he'd tested positive for the Venator gene, but he didn't really want to. Just the reminder that what he was made him unacceptable to them to the point where they felt they needed to have another child to replace him was enough to send him into a spiral. So he tried not to think about it.

It looked like all of that was over now though. Because Oliver had returned to Ironport and was running the Council of Creatures. Meaning Eric would have his face rubbed in what a fucking failure he was to the two people who were meant to love him unconditionally every fucking day. Especially if Oliver had decided it was appropriate to call him.

He held his breath, hoping and praying that Oliver wouldn't call again, wouldn't leave a voicemail. That he'd give up. There was nothing he had to say that Eric wanted to hear. A second later, Eric released a long exhale with a groan when a text notification popped up right below the missed call.

"Read it," he said, all but tossing the phone into Hunter's lap and easing off the breaks to go through the light.

"Motherfucker," Hunter hissed.

"What is it?" Tony asked, his words so strained, Eric was surprised he hadn't crawled into the front seat to sit in Hunter's lap so he could be closer to whatever train wreck they were all about to experience.

"Another mandatory Council of Creatures meeting." Hunter unlocked the phone so he could read the rest of it, his rings clicking against one another with the motion.

"When?" Eric's fingers tightened around the steering wheel, the leather creaking under his grip. This was going to fuck up their entire plan for the evening. It would throw off the timing of getting to the morgue just after closing. Their plan was to stake the place out so they could get their hands on the freshest turned vampires. Breaking and entering wasn't high on Eric's list of crimes he wanted to be arrested for—not that he wanted to be arrested for any of them—but he knew Kalla would look the other way.

Hunter lifted a hand to scrub at his face, a tired sigh leaving him. "An hour. It says you have to bring Tony with you."

"What the fuck am I? His keeper?" Eric growled at the same time Tony snarled, "Excuse the fuck out of me?"

A soft chuckle left Hunter as he shook his head. It didn't have much joy behind it though because he understood as well as Tony and Eric that they were all fucked. How much of this had been intentional, Eric couldn't be sure. It felt like there was a leak in his camp, but it could have been coincidence. Eric would much rather that be the case than to think someone at the dorm was feeding information to the Council of Creatures. Because if it wasn't Tony or Hunter—which it sure as shit wasn't—that left Janet and the kids. It couldn't be the kids.

"What do we do?" Tony threw himself back into the seat again, his arms crossing over his chest. His glare met Eric's in the rearview mirror. It was an act, Eric could see it. Tony was just as scared as he was. Rattled by the idea that the Council of Creatures might know what they were up to and might report it back to Dash. Maybe he was even afraid that Dash would show up at the meeting.

Eric would do everything in his power to protect Tony from having to face Dash ever again. The man had abused him, raped him. Used his power to twist Tony's will and turn him into a plaything. And when he'd refused to dance any further, Dash had threatened to hurt the people Tony cared about just to keep him quiet.

Rage raced through Eric so hot and sharp, his foot started to press harder on the gas, his beat-up old beamer racing down the main highway into Ironport. A warm, gentle pressure squeezing his forearm pulled him from his thoughts, and he eased off, looking over at Hunter, who was watching him with knowing eyes.

"What's the plan?" Hunter's voice was quiet, calm, and Eric appreciated it. One of them needed to be calm. One of them needed to keep them all on an even keel. Tony ran too hot under the collar—he was always on the edge of boiling, and that was even more true now that the wolf sat so close to the skin. And Eric . . . Well, it was hard to think rationally where Oliver was concerned.

Eric inhaled deeply, forcing himself to think about their options. They didn't have many. Sure, they could wait another night to put their plan into motion. But Eric wasn't willing to do that. Especially when he didn't know what the Council of Creatures was going to demand of them next.

"I'm going to drop you off at the morgue, and you're going to call Ava. Between the two of you, I'm sure you can figure out how to get in there." He didn't like it. Hunter and Ava weren't built for this the way he and Tony were. Anything could happen to them while they waited for Eric and Tony to get there. "We'll be there as soon as we can."

Hunter nodded, but out of the corner of Eric's eye he could see Hunter's hands fidgeting in his lap. Unsettled. Nervous.

"If you don't want to do it, we'll wait. We can always try again tomor—"

"No." Hunter barked the word then sighed, running his fingers through his curly hair. It caught in the rings. "No," he tried again, calmer this time. "Ava and I can handle this. We're just capturing a vampire, right? We've just got to hold them there until you come and get us. And in all probability, they won't be interested in either of us."

"Right, they're after Ricky's sweet, sweet—Ouch! Fuck you!" Tony swatted Eric's arm that he'd reached into the back to punch Tony's leg.

"Boys!" Hunter scolded through his laughter. Tension

eased away from his shoulders as he slumped further into his seat. "Not while we're driving."

"He started it," Eric grumbled.

Tony stuck his tongue out at Eric in the rearview mirror.

Eric snorted a laugh. It was hard not to let the immature, playful nature of their relationship take away the stress that had settled into Eric's bones. It would be easy to forget how well the three of them could get along with everything else going on. But thankfully, Tony had never been the sort to keep his fucking mouth shut, and in this instance, it was for the better.

The door shut behind Hunter, and Tony clambered over the center console to climb into the passenger seat and make an absolute nuisance of himself by dicking with the radio the whole way to the Council of Creatures meeting.

"Dude, could you just leave that alone?" Eric didn't really want him to stop. It was a good distraction, one that he needed. Desperately.

"Shut up, Jeeves," Tony snarked back without any real bite.

"If I'm a chauffeur, then you should be in the back." Eric cut him a side-eyed glance, but Tony seemed unbothered by everything happening. It was an act. One Eric wasn't going to call him on because it would only make things messier.

"What's that?" Tony called over the radio he'd just cranked to some infuriatingly loud old rock song. "Can't hear you!" Then he shouted along to the lyrics. And Eric . . . Well, Eric joined him.

They pulled up outside of the building, still practically screaming along to the radio, the windows rolled down to let in the cooling fall air. Eric cut the engine and looked over at the building where Oliver was standing, his hands in the pockets of his neatly pressed chinos, and the words died in his throat.

"You good?" Tony murmured as he sidled up to Eric's side, bumping their shoulders together lightly. Companionable. Supportive.

"I will be once we get this over with." Eric was glad Tony didn't press further. Tony could have demanded an answer. He could have asked what the fuck was up with Eric and his little brother. But he didn't. Maybe because Hunter had already given him the lowdown, or maybe because he was saving his questions. Letting them pile on his tongue where they could ferment and fester until he knew all of them were safe. Either way, Eric appreciated it.

"Eric," Oliver said, his head dipping in something that would have almost looked respectful if Eric didn't catch the disgusted lilt to his mouth.

Eric returned the nod and headed inside. He felt the warmth of Tony at his side, a hand on his lower back, protective and sure, and he settled into that feeling if only for a moment. Tony had him. So did Hunter. They were in this together. Even if right now it was the two of them against the Council of Creatures. He wasn't alone.

It took a bit for everyone to get into their places and get settled. But once they had, Eric pushed back his shoulders and pressed his mouth into a flat line, ready to take whatever Oliver said next on the chin.

"We appreciate that you brought McMahon," Oliver said, his eyes never wavering from where they watched Eric. As if he were looking for a tell. A chink in the armor.

"Didn't exactly give him much choice," Tony mumbled. Eric resisted the urge to elbow him in the stomach. It would draw more attention.

Oliver's eyebrow twitched, a clear indication that even

without a Venator's enhanced senses, he'd heard. But the smile that quirked at the corners of his lips was enough to tell Eric that whatever came out of Oliver's mouth next would be Tony's comeuppance for being such a little shit. "It is my great misfortune to tell you that from here on, Tony McMahon has been expelled from the Huntsmen community."

Tony stopped shifting, his head jerking from where he'd been watching Eric to narrow a glare on his brother instead. "Excuse me?"

"What does that mean?" Eric asked, giving Tony's hand a warning squeeze. They couldn't afford to tip the council off to everything they were doing. Couldn't afford to have them looking more closely at Eric and his class of Venator. If the council got it into their heads that Eric needed a minder, then all of this was over. Dash would get what he wanted, and that would be the end. Of the Venator classes. Of Eric. Of Tony. Of everything they cared for.

"It means he will no longer be permitted out on Venator patrols of the area. After hearing about how he shifted into a werewolf and ran through the streets of—"

"I've got better control over it now," Tony protested, but it sounded like a lie.

"That doesn't change the fact that you are no longer a Venator. And such activities are for Venator exclusively." Oliver shook his head as if saddened by this news when Eric could see he was anything but.

"What about Hun—"

Eric trod hard on the toes of Tony's shoes, grinding his heel into them. Tony yelped, but it stopped him from saying any more. "We understand," he said, praying to the Goddess that no one had noticed it. "Is that all?"

"No. That is not all." Oliver's brown eyes narrowed on Eric. He didn't know Eric from a hole in the wall. They weren't friends. They weren't even brothers outside of blood.

But he was suspicious, and Eric couldn't have that. "It is our understanding that your Venator class is patrolling in groups. That is unacceptable. They are all of an age where they should—"

"So are you." Eric glared, the expression mirroring his brother's, and took a step forward.

"Excuse me?" Oliver arched a brow.

"You are also of an age where you should be able to handle a patrol of Ironport."

"I'm not a Venator."

"Technically, neither are they. We've had this discussion once already. None of their genes are active. They're no more quick or strong than any other human being—than you. I cannot in good conscience, and will not, let them go into the field without teammates and supervision until their genes are active and they have the added benefits of being a full-fledged Venator to protect them. Or would you like the small force we have to protect Ironport when I'm gone be decimated before they're even really needed?"

"I'd say that there will be no other time they'd be needed outside of—"

"You'd say, but you don't know. Do you? Things are bad now, yes. Worse than they've ever been. But they can still get worse." Eric shrugged. "But sure, put those kids into a situation where they'll die, and see what happens. Maybe some of the older Huntsmen who never tested positive for the gene will start to. Maybe they'll even be activated. We both know what happens when there aren't enough Venator to keep up with the threat. More are made. It's in our nature. In our blood. In *your* blood."

It was mean. It was vindictive. And it may not even be true. Eric had no proof that people who had passed puberty could suddenly test positive as a Venator. But he had no proof that they *couldn't* either. And if there was one thing that would scare Oliver and the other Huntsmen into backing down, it was the idea that if Eric and his class were gone, they would be next.

"There have never been any reports of—"

"No. But we live in unprecedented times, don't we, Oliver? There's a first time for everything."

Oliver's hands clenched one another where they rested on the table in front of him, his whole face spasming with something between fear and fury. "Very well. The groups will remain. But if the threat continues to rise and you're unable to keep up with it, we will be revisiting this issue. And you will not take the wolf out on hunts, especially not this close to the full moon."

"Of course." Eric dipped his head in respect and spun on his heel, not waiting for the argument he was sure would come from Tony. They didn't have time for it. They had to get back to Hunter and Ava. Tony could yell at him once they were back in the car, away from anyone who might hear.

Chapter 25

"THEY CAN'T TELL me where the fuck I can be," Tony grumbled, throwing himself into the passenger seat of Eric's car, his head thumping against the headrest harder than he'd intended. He was pissed. Of course he was. But he was also undeniably horny. Watching Eric put the fear of the Goddess into that stuck-up brother of his was hot. It wasn't Tony's fault he reacted the way he did.

Eric didn't respond. He was busy trying to get his hands to stop shaking as he got the car started. There was something about that too—something about knowing that what Eric had just done rattled him to his core, but he'd done it anyway to protect the gremlins—that made Tony's skin tingle.

The wolf in his chest rumbled an agreement, and Tony rolled his eyes. Who would have guessed that the one thing they would be able to agree on was the fact that they needed to jump Eric Marcelino's bones at any free moment. Typical, really. There was no part of Tony that wasn't a horny bastard.

"Are you going to bench me?" Tony didn't think he wanted the answer. Eric would do what was best for all of them. He would do the thing that would protect the most of them, and there was nothing Tony could do to argue with that. Because if he did, he might put his own sister in danger. That was unacceptable.

"Only on the days of the full moon." Eric tilted his neck

one direction, then the other, the vertebrae popping loudly in the quiet of the night around them. "Three nights."

Arguing further wouldn't change Eric's mind. So Tony bit his tongue, settled in his seat, and waited until Eric had gotten the car into gear and they were headed back the way they'd come to ask, "Do you want to talk about it?"

"No." Eric didn't let his eyes drift from the road, his hands at ten and two like his life depended on driving properly. Maybe it did. Maybe it was the only thing holding him together.

Tony wished he was better at comforting. He wished he knew all of Eric's history and what to say to bring him out of this spiral. But he wasn't Hunter. That thought rankled more than he'd like. The jealous knot that had been curling in his belly grew. He really needed to solve that before he exploded about it. But there never seemed to be enough time. And even when there was, he didn't know where to start. He wasn't good at talking about his problems, especially not his emotional ones. He buried them deep inside of himself and let them fester until he eventually went off in a rage. No matter how unhealthy he knew that was.

Instead of saying whatever Hunter probably would have been able to, drawing Eric out of his shell and laying all their cards on the table, Tony chewed on his tongue in thought. Silence settled over them, thick and suffocating. A weighted blanket of soundlessness that made it hard to breathe.

Why wasn't he better at this? Why couldn't he at least pretend to not be so emotionally constipated? The wolf in his chest grumbled judgmentally, and it took everything Tony had not to snap back at it. How dare it judge him. How dare it act like it'd be better at comforting Eric. But at least that was another thing they agreed on—they wanted to reach out to Eric and make this better somehow.

Maybe he and the wolf had more common ground than he'd originally thought.

Tony opened his mouth as if to say something—what? he still wasn't sure yet—but before he got the chance, they pulled up outside of the morgue. The squat cement building was dark outside and in. The lights in the parking lot had either gone off on a timer, or someone had turned them off on purpose. The windows showed not even an emergency light to differentiate them from the rest of the building.

"Something's not right," Eric murmured, his body going so still, Tony thought he might not be breathing.

"What do you mean?" Tony frowned. He squinted through the windshield at the building and the way the head-lights flashed against the windows.

"You don't feel that?" Eric lifted an arm to show Tony how the hair all along his forearm had raised in alarm.

Wrinkling his nose, Tony closed his eyes and tried to feel whatever Eric felt, but he could only barely sense it. Like it was fading. Like soon he'd be cut off from that eerie sixth sense Venator had. His other senses were better than they'd ever been, but that thing that he'd never been able to explain, the one that told him when danger was right around the corner, would be gone soon. Maybe because wolves didn't have to worry as much as Venator did about not being the biggest, strongest thing prowling the night. They were further up the food chain and didn't have to be as aware. But it was the first time he'd noticed the difference between his abilities as a Venator and what he had now as a werewolf. He had to admit, he didn't like it.

"I smell decay," he said instead, lifting his nose to the air and inhaling deeply. Rot and blood was thick here. Likely because of being parked right in front of a morgue, which was why he hadn't thought much about it before.

"Vampire tinged?" Eric yanked the duffle from the back-seat and started pulling weapons from it, including a pair of sleek new wooden hair sticks, which he handed over to Tony.

"I have—"

Eric shook his head. "Silver ones. Don't think I haven't noticed that you haven't been wearing them. They burn now, don't they?"

Tony shrugged, ducking his head in embarrassment. It was true, he'd stopped using the silver hair sticks because they left his skin and scalp itchy like an allergic reaction. He hadn't developed hives from them yet, but it was just a matter of time. Without a word, he twirled his hair up into a messy bun and stuck the sticks through to hold it in place.

"Vampire?" Eric repeated, dropping several stakes into his lap where he presumably would stuff them into his pockets once he was out of the car.

"Can't tell." Which was never good news. Not knowing what they were heading into was a recipe for disaster. They hadn't known what they were heading into when they went into that house all those months back, and Tony had been nabbed then drugged until— He shook himself. "We'll have to be careful."

"I don't see Ava's car."

Fuck. Hunter was alone in there, with whatever Dash had raised from the dead.

That had Eric and Tony rolling from the car, stuffing stakes into their pockets as they ran toward the morgue.

Getting into the morgue wasn't the worst part of this whole experience.

Hunter had been a bit of a delinquent in his early teens. Breaking and entering a building with no intent to steal was low on the list of crimes he committed throughout his life. He was pretty sure drug possession would rank a lot higher. Plus that time he'd broken into a Denny's just to see if he could make the Moons Over My Hammy himself while high. Thankfully, as far as punishments for those things went, the police had never been called on the drug thing, and when they had been called while he was in the Denny's, the sheriff who picked him up knew his mom. Another witch in the community. And she'd taken him straight home to have his ass handed to him by his mother.

He'd never broken into a morgue before, though. So the breaking and entering part, he was familiar with. It was the morgue part that was proving to be . . .

Spooky was putting it lightly, okay?

It wasn't that Hunter had problems with dead bodies. He'd been around enough of them in his time working in the lab at Moondale U. There were some things scientists could only get from dead bodies. But he'd never been in an actual morgue before. Cold metal tables. Body drawers. A fridge full of . . . *stuff*. No, he wasn't looking at the labels on those jars, thanks.

And it was also the first time he'd been in a place by *himself* where he knew vampires were going to be.

The light from his phone burned his eyes as he lifted it to check if Ava had texted him back yet. It'd been several minutes at this point, and when he looked, he found that the first message didn't even have a read notice under it. That was unusual for Ava. She wasn't exactly attached to her phone, but she usually got back to him within a few minutes.

HUNTER

When are you getting here?

He waited, tapping his rings against the edge of the phone. She wouldn't leave him hanging. Even if she was on a date or something. And she had to have her phone. With everyone as on edge as they were right now, with the shit about to hit the fan for about the fifth time in as many weeks, she couldn't go off the grid. If anything, she'd probably turned her ringer on to make sure she wouldn't miss it if someone needed her.

So why wasn't she answering?

The texts looked like they'd been delivered . . .

A low groan broke Hunter from his thoughts. He gripped his phone tighter.

He squeezed his eyes shut as if not being able to see what was coming for him would keep it from happening. Like a child pulling the blanket over his head.

"I didn't just hear that. I did *not* just hear that," he sang to himself. Maybe if he was louder than the groaning, he could scare it away, show his dominance over the situation.

It didn't work.

Another groan came. Dry. Rasping. Like the sound of a door in a haunted house.

A chill ran down his spine, cold sweat starting at his temples. He was not equipped for this. He was too much of a fucking chicken. Why had he thought he could come in here alone? Why had he thought he could hold out until Tony and Eric got back? In a fucking morgue of all places.

The answer was that Ava was supposed to be on her way. He wasn't supposed to be alone. But . . .

Hunter frowned, pulling up a browser to do a Google search. The little spinning wheel spun, and spun, and spun. Nothing loaded.

The groan came again, this time accompanied by the thud of feet hitting the tiled floor.

It dawned on Hunter then, what this was. What he'd walked right into.

This was a fucking *trap*.

And just as the realization hit him, a puff of warm breath hit the back of his neck.

Hunter screamed and swiveled, his arms flying wildly to smack the vampire in the face. They snarled at him, teeth dripping in venom as they backed him step after step across the open space of the morgue.

Panic seized him by the throat. Any spell he might have used in defense flew from his mind. The only option was flight.

Hunter spun on his heel and hauled ass, putting as much distance between himself and the vampire as he could before slamming the inner office door behind himself, locking it, and then sliding under the desk to hide.

The vampire hissed, slamming their body over and over against the door. Rattling it on the hinges. The knob jiggled like it wanted to give. And all the while, Hunter's heart pounded in his ears, his body curling tighter and tighter around itself where he hid in the well between two sets of drawers in an old wooden desk.

How long could the door hold before the vampire got through?

Hunter nearly lost his grip on his phone as he pulled up his contact list and hit Eric's name. He couldn't get a text out. There was no internet. But maybe this would work? Maybe, *maybe* the Goddess would be on his side, and he could call for help?

The screen lit up, processing the request.

No ringing started.

CHAPTER 26

THE SILENCE that surrounded them when they walked into the morgue was damning. A ringing alert that Eric had failed. Whatever he'd been trying to do here, he'd failed. He wasn't even sure what his goal was anymore.

It didn't matter. Because Hunter was in trouble, might already be dead.

And it would be Eric's fault, just like everything else in this fucked-up city.

Goddess. Why the fuck had anyone ever entrusted themselves, their safety, to someone like him. Someone who even his parents thought was at—

"Eric!"

Nails like claws dug into his shoulders, ripping him back into the moment, and when Eric was able to focus again past the feeling of impending doom that had settled over him, he was faced with Tony's glowing green eyes. His blond brows were drawn up in concern, a frown marking his beautiful face.

"You good, baby boy?" Tony asked, his hand slipping from his shoulder to cup the back of Eric's head, a grounding pressure of claws on the back of his neck. He wondered if Tony realized he'd half shifted in his worry. It was probably better he not point it out, not when Tony was still struggling to come to terms with what he was.

Pressing his forehead into Tony's, Eric inhaled deeply. A mistake, he realized a moment later, as the scent of death and rot invaded his lungs, making them burn and ache. A grounding pain, like the pressure of Tony's slowly retracting claws on the back of his neck.

"Yeah. Fine," Eric said after another deep gulp of air.

Tony waited a beat, watching Eric until he seemed satisfied with what he saw, then he pressed his lips to Eric's forehead and pushed away.

A second later they heard the crash of a door being forced off its hinges, and both broke into a run in the direction of the sound. They skidded to a halt outside the main exam room to find a vampire struggling with the door to the office. It was hanging on by the lock that had been engaged and the upper hinge, making it wobble like a swinging door.

Eric didn't know what the vampire was after, but he could guess and there was no time to check his theories before he acted. Not with how determined the vampire was to get into the office.

"Hey!" It wasn't his best ploy to get the vampire's attention, but Eric didn't have anything better. He needed to get them away from that door, away from where he was almost positive Hunter was hiding. "Hey!"

The vampire whirled around, hissing like a cat at him, their eyes dilating as they stilled for a moment, sniffing the air.

"Are you lookin' for me?" Eric asked, tilting his head curiously. Then he smiled, sharp and dangerous, and took off at a run, praying to the Goddess that they'd follow him. He pushed past Tony, giving him a quick nod, an unspoken order to go to Hunter and take care of him while Eric dealt with the vampire.

He paused for a moment right outside the door and listened, waiting for the sound of the vampire scrambling after him. Then he started at a jog down the long dark hallway. His shoes squeaked on the tile floor, but he heard the vampire behind him, running, trying to keep up.

The door at the end of the hall burst open and Eric pushed out into the cool night air. He heard it slam shut behind the vampire again, and a subtle click echoed in the quiet of the night. They were both locked out. It wasn't much, a flimsy door between the vampire and Hunter and Tony, but it would give Eric the space he needed to run the vampire out while they got back to the car and set up the net.

It would be easier to slay the vampire, but they couldn't waste the chance they'd been given.

His breath came in hard pants as Eric looked over his shoulder. The vampire was still behind him, running mindlessly after. They didn't seem to realize he was leading them in a circle around the building. Good. That would give him room to breathe.

Hunter wasn't sure when he'd started trembling. Was it before or after his phone battery died? There was no way to tell. But as the dark closed in on him, he shook so hard he jammed his shoulder against the desk. It would bruise. But he hardly felt it.

Just like he hardly heard the shout that came from the main part of the morgue shortly after the vampire managed to break through the door. His breath was shallow, his heart was in his ears, and what little light came through the windows from the near-full moon outside did nothing but make his fear ratchet up another notch with the view it revealed.

The door half hung off its hinges and the vampire had one arm through, taloned fingers clawing at the air as they tried to force their way into the room. It wouldn't be long now. Then the vampire would be on him. They would drag him from under the desk, and this would all be over.

He'd be with Britt again, at least. But what about Eric? What about Tony? Chase? The other kids? Would they be all right without him? Would—

"Hey there, handsome." A soft, rumbling voice ripped Hunter from his thoughts, and he focused to find Tony crouched in the opening of the desk, his hand extended like some savior from a movie. Goddess, he looked beautiful like this. "Are you back with me?"

"I—I uh." Hunter swallowed. His heart was still hammering so hard, he felt it throbbing at his temples. He clamped his phone so tight in his hand, he was sure it would leave behind a permanent indent. Fear gripped him tightly. But he was safe now. Tony was here. Eric probably was too. "Yeah." He nodded, forcing himself to reach out with his free hand for Tony's and letting the other man guide him carefully from under the desk, a hand on top of his head to make sure he didn't crack it against the underside. "Yeah, I'm okay."

Tony's brows were pulled together in the center like he didn't quite believe Hunter, but he didn't say so. He also didn't let go of Hunter's hand. His grip dry and calloused. A silent assurance that he was there. That Hunter was safe. Hunter felt that grip like a zing up his spine, doing nothing to settle his heart. Only now it was rabbiting in his chest for an entirely different reason. Goddess, he was pathetic. Getting this worked up over *holding hands*.

"What happened to the vampire?" Not that it really mattered at this point.

"Eric led it away. We've got to get out to the car to get the net laid out. Once you get your legs under you again." Tony pressed his other hand into the small of Hunter's back, and the pressure there felt like a brand. Hunter wanted to lean into it. To curl up against Tony and let him provide any small comforts he could. It was so . . . unlike him. Usually, Hunter was the one doing that for Eric, for Britt. But there was something different about Tony he couldn't put his finger on.

"I'm good."

"Your knees are still shaking, sweetheart. You're not good." Tony snorted. He nudged Hunter closer, lending his support in any way he could. "Take a breath, get your heart rate under control."

Okay. Well. That wasn't going to happen. Not with Tony so close.

Hunter swallowed roughly, willing himself to inhale deeply, hoping it would calm his pounding heart. It didn't. But it did make him feel a bit steadier. He also realized, belatedly, that it had stopped the ringing in his ears and settled his stomach. Had he been holding his breath this whole time? Maybe. It was hard to tell.

"Better," Tony murmured, a gentleness to his tone that made Hunter's stomach twist for a whole other reason. Tony wasn't usually like this. He wasn't generally the caring sort. It looked good on him, but it was also doing funny things to Hunter's insides.

"We shouldn't leave Eric out there by himself."

"It's just one vampire. He can handle one vampire."

The reminder of that made Hunter's stomach drop. Just one. One vampire, and no cell reception. One vampire, and all the lights out. One vampire, and no way to reach out if he needed help. There was something wrong going on, and Hunter just didn't know what. This had been a trap. But the end goal was still unclear. But explaining that to Tony would take too much time. "C'mon, we need to catch the vampire and get back to campus."

Tony frowned at him. He looked like he wanted to ask what the rush was, but whatever he read in Hunter's expression made him change his mind. He nodded. "Okay. Let's go."

Then he tugged Hunter along. Through the broken door, out into the morgue, and into the cool night.

Tony didn't need to know what had Hunter so freaked out, he just needed to know that something about this situation made Hunter hyper alert of some unseen danger. He trusted Hunter's instincts as much as he trusted his own, and Eric's. And wasn't that a thought he'd have to ponder over more later. Because it was weird, wasn't it? To trust someone so wholeheartedly that he was also supremely jealous of? Those two emotions were so in contrast with one another that he wasn't sure how they fit inside his chest.

But it didn't matter. What mattered was that Hunter was positive they needed to catch the vampire and get the fuck out of there. So that's what they were going to do.

He held up a hand, poking his head out the door to ensure the vampire and Eric weren't right there in case the vamp decided to veer toward Hunter again. He didn't think it would. It, like all the others, seemed to get the scent of Eric and lose all sense of anything else. But he wasn't willing to take that chance with Hunter's safety.

The coast clear, he motioned for Hunter to stick close as they made their way across the parking lot to Eric's car. They had only the light of the near-full moon to see by, but it was enough to pop the trunk, get the net out, and lay the trap.

Now all they needed was Eric and the vampire.

"You should get in the car. The wards will keep you safe." Tony ushered Hunter toward the back seat. The wolf rumbled approvingly in his chest. He didn't want to know what that was about. Not when there was so much else to bother with.

Hunter shook his head, brushing off Tony's careful hands. "You might need my magic to stun them."

He was right, as much as Tony didn't like it. As much as something protective had seized hold of him where it came to Hunter, he couldn't argue that Hunter was right. And to ignore him might put Eric in danger. That wasn't something Tony could ever do. So he nodded, brushing his fingers through his hair, and turned back to the parking lot at large.

"Yo! Pretty boy!" Tony shouted, his hands cupped around his mouth to make the sound carry further. "We're all set."

"Headed your way!" Eric shouted as he rounded the corner of the morgue, the vampire hot on his tail. He leapt over the net, almost as if he was afraid that walking on it would capture him too, and the vampire followed close behind, trudging along until it was stopped by the net's containment magic.

Hunter didn't waste any time. Magic sparked from his fingers like electricity in a static ball, forming a knot that he hurled at the vampire. The spell hit. The vampire slumped. Then Eric and Tony hauled it into the trunk of the car.

"Let's get the fuck out of here," Hunter rushed, bouncing on his toes behind them, nervousness rolling off him in waves, making his scent sour with panic.

"What's the rush?" Tony asked.

Hunter shook his head, and no one spoke again until they were all loaded in the car and on the road. Then he said, "I couldn't get any calls or anything out. It was like something was blocking the signal. And then my battery died."

"You think it was a trap," Eric said.

Tony's shoulders tightened.

"To what end?" Tony asked, not really wanting the answer.

"I'm not sure yet. But the sooner we've gotten rid of this vampire, the better."

# CHAPTER 27

"I'M GOING to need you to sit the fuck down and stop pacing." Hunter didn't look up from his work, his back hunched, his shoulders rounded, as he examined the latest sample from the vampire with a microscope. Skin this time, and it was doing the exact same thing the blood had. It was as fascinating as it was terrifying.

"I don't think that's the right order." The stool creaked under Tony's weight as he settled in, and Hunter let out a small breath of relief. It was worse somehow, doing this work with a wolf prowling back and forth in the basement lab. It made the air feel thicker, like he was breathing through molasses.

"Your witticisms aren't helping right now, sweetheart." Hunter kind of wished Eric could be down there with them. But he was busy elsewhere, dealing with the kids, trying to find out how the Council of Creatures knew what was going on under their roof.

They couldn't all lock themselves in the basement until this was over, as much as Hunter wanted to. But the desire to do so was so strong, Hunter could hardly think past it sometimes. It would be easy. Hide away here until Dash got bored. They were relatively safe on campus, more so than anywhere else in Ironport. Maybe when they came up for air, the city itself would be gone. But that mattered little to Hunter at this point.

He shook himself. Goddess, he'd somehow gotten *more* protective of late. It likely had something to do with the loss of Britt. With the guilt and the sadness that still occasionally blindsided him in the middle of the day.

"Anything?" Tony asked, ripping Hunter from his thoughts.

"The skin samples are the same. It's so strange, I've never seen anything like it. Even when I studied parasites years ago, I never saw something that would constantly eat itself over and over again. It's worse than how cancer mutates cells. And so much quicker." It was sick to watch. Like a car crash. He couldn't look away, but every moment he spent watching, his stomach twisted more and more violently.

"So, there's no DNA left from Dash?" Tony was closer now. Hunter didn't know when he'd gotten up from his stool to peer over his shoulder, but his warmth was there now. A comforting, heavy presence against Hunter's back.

Hunter flicked the switch on the microscope that made it display what he was seeing on the screen to his right so Tony could watch it too. It was mesmerizing.

"None. I think we'd have to get a vampire right after they'd been turned to get a viable sample of his DNA for the tracer to track." If they were going to do that, they might as well just trap Dash and use *his* DNA. Which would defeat the entire purpose of this exercise.

"What about saliva?"

"It's the same."

"Spinal fluid?"

"The same. I've taken a sample of anything and every-thing that could possibly hold DNA, and there's not a single string of Dash left in this vampire. They're wholly their own." Which didn't make a whole lot of sense to Hunter. He'd have thought that because Dash was the parasite, and his DNA was the one taking over the body of a human, that eventually the human's DNA would all be Dash's. That would make more sense. Nothing about vampirism followed traditional science. It set Hunter's teeth on edge.

"Does it ever stop?" There was a strained awe in Tony's voice that Hunter completely understood.

"Not that I've seen. I'd have to look at the samples periodically over the next few months. Maybe it slows down? But . . ." He bit his lip, his eyes fixed on the cells slowly morphing, eating themselves, reproducing, over and over. "This is probably why vampires are immortal. Their cells never stop replicating."

Tony made a soft noise in the back of his throat, like agreement or wonder, Hunter couldn't tell. "But isn't that also what happens with cancer? Cells replicate and replicate and mutate, and then the mutated cells replicate?"

"Same concept, but with vampiric cells and on a much faster time frame." Hunter nodded. "Explains the dramatically quick healing factor as well. For example"—Hunter reached over and pulled a petri dish labeled *Eric* from the fridge on the counter, swapping it out for the vampiric sample he'd just been working with—"this is how a Venator's cells work."

The cells on the screen were doing the same thing as the vampire cells, just much slower. Taking minutes instead of seconds to regenerate. It was amazing to see the similarities but also the differences. Hunter would love to make a full study of this. To see the way the many species of folk were different and yet similar to one another. To look at magic on a cellular level, instead of on the macro level the magical community had always used. Why were there so many different types of fae? When a werewolf shifted, were they different on a cellular level? Did they always have the DNA of a canine after being turned, or only when they were in their wolf form? How did a medium look different from a witch with seeing magic?

There were so many avenues to go down. So many things to learn!

Hunter was breathless just thinking about it.

But they had to solve the problem of Dashfield B.M. Chadwick first, then hopefully he'd have the time to explore this further. Once they were safe. Once he knew he didn't have to worry every night whether Eric would come home or not. Then he could let his scientific imagination go on a roll.

Likewise, then he could better explore this thing happening between him and Tony. He wanted to lean into Tony's warmth at his side. Let the other man take some of the weight off his shoulders so he didn't have to bear it alone.

"Did you figure out what Dash has done to them to make them so . . ." Tony gestured back to the vampire on the table with their bruised wrists and tousled clothing. They had jerked around so much on the table that it had nearly fallen over before Hunter subdued them.

"Rabid?" Hunter frowned, spinning on his stool so he could look at the vampire, who was so still they might be asleep. Did vampires sleep? He wasn't sure. They'd only captured two so far, and neither of them had. He supposed he could ask Janet, but she liked to lie just for the fun of it. "I don't know. I don't have a vampire that isn't like this to test against, unless you count Janet, but she's—"

"A weird one," Tony finished for him.

"Right. I do want to take some samples from her eventually. See how her vegetarian lifestyle changes things for her, versus a vampire who drinks blood from people regularly. I just wish I had more time to experiment." Hunter pushed his glasses into his hair and scrubbed at his face. He'd taken his rings off to get samples, making his hands look terribly bare.

"You'll get time," Tony murmured gently, reaching for Hunter's cheek, hesitant and slow. Like he was unsure if he was allowed to touch. Unsure if he was the one who should provide such comfort.

Hunter met him halfway, leaning his cheek into Tony's palm, soaking up any small bit of warmth provided. It eased something in his chest he didn't know was tight, his shoulders drooping at the reminder that this would all be okay. It had to be. There was no other option. And even if Hunter couldn't ensure that outcome by himself, he wasn't alone in this. He had Eric. He had the kids. He had Ava and Kalla. And he had Tony.

Tony's thumb brushed the skin along his cheekbone, and Hunter swallowed a happy trill that threatened to crawl up his throat. He didn't want to scare Tony off. Not when all of this was so new. Better not to push it. He hardly breathed, almost afraid Tony would realize what he was doing.

The moment stretched between them. The warmth of Tony's palm seeped into Hunter's skin, color slowly rising on Tony's cheeks, making his freckles turn a darker shade against the redness. Then he cleared his throat and pulled back, his eyes averted to the vampire once more, embarrassed.

"Did you . . ." He cleared his throat. "Why did Dash plan to trap Eric in the morgue with this one?"

"Unclear." Hunter shrugged, scrubbing at his nose to hide the smile that threatened to take over his face. He couldn't help it, Tony was so cute like this. All blushing and shy. Nothing like the brazen way he'd pursued Eric. One day Hunter would ask him why, after they'd gotten over this strange bump in the road where Tony didn't think he was allowed to have this with Hunter. "Nothing I've seen from this one is any different from the last."

"Could it have been a coincidence that the cell service was blocked there? Maybe a weird dead zone? Maybe they have a blocker in the building to keep staff from using their phones at work?" Tony tilted his head at the vampire. They were starting to stir, their eyes blinking harder than before, their fingers twitching.

"I don't think so."

"What are we going to do with it?"

"Them," Hunter corrected gently. "They're a person still, Tony. Even if they've been taken over by this . . . disease."

Tony turned to blink at him, eyes wide and brows drawn up like no one had ever corrected him about this before. Like maybe he'd never thought about how the language he used demonized an entire species of folk.

"Rus said most vampires abroad aren't like the ones here," Hunter explained calmly. "It's hard not to think of them as people once you know that." Although he knew Eric had been doing it for decades. Eric saw too much of himself in the vampires, and now that Hunter had examined a vampire versus a Venator on a cellular level, he could see why. They had more commonalities than differences.

"Right. Sorry." Tony dipped his head in acknowledgment and understanding. It would no doubt take him time to get used to the shift in mindset, but this was a start. "What are we going to do with them?"

A bone-deep ache settled into Hunter's joints at the thought of what they were going to have to do. This was so different from the last vampire he'd had on his lab table—the one that had been decaying, more dead than alive. This vampire was so close to being *human*. He knew there wasn't any choice. He couldn't keep the vampire subdued indefinitely while he searched for a cure to what Dash had done to them. Especially when he didn't *know* what Dash had done to them.

Tony didn't seem to need an answer. He understood what Hunter was thinking without him having to say anything. Which was a relief, although it didn't make the situation any less bad. It still felt like murder. Even more so now that Hunter had seen how close the vampire's cells resembled

Eric's. But they couldn't let the vampire continue to live in this state. They were too dangerous, and they were no doubt miserable, half out of their mind.

"I'll do it," Tony said gently, reaching for the stake. "We've gotten everything we can, right?"

"Yeah." He wanted to turn around. He wanted to not have to watch as Tony turned the vampire to dust, but that would be disrespectful. The vampire deserved for Hunter to acknowledge them and their suffering. So he watched, his eyes burning with tears as Tony buried the stake in their chest, and a moment later the vampire burst into dust.

Red. Dust.

The fan over the vampire wheezed. The lights flickered. The breaker flipped and they were cast in darkness before an alarm started blaring, red lights flashing from the sensor Hunter had installed some weeks back over the worktable.

"That's not good," Hunter whispered, then he started to cough, his body too hot. Too cold. His stomach twisting.

Tony lurched forward and vomited on the floor, then fell to his knees.

"What the fuck is going on down there?" Eric called from the top of the steps.

"Don't come down here!" Hunter shouted, already running to the door at the bottom of the steps and locking it to keep Eric out. "We've been contaminated!"

"Contaminated by *what*?" Eric banged his fists against the door. "Hunter, let me in."

"Not until the air is clear!" He stumbled across the floor, his legs wobbly. Tony sidled up to his side, but he wasn't much better. "The breaker. We need to flip the breaker back on, get the fan going to dispel it."

Tony nodded, and between the two of them they managed to get to the switchboard on the wall. With shaking fingers, they both flipped breakers off then back on in a rush. Sweat slicked Hunter's body, cooling. But the fan eventually kicked on, sucking the dust into it as it rattled.

"What will happen to it?" Tony asked.

"It'll be contained for the—" Hunter coughed, tasting something metallic on his tongue. It could be blood. It could be cold. There was no way to tell unless he looked, and he didn't want to. "For the moment. I'll have to purify the air. But first—" He wheezed, his body slumping further against Tony, who seemed to be fairing a bit better—likely because of his werewolf nature—but was also trembling violently. "But first I need to figure out what the fuck that was. And if we're contagious."

"Hunter! Tony!" Eric shouted, still pounding on the door.

"Not yet!" Tony barked, his voice too loud in Hunter's ears. "Go check on the kids, pretty boy. We've got this covered. We're okay."

"I'm coming right back!" The stairs groaned under Eric's weight as he went up to the main house to check in with everyone else.

"*Are* we okay?" Tony whispered.

"I don't know yet."

CHAPTER 28

"HOW DO we know we aren't contagious?" Tony's voice was weak, thready. There was a sheen of sweat on his brow that Eric could see even from across the room where he was currently pacing in front of the door.

He'd managed, somehow, to lug them both up the stairs and tuck them into the tiny bed in his room. It wasn't ideal, but it was the only bedroom in the house with an ensuite bathroom, and the less they exposed the kids, the better. Taking chances with his own health was fine—he was sure his Venator system could take it. Taking chances with the kids was not. Which is why Chase and Lu were locked out, likely pacing the hall at that point.

"I don't care if you *are*," Eric snarled, his words muffled by the medical mask he'd put on before going into the basement to retrieve his idiot boyfriends. His gaze narrowed on where Tony was sitting against the headboard, his body pressed so close to Hunter's, they had to be touching under the covers. Good. Maybe being laid up in bed together would mean they finally talked to each other about what the fuck was going on between them.

"Eric." Hunter breathed out the word, exasperated, exhausted. His skin had taken on a paler hue, the normally rich brown gone washed out with illness. His bright eyes were glassy in a way Eric had never seen before.

Fear crawled up Eric's spine, threatening to paralyze him. What if he lost them? What if whatever illness had been spread to them from that vampire was enough to kill them? He couldn't—he couldn't think like that. This would be fine. It wasn't deadly, he was sure of that. Dash wouldn't have wanted to take the risk that the virus, or whatever it was, would kill Eric before he had a chance to do it himself. It was meant to slow him down, meant to weaken him. Make him an easy target.

"Don't *Eric* me!" Eric snapped, fixing Hunter with the same heated expression. "You knew something was wrong, and you didn't take any precautions. I'm furious with both of you."

He wasn't really. He was just . . . *scared*. But it was easier to be angry than to let the terror take him. At least he knew what to do with anger. It was an emotion he was familiar with. Fear . . . Well, honestly, he was familiar with that one too. But he'd never really learned how to handle it. Not in all the years he'd been doing this. So he'd stick with the one he knew how to deal with.

"We had the fan on," Tony grumbled, rolling his eyes. "Not our fault the dust kicked it off."

"It is your fault you weren't wearing any protective gear." Eric bit the words out, his jaw ticking with every one. It wasn't fair of him to expect that they'd have done that. They couldn't have known. This circumstance was completely unprecedented.

"I need to be in the lab." Hunter struggled against his weakness to push himself up to a seat beside Tony. The movement was accompanied by a soft whine and a shiver. Tony reached over to help him, and between the two of them, they managed to get Hunter into an upright position. Although they were both panting and sweating once it was done. "I need to figure out what this is so I can fix it."

"Absolutely. Not." Goddess, he was giving himself a fucking migraine grinding his teeth. He needed to get his heart rate down before it got to the point of incapacitating him. There wasn't time for that. But he couldn't seem to get control over himself. Every time he thought he might have, he looked at Tony and Hunter lying there in his bed, looking so shaky, so small, and he lost control again.

But Hunter had a point. They needed to work on a cure for this thing, and fast. He couldn't afford for this to permanently damage Hunter's and Tony's health, and not just because of his feelings toward them. He needed them. They were crucial to his fight against the vampires, something the Council of Creatures and his brother seemed unable to understand.

"Eric." Goddess, Hunter sounded so fucking tired. Like he'd been ill for months instead of less than an hour.

Eric's heart clenched in his chest. "Ava will be here within the hour," he said, not giving Tony nor Hunter a moment to argue. "She's bringing Icarus. Between them and Bert, I'm sure they'll figure this thing out. I know no one has the kind of knowledge you do about the magical body, but Bert will set up a video call between you and the lab. That'll have to be enough."

Hunter's hands clenched around the blanket in his lap, his mouth pursed in a hard line. He was pissed. Eric could see it. Hell, he could even understand it. But there was no moving him on this. "It would get done faster if—"

"I don't fucking *care!*" Eric's voice broke on the last word, the fear finally gripping his throat so tightly, the words came out strangled as tears burned his eyes. He couldn't take much more of this.

There was a tipping point, a precipice, a cliff, and he was standing on it, waiting for one more thing to push him over the edge. It had been— Fuck, he'd been doing this since he was thirteen. Over two decades now. Over half his *life. Most* of his life, if he were to sit down and do the percentages, probably. Not that he was going to—it would make all of this worse.

But in all those years, it had only ever been his neck on the line. The safety of the people he loved was never up for question because he was able to keep them out of the fight. Push them far enough away, be alone when he had to, to protect them. Then Tony arrived, and all of that came down around Eric's ears. They were in this now. This wasn't just his fight anymore. It was *theirs.*

Still. Enough was enough.

"I'm the leader of this group, and this is how it's going to work," Eric said, his words hard, stiff. He didn't like pulling rank like this. It had never been his way. And he knew Hunter had a point, that having him down there would make this all go so much faster. But he couldn't stand the thought of Hunter or Tony leaving the bed when they both could hardly sit up. What if they fell down the stairs? What if they passed out? They could hit their heads! "You two will stay in this bed and let the others act as your hands to find a solution to this. Have I made myself clear?"

Hunter and Tony both blinked at him, green and brown eyes different in color but matching in that wide-eyed expression. Eric would like to say it made him feel powerful—in charge—but it didn't. His shoulders curled in tighter around his chest, and he ducked his head, making himself a smaller target for whatever those looks meant. He wasn't sure. They were so dissimilar to anything he'd ever seen on Hunter's and Tony's faces before.

"You've made yourself perfectly clear, pretty boy," Tony said, gentle, soft. Like he could see through all of Eric's bravado into the panicking core of him. He probably could. Tony tended to be brash and obnoxious at times, but he knew people and he'd always been able to see Eric for what he was. Or at least, that's how Eric felt anyway.

"Okay. Good." Eric nodded then lifted his chin, his confidence returning. But the moment he got a good look at Tony and Hunter again, the realization sunk in.

He needed to do something about Dashfield B.M. Chadwick before he came for the people Eric loved again. Even if this hadn't been a direct attack against them. Even if this trap was meant for *him*. Eric wasn't going to let Chadwick near them ever again. He would—

He would put an end to this.

"I'm going to run to the store," he found himself saying before he'd fully processed the plan forming in his mind. "Do you two need anything? Cold medicine? Extra blankets?"

Tony tilted his head, confusion drawing his brows together.

"Eric," Hunter said, the tone a warning, but Eric was already backing toward the door. He wasn't at all surprised that Hunter saw through what he was doing. If either of them was going to, even when they were sick like this, it would be Hunter. He knew Eric too well.

"Vitamin C would help, right? I mean, I know this thing isn't like a typical cold, but Vitamin C can never go amiss, right?" What the fuck was he even *talking* about? It didn't matter. He just needed to get out of the room, out of the house, before Hunter managed to get out of bed and Tony realized what was going on.

"Eric, don't you fucking *dare*." Hunter pushed against the headboard. His arm gave out from under him, but he didn't stop struggling. He kicked against the covers to try to get his feet on the ground. "Eric Salvatore Marcelino, I'm not fucking around!"

"Orange juice," Eric concluded, nodding as he took hold of the knob in preparation to shut the door behind him. He could take off at a run once he had it between him and the room. He just needed to get there. "You definitely need orange juice. Two bottles. One with no pulp, the other with extra pulp."

"What's he doing?" Tony asked, but he hadn't moved yet. He was watching Eric like a predator might prey. Thankfully, Eric was used to that feeling and it didn't slow him down at all.

"You boys sit tight. I'll be back in an hour, maybe two." He waved and slammed the door behind him. "Keep an eye on them," he told Lu and Chase, who were leaning against the wall outside. "And don't go in there."

They both blinked at him, confused.

"ERIC!" Hunter shouted after him, then he broke out into a coughing fit so violent, Eric's stomach lurched. All he wanted was to go back into that room and comfort them. To sit with them. To wait on them hand and foot while they got over this thing, together.

He couldn't.

Because the quickest way to ensure they were both safe was to capture Dashfield B.M. Chadwick. To force that son of a bitch to tell him what he'd done to that vampire that would cause an illness like this.

And that's what Eric was going to do.

His heart hammered in his chest, a thin sheen of sweat gathering on his lower back as he leapt down the steps two at a time. He didn't pause at the foot of the steps, or on the first floor, to tell the others where he was going. Too much chance that Tony and Hunter would get their feet under them while he wasted time. Too much chance that one of the kids would try to stop him.

He trusted Ava to have this well in hand. To do everything she could to understand what the fuck was going on. Or at the very least, to keep Hunter and Tony from hurting themselves further while he went after the culprit of all of this.

The world outside was turning to dusk, the evening closing in around him, cool and windy. Summer was dying on the vine, finally, after clinging for so long, giving over to fall. Not the ideal weather for drawing a vampire out into the open, but Eric wasn't going to complain.

After all, he'd always liked this time of year growing up. Before he'd become a Venator. Before all he became to his parents was an exterminator. He remembered—the memories blurry and soft—the last dregs of warm weather at the beach with his parents. He remembered his mother in a striped one piece, hiding under a big umbrella, looking like the first Barbie. He remembered his father chasing him into the water as he ran screaming, the surf biting at his ankles as it slowly warmed for the day.

It was the happiest he had ever been.

Early fall was also when he'd first tested positive for his Venator gene.

The doctor's cold sterile room, a jarring contrast to the sunshine and warmth of the outside. The table hard, cutting into his thighs. His mother standing at his side, holding his hand, telling him everything would be okay. Telling him there was no reason to think that he'd have the gene. She didn't. His father didn't. Why should he?

But the room wasn't the worst part. The anxiety leading up to the needle in his arm, the news that he was positive for a Venator gene . . . None of that was the worst part. Not even the way his mother dropped his hand and took a visible step back like he was contagious.

The worst part was that that year, his parents went to the beach without him.

Fitting then, that this confrontation with Dash would happen now.

With fall well and truly setting in, and lingering traces of summer blown away on the wind. With the cool breeze cutting through his jacket and tasting of brackish water, and the world winding itself down for a season full of early nights and cozy blankets.

Maybe if he survived this, he'd take the kids to the beach next summer.

They deserved a break.

CHAPTER 29

"WHAT'S HE DOING?" Tony's throat was tight, his eyes darting around Hunter's shocked face. Searching. He wished he understood Eric half as well as Hunter did, but at the same time, Tony recognized that knowing him that well might give him gray hairs or make him go bald early, if the look of pure fear on Hunter's face was anything to go by. "Hunter. What is Eric doing?"

He had some inkling of what Eric was up to. Because Eric was just as rash, just as stupid, at times as he himself was. But that couldn't prepare him for what Hunter said to him next.

"He's going after Dash by himself," Hunter whispered. He was still staring at the door, his hands tightened into fists, his knuckles going white.

Tony's heart plummeted, swooping toward his stomach in a way that made him heave like he might throw up again. Fear caught him in its net, winding around him like a puppet on strings. "What are we going to do?"

Hunter shook himself finally. He still looked shaky, sick. It was amazing he was sitting up at all, given the fact that witches didn't have any added strength or resilience. They were just long-lived humans with magic. But, Tony supposed, the need to keep Eric from doing something stupid enough to get him killed would be strong enough to get him up and moving even when he was deathly ill too. There was something about Eric Marcelino that called to a person to protect him. Likely because he'd spent his entire life looking out for other people.

"Hunter," Tony tried again, his fingers twitching at his sides. He needed to get up. He needed to move. Even as the weakness weighed him down. Even as his eyes drooped with exhaustion. There wasn't anything he could do, not that he could think of, but the desire was so strong, his muscles jerked with it. Or maybe that was whatever sickness he'd been infected with slowly shutting his body down. He didn't know. It didn't matter. What mattered was dragging Eric back before he got himself fucking killed. "Hunter, what are we going to do?"

Hunter breathed in deep through his nose and let it out through his mouth. His hands trembled as he grabbed his phone from the nightstand. It fell to the bed with a dull thunk, and Tony reached to hand it back, gentle, calm, even as his heart hammered against his chest and panic gripped his throat. After another moment, Hunter managed to get the phone open and call someone. He put it on speaker so Tony could hear everything.

"We're on our way. Chill out," Ava said, sounding exhausted and worn thin.

"I know. But . . ." Hunter chewed on his lip, the ring pierced through the flesh flashing in the low lights. "Eric has gone after Dash."

"You've got be fucking *kidding* me," Ava hissed.

"What is it?" Someone asked in the background, but the voice was so muffled, Tony couldn't tell if it was Icarus or Vanessa Cochburn.

"Eric has gone after Dash," Ava repeated dutifully before returning her attention to Hunter. "We'll be there in five. I'm going as fast as I can. Do you think Kalla could get me out of a speeding ticket if I got caught?"

"If she doesn't, I'll hex her myself." Hunter breathed out a sigh of relief. "We're going to get down to the lab to help you guys. Even if it's just to oversee things."

"Eric isn't going to like that." But Ava sounded like she approved. "How quick do you think we can have this thing solved?"

Hunter's shoulders hunched toward his ears, his expression cagey, closed off, like he didn't want to answer. Tony held his breath, his body tensing. "The quicker you get here, the quicker we can get to work."

"Right." Ava's tone was clipped, worried. "We'll be there soon."

Then she hung up, the line going dead, and Hunter slumped back against the headboard again. Sweat clung to his brows, making his curls stick there, and he was breathing heavily. "All right, up," he said, and Tony thought he meant it more for himself than for anyone else.

"Maybe you should give yourself a—"

Hunter jerked his head to fix Tony with a hard glare, and Tony held his hands up in surrender.

"I'm just saying, breathe. We've got a bit to get downstairs, we should take our time."

"We don't *have* time!" Hunter snarled, showing teeth. Magic skittered across his skin like a static ball, out of control and sharp smelling. "We don't have time to fuck around, Tony. We need to get this shit out of our system so we can go after him. Don't tell me to sit back and watch another person I love die. Don't you fucking *dare*."

"Okay." Tony nodded. He knew all this, of course. It was just a struggle to see Hunter so weak and tired when, from his perspective, Hunter had been the rock that held them all up. There were times shortly after Britt died when Hunter had been more vulnerable, but Tony wasn't around for those. All he'd ever seen of Hunter was the man Eric relied on to keep him together, to bolster him. The one Eric trusted above all others. It was unimaginable to think that the one who lifted Eric up was also the least powerful of them. The one who was the most human.

"Okay." Tony sucked in a breath, swallowing his nausea. "Let me help you."

From there, it was a struggle against his own weakness to get Hunter on his feet and toward the door. They had to pause every few minutes to breathe through the exhaustion and the dizziness, but they didn't stop. Even when Tony wanted to, more than anything. Even when his bed called his name and his knees shook under him.

"Hey! Where do you two think you're going?" Lu called across the living room, her slippers already scuffing as she marched over to where they'd just reached the bottom of the steps. The kids had congregated there, it seemed. All of them together, trying to comfort one another maybe, in the wake of everything going on.

"Eric said you needed to stay in bed," Chase agreed in his quiet, gentle way.

"Well Eric isn't here, is he?" Tony sniped, feral and sharp, and he felt bad about it. He did. But Goddess, it was exhausting holding himself and Hunter up now that they had stopped moving.

"No, but he'll be back!" Bert joined them, blocking the path to the basement. "He just went—"

"He didn't go to the store, kid," Hunter murmured, far gentler. "He went after Dash. He's planning a suicide mission."

Chase jerked as if he'd been slapped. "What is he—"

"Why would he *do* that?!" Bert's face lost some of its color, the eyes behind his glasses darting around as if he could find some indication that Hunter was lying to him.

"Because he's a fucking idiot. That's why," Tony snarled. "Now, are you going to help us? Or get in the way? Cause I gotta say, kid, I'm over—"

"I'll help." Bert nodded firmly, and the others joined in, already rising from the couches in the living room.

"We'll see if we can track his phone, see where he's gone," Lu said.

"I'll call Kalla, send someone that way. Maybe she can cut him off at the pass," Kate volunteered.

"Good idea." Hunter nodded then groaned, holding his head. "And when Ava and the others get here, send them down. We're going to get to work on a cure for whatever this bullshit is that was in the vampire."

"I could—" Bert's jaw worked for a moment as if he were chewing on his words, on the offer. "We could go out after him."

"No!" Hunter and Tony shouted at the same time, both so loud and afraid that Bert jolted.

"If you go out there, you'll put yourselves and him in more danger," Hunter said, his tone soft and reasonable suddenly.

Bert's brows lifted, a frown tugging at the corners of his mouth, clearly displeased with this accusation.

"He'll be too worried about keeping you all from getting killed to look after himself," Tony added to waylay whatever bullshit the kids might think of getting up to.

"Just give us a couple of hours," Hunter pled. "We'll get this sorted and then we'll go after him ourselves."

Bert's jaw clacked shut and the lot of them nodded, scattering to deal with their respective tasks.

When they finally made it to the basement and found it mostly cleaned up since they'd been relegated to bed, Tony asked, "Do we *have* a couple of hours?"

"I don't know." Hunter slumped onto the stool at the counter along the wall, his fingers fiddling with an empty petri dish. "It'll take him a bit to get down the mountain."

"And the sun hasn't fully set yet."

"Right, but that won't stop Dash."

"No, but I doubt he'd attack Eric in broad daylight. He'll want to do it in the dark." Tony leaned back against the metal worktable, his hands leaving behind sweaty prints. "Less chance of someone seeing."

Hunter nodded, taking another deep breath before he pushed to his feet. "It'll take Eric time to find the best place to lay his trap, he won't want a chance of Dash escaping once he has him. He'll use the net."

"You think that's what he'll do?" It was the smartest method, Tony had to admit. It's what he'd do were he in Eric's place. But how clearly was Eric thinking with every-thing that had happened? Could he be trusted to make a wise tactical choice right that second? No. Clearly not. If he could, then he wouldn't have left the house without backup.

"I *hope* that's what he'll do," Hunter said like a confession as he crossed the room to a box set against the wall. It was connected by tubing that Tony hadn't noticed before to the fan above the table.

"And if it's not?" Tony didn't want the answer to that question. He knew he didn't. But he was going to ask it anyway, because he had to. He needed to be prepared for the worst-case scenario, and Hunter knew Eric best.

"Then we're all fucked." Hunter sighed, his shoulder hitting the wall with a hard *thunk*. His head was tilted down-ward, his face hidden by a curtain of curly black hair that hung in gnarled strands from the sweat and the sickness. A rattle sounded when he breathed. How much longer could he do this? Would this thing kill him? "Come help me with this."

"We should put on protective gear." The metal table shook as he pushed off it to stand upright again, his knees knocking beneath him.

"We've already been exposed." A shrug accompanied the words, like Hunter didn't really care about his illness. Like all that mattered was getting to Eric before he got himself killed. Tony could understand that feeling, probably more than anyone else. But he couldn't give in to it. And he wouldn't let Hunter either.

"And what if this makes it worse, huh?" Tony grabbed him by the arm and pulled him away from the container holding the ashes of the vampire that caused all of this.

"I'll take that chance." Hunter jerked his arm, but he was so weak that even if Tony was just as sick, he couldn't pull away.

"I won't. C'mon, it'll take two minutes to put on a mask." He pulled Hunter toward the metal cabinet in the corner where the supplies were kept. He'd seen a couple of masks and things in there when he'd helped Hunter with their experiments before.

"You're a pushy bastard, aren't you?" Hunter snapped, but he took the respirator mask and put it over his face, the straps getting caught in his hair. His hands trembled to the point that Tony snatched the mask from him.

"You're going to make yourself bald like that, asshole. Let me help." He didn't wait for an answer before he was gently tying Hunters curls up in a hair tie from his own wrist. He carefully pulled the mask straps over Hunter's ears then did the same with his own. "There. Now. What do you need me to do?"

"Let's get this thing emptied. Then we can see what we're working with here." Hunter bent down, his balance wavering, and Tony had to grab him before he fell over.

"Let me." Tony patted him lightly then bent to retrieve the sealed bin at the bottom. It reminded him a lot of the dehumidifier he and Lu had to use to keep their basement dry when they lived in Miami. He wobbled on his feet as he headed to the counter with Hunter behind him, then set it down. "Now what?"

"Now we hope that whatever is left of the vampire is viable and whatever Dash used is easily identifiable."

"And if it's not?"

"We'll cross that bridge when we come to it." Hunter mumbled through the mask.

Chapter 30

SOME PLANS WERE shit from the get-go. Eric knew that better than most. A lot of his plans, as it turned out, were. But this one, he thought, took the cake.

Was that going to stop him? Absolutely not.

If he had more time, maybe he'd think up something else. Give himself a minute to ponder over all the problems that might arise from this one stupid-as-fuck decision. But there was no time. Not with Tony and Hunter as sick as they were. Not with the mystery of what caused their illness hanging over their heads.

Capturing Dash was the simplest, quickest way to get answers on what he'd done to the vampire to make it so dangerous after it was staked. What Eric would do with Dash once he'd trapped him, he didn't know yet. He didn't have Hunter's magic to incapacitate him. And there was no Tony there to help him shove the vampire in the trunk.

He'd figure something out.

He just needed to get Dash to chase him into the net and get stuck there first.

But before all of that, he had to draw Dash out. Easier said than done. Eric had no idea where the bastard had holed himself up. No way to reach him since the number he'd used when he'd been playing at being an everyday citizen of Ironport was disconnected.

So, Eric was going to have to drop a couple of hooks and hope one of them caught a fish. Not completely out of the ordinary, honestly.

First and foremost, a call to Oliver.

There was no proof at all that his brother was working with Dash, but there was no proof that he wasn't either. And what was the worst that could happen if he tried this and Oliver wasn't actually working with Dash? Oliver would be kind of annoyed. Which was less than Oliver deserved.

"If you're calling to state your case on why that *dog* should be allowed out on patrols with you, you're wasting both our time," Oliver said as soon as the line clicked through.

"I'm not, actually. But I think the werewolf on the Council of Creatures would find it interesting that you're referring to a member of her species as a dog. What was her name again? Melinda? Maybe I'll just—"

"What the fuck do you *want*, Eric?"

Eric chewed on his lower lip thoughtfully. He hadn't really thought of a lie to use on Oliver yet. He hoped that he'd come up with something once he had him on the phone. The problem was that talking to Oliver was like running through the quicksand in that *NeverEnding Story* movie the kids made him watch a few weeks back. It bogged down his brain. It made his muscles feel heavy and tired. And every second he spent doing it reminded him of the difference between himself and Oliver in upbringing, in status, and in the love their parents showed them.

"Spit it out *brother*, I'm busy." The word *brother* was said with as much disgust and disdain as the word *dog* had been. Like Oliver couldn't fathom how he was related to a creature so lowly.

"I'm headed to the morgue. We picked up a vampire from there last night, and there was something going on with it. I figured I'd drop in, check for clues." His fingers tightened on the steering wheel, mind racing. What could he say to explain why he needed to tell Oliver this? What lie would make this seem normal? The sun beat through the windshield on its way toward the horizon, burning Eric's eyes. He needed a lie. A good one.

"*So?*" The annoyance was evident in Oliver's voice. There was a subtle sound of murmured chatter behind it. Like he was in a coffee house or a restaurant or something. Probably someplace overpriced, given the nature of their family. "I'm out to dinner right now. If you can't get to a point—"

"I just thought you'd like to know since you seemed so interested in what was going on with the Venator," Eric snapped. It wasn't his best idea, but he couldn't think of another one. At least it got the information to Oliver without inviting him to the location. Not that he thought Oliver would show up even if Eric asked, but Eric wasn't willing to take that chance. Even if he hated his brother. The goal here was to save lives, not put more in danger.

Oliver scoffed, a sound likely accompanied with an eye roll from what little Eric knew of his brother. "You called to be a petty bitch about my decision then?"

"Pretty much." Eric did his best to sound flippant. It would be better if Oliver didn't suspect what was really going on. "Wouldn't want my new *boss* to think I was slacking on my job, would I?"

"I presume you're not taking the children with you?"

The question set Eric's instincts on high alert. Was Oliver checking to see if Eric would have backup with him? Or was he just being an asshole? There wasn't any real way to tell. He didn't know his brother well enough, especially with a phone between them. "No. I'm not bringing Tony or Hunter or any of the others either, before you ask. I figured I didn't need all that backup for a fact-finding mission."

Oliver hummed softly as if he found this all very interesting. Eric thought that *might* mean he was logging the information mentally for someone else, or at the very least for a future date. This whole conversation would probably come back to bite Eric in the ass . . . if he lived long enough for that to happen. He could only be so lucky.

"I see," Oliver said after a moment. "Well. I wish you luck, brother."

"Yeah. Thanks." Goddess, this had gotten fucking awkward quick. He hadn't been expecting that. Stupid really. He should know better.

"Is that all?"

"Yeah. Whatever. That's it." He should hang up. That would be easier. But as much as Eric didn't get along with his brother, as poorly as Oliver and the rest of Eric's family had treated him, there was a bit of politeness engrained in him that wouldn't allow him to. That kept him on the line until Oliver said he could hang up.

Oliver, it seemed, didn't stand on such ceremony. He simply said, "Good" and then the line cut out.

A long slow breath exited Eric's mouth, ruffling his bangs, and he let himself relax into his seat. There was no guarantee that the information would get back to Dash via Oliver, but he wasn't the only one who knew where Eric was going. He'd been sure to let Janet know on the way out the door too. And then there was the matter that he wouldn't be surprised at all to find some kind of warding at the morgue set up to let Dash know when Eric was there. Dash did have a witch on his payroll, after all.

Still, Eric wound down the windows to his car, pulled a knife from the duffle bag on the passenger seat, and cut a long line into his palm. It hurt like a bitch, his heartbeat settling into the wound to leave it throbbing, and the scent of blood made his nose itch as it clogged the air in his car. But that was all right. The more he bled, the stronger the scent, the better the trail he left for Dash to follow.

Now he just had to drive slow enough through Ironport to make sure the smell settled into the air.

The city rose like a mirage. Warped and hazy in the twilight hours. Unfortunate, really, that it was real. Eric tapped his breaks, his car slowing to a crawl that he knew would drive anyone who got behind him to fury. But that was fine. Let them think he was a student driver or some little old lady. He needed to set the line, just like he'd done once upon a time when his grandmother took him crabbing.

He crept through the party district, the warehouses, the neighborhood where Dash used to live, by the houses the vampires used as safe houses for a while, the marina . . . all the places Dash had ever shown up at or had his people show up at. Months and months of locations. Places Eric had hoped that he'd never have to see again since they held some of his worst memories.

All of them looked soft in the slowly dwindling sunshine. Innocuous. Like they'd never been the spot of his near drowning, or the place where Tony had been abducted. It was jarring. His skin crawled.

Eventually, he had to cut his hand again to keep the bleeding going. He hoped he wouldn't wind up needing to hold anything. His hand would no doubt still be sore once he reached the morgue, even with the increased healing time being a Venator provided. Although, with the way his luck was running . . .

His phone started vibrating the moment he got to the morgue.

Sighing, Eric grabbed it and answered the call, even as his brain registered the picture on the screen as Bert.

"Not now, Bert," he said, hoping he could head Bert off before he got into whatever thing he'd called about. Eric didn't have time for this. He had a net to set up. A vampire to trap.

"Tony and Hunter are out of bed," Bert whispered like he was afraid to be overheard.

"Are you fucking *tattling* on them now?" Rubbing at the

stubble that lined his jaw, Eric threw the car into park and leaned forward. Why couldn't those two idiots do what they were told? Why couldn't they sit still?

"I thought you'd like to know." Bert's tone was a verbal shrug, and Eric felt a headache pulse at his temples from the combination of blood loss, the stress of his idiot boyfriends, and the pain in his palms.

Eric had the sinking suspicion that Bert wasn't really calling to get Hunter and Tony in trouble, but to convince Eric that he should turn the car around and head back to look after them. There was something distinctly manipulative about the timing and the fact that it was Bert. "Did they put you up to this?"

"What? No!" The affront wasn't enough to cover the lie that Eric could hear in his voice. He'd known Bert too long to not notice.

"You're a shit liar, Bert." Eric lifted his head to stare at the morgue he was parked in front of. It was quiet, just like the night before. The lights in the parking lot were turned off, the building dark. All he'd have to keep him from tripping over something was the near-full moon. It would have to be enough.

"They know what you're up to. Hunter has you all figured out," Bert accused, more confident now that he'd been called out.

Goddess, Eric was so fucking tired. He could imagine the way Hunter and Tony were losing their fucking minds over this. "They're not coming out here, are they? They're too sick, Bert. I just— You get it, right? I'm doing what I have to."

"I get it." Bert shifted. Wherever he was, he wasn't around anyone else. Maybe he'd gone up into his room to call Eric. Hopefully that meant that no one would hear what they were saying. "They're not leaving the house yet."

"Yet? What do you mean *yet*?" Eric ground his teeth. The

light had almost entirely faded by this point. He didn't have time to fuck with this shit anymore. He needed to get set up.

"They think they can get this thing sorted out before you get yourself into too much trouble. But Eric, if you need us, you need to call me. You should put in your earpiece and—"

"Listen, Bert, I've got to go." Eric didn't wait for Bert to argue further. He hung up, turned off his phone, and got out of the car.

CHAPTER 31

EVERY MUSCLE in Hunter's body screamed for him to stop. Lie down. Rest. Play dead. He ached down to his fucking *marrow* in a way he'd never experienced before, and Tony didn't seem to be fairing much better.

But they were upright. They were standing. They were working. And that was more than he could have hoped for given the circumstances.

The only thing worse than the ache that had him grinding his teeth and gasping for breath anytime he moved wrong, was the lack of progress. Half an hour, and nothing to show for it. He was going to lose Eric. Just like he'd lost Britt. Just like he'd lost his mother. He was sure of it.

The failure caught in his lungs, made him cough, retch.

"All right, that's enough microscope time for you buddy. Let Rus have a turn," Ava said, shooing him off his stool like she'd read the hopelessness in every line of his body and decided it was her job to fix it.

Hunter didn't know when they'd gotten there, but the four women—Rus, Vanessa, Ava, and Azure—had crowded into his workspace in the basement and made themselves at home. Each one of them took on some task he hadn't gotten to yet: replacing the filter in the vent above the worktable, reorganizing his samples, going over the data he'd already collected. They worked like a well-oiled machine. A coven.

Hunter had never been so grateful for a group of busybody witches in his life.

"There's nothing there," he told Rus as he pressed his hip into the counter next to where she peered into the microscope. "On a cellular level, it's exactly the same as the other vampires we've interacted with recently."

"Did you stake any of those in this room?" Vanessa asked from where she was carefully going through his recent samples, her keen gaze searching for something none of them could see with the naked eye.

"One," Tony volunteered. "Nothing happened."

"Do you have samples from that vampire?" Rus held out her hand, not taking her eyes away from the dust on the slide. It reacted the same way the blood had, although it looked more like that sand monster from the Mummy, constantly rolling and twisting and eating itself, than like the cells of a being.

Azure handed her the sample without a word. The petri dish clacked lightly as Rus loaded it into a second microscope then flicked the switch so they could all lean in close and look at the differences between the two samples side by side.

Hunter's gut churned at what he saw. Although the substances were different in texture, they were the same in everything else. A chemical breakdown of what they were made of appeared on the screen between the two pictures, showing that they were virtually identical.

"So if they're the same," Tony murmured, as if he were worried that if he spoke too loudly he would give away their location to their enemies, "what does that mean?"

"It means what you're experiencing wasn't caused by something chemical or biological." Rus's voice was oddly calm, almost detached. "It was magic."

"An airborne hex or curse?" Vanessa frowned.

"Is that possible?" Hunter couldn't help but ask. His knowledge of magic was limited, but magic usually needed something more solid to cling to, didn't it? It was why they were working with the tattoos to join Rus's coven. Why they had to go to the Heart of Moondale to receive the benefits the town bestowed on its own. Magic, like electricity, needed something to ground it.

"It's a difficult bit of spellwork." Rus scrubbed at her nose, her fingers twitching against the keyboard under her hand. She was unsettled, perhaps more so than Hunter had seen her in the limited span of their friendship. "But it's not impossible."

"You've seen it before. You know how to combat it," Azure said with a surety to her voice that Hunter envied.

Hunter had faith in a good many things, and people. He trusted Eric to always have his back, to do whatever he could to protect him. He had faith in Tony's ability to adapt and overcome. There was never a shadow of a doubt in his mind that Eric's class of Venator would grow to be strong, capable fighters. Belief seemed to be all he'd had once he lost Britt.

But he didn't think he could figure this out. Not in time. Not on his own.

And he envied Azure the space she had to feel certain of such a thing, even if that thing was the woman she loved.

"I've seen something *like* it before," Rus corrected gently, color rising high on her cheeks and in her ears. "But no, I don't know how to combat it. Jeesh, Az, I'm not as all-knowing as you seem to think I am."

"Nonsense," Azure scoffed.

Rus rolled her eyes, pushing back from the counter so she could spin around on the stool. When Hunter got a better look at her, there was a confident glint in her eye. The kind that set him at ease. If Rus felt like she could solve this, then they would be okay. He'd seen enough of Icarus Ashthorne and her powers over the last couple of months to know she was a strong, capable witch.

"Well?" Tony pressed, clearly annoyed with the dramatics. "You've seen something like it, what does that mean for us?"

"It means," Rus said, lifting her hips so she could pull her phone from her pocket, "I don't know exactly what we're looking at here, but I know someone who does."

"You know someone who specializes in airborne curse magic?" Ava's tone was doubtful, but when Hunter glanced at her, he saw a glint in her eyes that said she was impressed.

Rus shrugged. "I traveled all over the place before I came back to Moondale. I met a lot of people."

"You met an airborne curse specialist on the *road*?" Vanessa lifted a brow in amusement. "Where?"

"Cairo. Where else?" Rus ducked her head to start flipping through her contacts, and Hunter couldn't take his eyes off her.

He'd known Rus was a badass before he ever met her. Ava had dug up what could pass for her background at one point before they'd reached out to her about needing help tracking the vampires. But after seeing the way she was able to combine magic with tech, the way she handled herself when faced with terrifying ghost after terrifying ghost, he had to say he was glad she'd invited him to join her coven. He looked forward to learning anything and everything she had to teach him.

"*Which* contact from Cairo?" Azure asked, her dark eyes narrowing.

Rus laughed, waving her hand in the air. "Oh, Az, don't be like that. Bat's good people."

"Bat is a grifter." Azure sounded annoyed, poking out her lower lip.

"In this economy? Can you blame her?" Rus tilted her head in question.

"A grifter?" Hunter turned away from them as a tickle started in his throat again, and he found himself hacking so hard his whole body shook, his knees jerking beneath him. It was only through the grace of Tony sidling close and offering his strength that Hunter didn't keel right over.

Without a word, Ava pulled two more stools from against the wall and pushed the men onto them via a grip on their shoulders.

"Thanks," Tony mumbled.

Once they'd settled, Rus fixed Hunter with a mischievous grin. "Bat sells tours to haunted locations around the world. She takes rich assholes who have more money than sense to places that are famously 'haunted' and works a little magic to scare the bejeezus out of them so they get their money's worth."

"And that works?" Tony sounded impressed.

"It's a living." Rus shrugged. "Ah, there she is!" Rus crowed after a few moments. "Az, when we get home, remind me to go through my contacts, would you? I don't remember who half these people are."

"I'll set a reminder," Azure said, pulling out her own phone to do just that while Rus's started to ring.

She put it on speaker, holding the phone up toward her mouth, her eyes hooded as she stared down at the screen. It rang for a long time, but Rus didn't seem bothered by the wait. It was like she expected for this to take a minute. When it finally kicked over to voicemail, Rus hung up and called again.

This time the line picked up on the second ring. "Do you know what time it is, Ashthorne?" a groggy, annoyed voice asked from the other side. The person sounded like they wanted to reach through the phone and throttle Rus.

"Bat!" Rus cheered with no outward sign that she feared for her life.

"It's 2:30 in the fucking morning, *Ashthorne*."

"And you've been asleep? Oof, Bat, darling, you must be slipping."

"I was at a job the night before last. Someone wanted to do

Lennox Castle *again*. Fucking amateurs. Just *once* I'd like to take someone on a tour someplace that's *actually* haunted," Bat griped. She sounded more awake now, fabric rustling in the background as if she was sitting up in bed.

"Careful what you wish for, Batty-Bat. Putting that shit out into the universe is a good way to get exactly what you ask for," Rus chided playfully, and Hunter heard Bat let out a soft indignant scoff.

"What do you *want*, Ashthorne?"

Rus straightened on her stool, her gray eyes hardening, all business again. "I'm here in Ironport with a couple of folk who've been effected by some kind of airborne curse magic."

"Ironport, Maryland?" That seemed to pique Bat's interest. "You came across airborne curse magic in Ironport, *Maryland*? Fuck, Ashthorne, the life you lead. How do I get a ticket on that ride?"

"You don't," Azure muttered, clearly irritated.

"The magic," Hunter said, a reminder of what they were here for. He leaned more heavily against Tony. His shivering had subsided for a bit there, but it was getting to the point of near teeth chattering again. "The curse."

"You didn't tell me you had me on speaker, you asshole!" Bat hissed into the mic, then let out a loud groan. "You're such a dick, Ashthorne."

"Yeah, yeah." Rus flapped her hand through the air.

"What are their symptoms?" Fabric shuffled again on the other end of the line, followed by the crinkling of paper.

"Fever. Vomiting. Aches," Hunter reported.

"It's like the fuckin' flu," Tony added.

"Weakness? Fatigue?" Bat asked, clearly running down some kind of mental checklist.

"Yes, and yes. We've also had some dizziness." Hunter glanced around at the others in the room, the coven of witches who'd come together to help him and Tony so they could get back to Eric. There was some relief going through them now. Speaking to someone who knew what they were doing seemed to help. Goddess, he'd gotten so lucky finding Rus, and befriending her.

"Okay. So. You're either dying—"

"What the *fuck*?!" Tony shouted, his voice echoing off the cement walls of the basement and Hunter's aching head.

"*Or* you'll be fine in a couple of hours," Bat continued, undeterred by Tony's outburst. "Oh! What color are the whites of their eyes?"

Ava lifted the flashlight to her phone so she could check, and Hunter and Tony both hissed away from the brightness. "Bloodshot as all hell, but the normal color otherwise," she reported.

"Right, then you're gonna be fine. Unless you're human. You're not human, are you?"

"Werewolf and witch," Rus offered. "Newly turned, will that make a difference?"

"Nah. So long as they have magic in their blood, they're good." Bat's tone was a verbal shrug. "It's mostly humans who die from these low-level types of hexes."

"How do you know it's low-level without seeing it?" Azure sounded like she didn't put much stock in anything Bat had to say.

"I've dealt with enough crypts and shit to see the full breadth of airborne magic." Confidence came easy to Bat. The note of arrogance in her tone seemed to make Azure's hackles rise as her shoulders lifted.

Rus reached for Az and gave her forearm a squeeze that seemed to calm her. "Anyway, to counteract the hex and speed along the healing process . . . ?"

"No idea without seeing it up close and personal. Out of curiosity, where did they pick this thing up? Did you break into someone's tomb or something?" Bat sounded fully awake now. Whatever long night she'd had the day before was washed away by her curiosity, and the more she talked, the more Hunter could see how she and Rus had become friends. Two folk with a thirst for knowledge that wouldn't be quenched.

Maybe he could get her number off Rus and get in touch with Bat himself. The things she knew about the wider world of magic would be invaluable for his research.

"Booby-trapped vampire," Tony grunted.

"Huh. That's a new one."

"For us too," Hunter couldn't help but add with a laugh. A weight lifted off his chest and he could breathe easier for the first time in what felt like days. He'd fucked up, sure, but not so badly that he and Tony were going to die from his mistake.

"Right. Well. We'll keep you posted, Bat," Rus said, clearly gearing up to end the call.

"Hmmm. Do." Bat sounded like she was still deep in thought, her mind working as fast and as hard as Hunter's tended to when he was presented with something he found supremely interesting. "And if you can find a way to send samples . . ."

"We will," Hunter promised. It was tough to say no to a like mind.

"I look forward to hearing from you then. Whoever you are."

"Hunter Delacroix."

"A pleasure." Bat's voice ticked up like she was smiling. "I'm going back to bed now." Then she hung up.

"So we're just supposed to wait until this thing works its way out of their systems?" Ava asked. She shifted her weight from one foot to the other. Nervous. Unsettled.

"Like hell we are," Tony growled.

CHAPTER 32

ERIC HAD NEVER BEEN PARTICULARLY good at fishing.

He understood the theory behind it. The patience. The waiting. The needing to know how and when to jerk the line to hook the fish right through the gills.

He appreciated the ritual of what came afterward too. The methodical gutting and cleaning.

The hunt. The kill. The cleanup.

Those were all things he understood as easy as breathing. It was the fucking *patience* that got him. Sitting still. Staying quiet. Letting the fish come to him. *That's* what got him. Every. Time.

His inability to be patient got him this time too, Eric realized belatedly. But that came after. What came before was . . .

The trap was set. The bait was in place. All that was left to do was wait and hope to the Goddess that Hunter and Tony wouldn't get it into their heads to come after him before this was all over. He couldn't watch their backs and his own too.

Eric sat in the autopsy tech's office just off the room with all the tables and medical equipment. A big window looked out over the parking lot, and he could see where he'd placed the net from the wheelie chair as he twisted back and forth in it, picking at the bandages he'd put on his hands.

The wind picked up. A door down the hall slammed open

then closed again, but the hairs on the back of Eric's neck didn't rise. None of his senses whispered *danger* in the back of his mind. He squinted through the dark into the parking lot. Still no sign of his prey.

Where *was* he? A few weeks back, Eric couldn't fucking get rid of Dash. He was around every corner. Taking Tony out to dinner. Showing up at Council of Creatures meetings. Being showy and full of himself. And now he was just gone? When Eric had about as good as sent a personal invite?

No way.

Dash wouldn't miss the chance to finally put Eric out of his misery. To get everything he'd wanted for months, possibly years. Eric was the missing piece, the only thing standing between Dash and some kind of weird domination over the vampires of America. Eric wasn't clear on the details, but he remembered what Janet said.

Then what was taking him so fucking long?

The clock on the wall ticked loudly.

Tick. Tock.

One minute. Two.

The longer Eric sat there watching the net, the more likely that the kids or his friends or his boyfriends came after him and put their lives in danger. It had already been a half an hour since he'd hung up on Bert, and he didn't doubt for a single second that the kid had held him on the line so he could track Eric's phone.

It was only a matter of time before they started down the mountain. Maybe they already had. If they left as soon as Eric hung up, that would give him about forty-five minutes before they descended upon him and made a mess of his plans.

He glanced at the clock. There were only fourteen minutes left to that.

A fight with Dash couldn't take more than ten. Probably not even that.

He had time.

He could wait.

Tick. Tock.

But what if Dash was already there? What if he was lying in wait for Eric to come out of hiding so he could do him in? What if when the kids and Tony and Hunter arrived, Dash melted out of the woods to the left of the morgue with his army of the undead like a pack of fucking jackals and tore them apart?

It would take Eric too long to get to them if that were the case.

He'd have to trip over the tables in the main area of this office. Run down the long hall, past the storage and disposal areas. Get out to the parking lot. That was at least a minute of time he'd waste just getting out there. By then, they'd be surrounded. By then, some of them might be dead.

Tick. Tock.

He didn't feel the tell-tale buzz of his senses warning him that a vampire army was close, but Dash had learned cloaking magic from someone. There was no telling what else he knew how to do. Maybe he was standing in the parking lot right that second, invisible to the naked eye, waiting for Eric's friends to show up to help him.

He'd wait a little longer. There was no reason to think that they'd come right away. Tony and Hunter were sick.

Tick. Tock.

Tony and Hunter were *sick*. The kids were untrained. They wouldn't be stupid enough to follow him here, even if they knew what he was doing. And he was under no illusion that they didn't. Otherwise, why would Bert have called?

Tick. Tock.

His friends were coming. His friends, the people he loved, the family he'd built, were going to get here.

Tick. Tock.

They would be here soon.

Tick. Tock.

Eric flung himself from the chair, heedless of the way it skittered across the floor in his wake, and stormed out of the office, past the tables, down the long hallway, and into the cool night.

The moment his tennis shoe touched the cement of the parking lot, he felt it: a prickle of the skin at the nape of his neck. His hair rising in alarm. *Danger.*

"Took you long enough," a voice murmured, giving Eric just enough time to duck the first slash of a clawed hand.

Laughter echoed through the dark, Dash's deep voice bouncing off the trees, the buildings, everything, making him hard to pin down. The moon had gone behind the clouds at some point, although Eric didn't remember that having been the case before he'd left the office. Maybe it was some kind of spell. A dampener put in place to dull his senses and make him easier to kill.

Just like the illness that now had his boyfriends bedridden.

"Why don't we stop playing games?" Eric called into the shadows. He inched across the parking lot, careful steps to keep himself from tripping over something, a stake in each hand. He needed to lure Dash to the net. That was all. It would hold him—hopefully—until the others came, and then they could use their magic and the power of teamwork to get answers right before they got rid of him.

He just had to get to the net.

"Who's playing games, Big Ricky?" Dash asked. His voice sounded like it was coming from everywhere and nowhere at the same time. This had to be some sort of magic. There was no other explanation. Eric couldn't even see the stars above his head, or the near-full moon. This wasn't just cloud cover.

"At least I don't have to hide behind cheap parlor tricks. Did your pet witch do up this one?" Maybe if he was demeaning enough, snarky enough, Dash would get sick of his shit and come out of hiding. Eric could hope. It had worked well enough for him in the past.

There was a snort off to his right, and Eric swiped out with his stake. He felt more than saw the wood swish past someone, just missing them.

Close. Dash was sticking close.

Good. If he wanted to keep Eric within arm's reach, then Eric would have an easier time leading him where he wanted him to be.

Even in the dark, he was able to orient himself toward his car and the trap he'd laid. Some innate sixth sense drew him toward it.

And all the while, Dash followed.

A breath on Eric's neck. A claw scraping up his back.

Some fucked-up game of cat and mouse. Eric wondered how long Dash would toy with him before he decided to finally take what he wanted. Not long, probably. He'd have to be quick.

The net was uneven beneath his shoes, like a wrinkle in the cement. One pace, two, three, and he was at the center of it. His feet planted. His arms at the ready. The net's magic dragged at his senses, weighing him down, threatening to keep him and suck him under like so much quicksand. He shook it off. Focused.

"All right, you fucker, come and get me," he murmured.

Dash didn't leave him waiting long.

"Oh. I'm going to enjoy this," Dash whispered right before he lunged.

Eric hit the cement so hard, he felt a rib crack, the wind rushing out of him, leaving him choking on nothing. It didn't stop him. Nothing would. Nothing could. His friends were coming, they'd be here soon, and he'd done what he was meant to. He'd trapped the Big Bad Vampire. Now he had to get the fuck out of his own trap.

The point of one of the stakes burned a hole through

Dash's side, his skin sizzling as he sunk his teeth into Eric's neck. Pain blossomed all along Eric's veins, burning through him like wildfire—the exact opposite of the venom he'd endured in the past. It threatened to blot out his mind, his motives. He couldn't see. He couldn't hear.

He could feel. He could feel and he wouldn't forget what he was there for.

He jammed the other stake into Dash's other side, just under the ribs. Close. Too close for the vampire who jerked away and rolled off Eric, taking his stakes with him.

Eric got onto his hands and knees and crawled toward the edge of the net. There wasn't time to think about how ridiculous he looked. Dash would get the stakes out soon and he'd be fucked. He needed to put enough distance between himself and Dash to be safe. His friends would come. They'd help finish Dash off then.

He just needed—

His head bumped into something solid. Like running into a wall.

"What the fuck?" With trembling fingers, Eric lifted his hand to push against the wall in front of him. It wouldn't budge. He was . . . he was trapped. He was trapped in the fucking trap *he'd* set with the vampire trying to kill him. So much for getting information out of Dash, it was kill or be killed.

Dash laughed, long and loud. The stakes Eric used to get him away clattered to the parking lot outside of the net array, out of reach. "Didn't think you'd get stuck in here with me, did you?"

A scream left Eric, the pulse of Dash's venom in his veins still making everything burn, even as the world burst forth with light again. The parking lot was all there like he remembered. The near-full moon above. Whatever magic Dash had used was gone now, or maybe he'd been abandoned by his witch.

It didn't matter.

Dash was alone. He was weaponless. He wouldn't go down without a fight.

"It's a fight to the death you want, is it?" Dash asked from where he stood at the center of the net, picking his teeth with a pointed fingernail. "Happy to oblige."

What happened next happened too quickly for Eric to fully comprehend. Dash was across the space between them, on top of Eric again. They were wrestling on the ground. Eric kicked, screamed, punched, clawed. Did everything and anything he could to keep the vampire's fangs at bay.

He pulled his Cross from his shirt, the pendant flashing in the moonlight, and it gave him some space. Not much. Dash didn't get off him, but it was like a barrier had gone up. He gnashed his teeth at the edge of it but couldn't get his face any closer to Eric.

The silver was hot against Eric's hands, bloodstained from years of wearing it in battle. Wrapping the chain around his fingers, Eric lifted off the ground, his abdominal muscles screaming. Dash fell onto his ass and scrambled back, but not quick enough. Not before Eric got the chain wrapped around his neck and pulled.

Dash howled, his nails scrabbling at Eric's face. His neck. His arms. Anywhere he could reach. His skin shifted under Eric's touch as if he was trying to turn to mist again, but he couldn't manage with the silver wrapped around his throat.

Eric tightened his grip, the chain digging in, slicing through Dash's flesh.

Talons nicked something important. Eric realized it the moment it happened. His head swam with pain and blood gushed down his neck. Too hot. Too fast.

His vision swam, darkening around the edges.

He was almost there though. The silver had cut half through Dash's neck. The vampire screamed. Wailed. Choked. Sobbed. Growing weaker and weaker by the second even as he pummeled Eric. Leaving behind gashes and bruises.

Every second, Eric was one inch closer to removing Dash's head.

Every second, another gush of blood soaked his collar.

That was fine. He always knew he was going to die this way.

The least he could do was make sure he took Dashfield B.M. Chadwick with him.

Eric didn't know how long it took. How much blood he'd lost. Or how close he was to death.

But eventually, it was done.

It was finally done.

The chain cut through. Dashfield's head toppled from his shoulders, rolling across the ground for a second before his entire body burst into ash.

Eric slumped back onto the cement, the world spinning around him. Darkness closed in. It was cold. Everything was cold. His ears rang. His vision blurred.

The sky had never looked so pretty.

THEY WERE HOLDING each other up, leaning on each other so heavily that Hunter's shoulder dug into Tony's chest. But it didn't matter. Nothing mattered.

Nothing apart from the need to get across the parking lot as quickly as they could. To reach Eric before it was too fucking late.

Together.

They hobbled across the cement, keeping each other from stumbling, falling. They both dropped to the ground beside Eric's body. Hard pavement dug into their knees. Their bodies still shook from the illness, from the exertion, from the fear.

"Talk to me, pretty boy," Tony whispered, his hand trembling when he reached for Eric.

There was so much blood. Red. And vicious. It stained Eric's mole-dotted skin. The parking lot. The net.

Too much of it.

Was it still flowing? Had it clotted? Eric's chest wasn't moving. Or maybe Tony just couldn't tell in the dark. Maybe—

"Eric. Eric," Hunter gasped, his voice strangled. He reached for Eric and gave him a nudge. "Come on, baby, this isn't funny. Get up." A shake, Eric's head lolling with the movement. "Get up!"

"Is he breathing?" Tony asked. He didn't want the answer.

Because he already knew, down to his marrow, that Eric wasn't breathing. His heart wasn't beating. He was gone. Gone so far that Tony would never be able to find him again, never be able to bring him back. Tony could see it in his eyes now that he was close. There was a blankness that had never been there before, a dullness.

He'd probably known it from across the parking lot, he just hadn't wanted to admit it. And he felt—

Numb.

"Eric. Hon." Hunter grabbed Eric by the shoulders, pulling his torso into his chest, leaning back so he rested against Tony. Tony's hands moved without him saying so. He held Hunter close. Brushed sweaty hair back from a face stained with tears. Kept moving. Kept his eyes on the person who was living, breathing. He couldn't look at Eric. Not with how still he was. He just . . . He *couldn't.* "Sweetheart. No. No."

"He's gone, Hunter." Speaking the words, putting them out into the air, made them real. Tony wished he could snatch them back. Rip them from his own throat and crush them under his boot. Even if they were true. Even if someone needed to say it.

Blood soaked into the knees of his sweatpants. It was cold. Thick. Congealing.

How long had Eric lain there before they reached him?

He'd died alone.

A howl crawled up his throat, but Tony swallowed around it.

"No," Hunter snapped, and he dropped Eric to the ground, already moving to start CPR. To try to push life back into a heart that hadn't been beating for several minutes by that point. "No! You're not leaving me! You're not fucking doing that! You wake the fuck up! You get up, and you look at me!"

Tony's heart constricted in his chest, his face hot with tears he hadn't realized he was shedding until he had to all but rip Hunter away from where he was practically beating on Eric's chest, ribs snapping under the force. "He's gone, Hunter. Stop. Stop!"

Hunter wailed and threw himself into Tony, and Tony caught him, held him close. What else was there to do? He couldn't bring Eric back. Neither of them—

Tony wheeled around at the sound of footsteps behind them, his eyes zeroing in on the pink-haired necromancer. He couldn't force Eric back into his body. But *she* could. And in that moment, it didn't matter to him what it cost or how she did it. So long as Eric was back with them, so long as Tony didn't have to hold the pieces of Hunter together while they both shattered.

"Bring him back," he said to Icarus Ashthorne, his green eyes narrowed on the woman. Everything fell away apart from her, and Hunter was heavy in his arms, hiccupping sobs wracking his chest.

"What?" Rus asked.

"I want you to bring him back." Tony peeled his lips back from his elongated teeth, snarling. Threatening. Not the best idea when he was asking someone to do him such a big favor, but he couldn't seem to help it. "Bring him back!"

"I can't. I—I shouldn't." Rus turned to look at the woman at her side. Azure, her partner. "He wouldn't want—"

"Tony." Ava was suddenly beside him, her tone gentle even as she shook with guilt, with grief. She reached for him as if she might take Hunter and Eric from his arms.

Tony snapped his teeth at her, feral. "They're *mine*." As soon as he said it, it was like something in his chest had unlocked. He breathed easier. A calm swept through him, his hands steadying, his breathing going deeper.

The wolf perked his head up, a soft whine echoing through Tony's mind. And Tony . . . He understood what the wolf meant, what he was trying to say. *Pack. Mates.* Hunter and Eric were his pack. Both of them.

"They're *mine*. You can't have them. And neither can the After. You will bring him back to us, Ashthorne!"

"This isn't what he'd—"

"I don't give a flying fuck what he'd want! You bring him *back* to *us*!" He felt his teeth growing sharper in his mouth, hair growing thicker along his arms. The wolf in his chest rumbled his approval, his encouragement, as if he too had decided that Eric and Hunter belonged to them, and they were not letting go of either of them.

Rus looked at Azure again, a question in her raised brows. The pair of them stared at each other for a long moment, silently communicating in a way Tony had hoped to one day be able to with Eric, with Hunter. In a way he might never get to if Rus said no. Because Eric would be gone, forever, and this would break Hunter. And then Tony wouldn't have either of them.

Azure inclined her head, her chin lifting.

"Okay," Rus said with a nod, and returned her attention to Tony. "Get him into the car. We'll have to go back to Moondale for this. I'll need her power."

"What else will you need?" Ava rose to her feet, already in motion, not even bothering to question what they were doing. Good. Tony didn't have it in him to convince someone else. Not now that he'd gotten the necromancer on board.

"A large mammal. Alive. If you can get me a cow or a horse, that'd be best." Rus scrubbed at her face. "And . . ."

She started listing off ingredients and supplies, and Tony tuned her out. Let the witches take care of that bit of it. Right now, he needed to focus on getting Hunter and Eric into the car.

"Hunter," he whispered to the man still shaking in his arms.

Hunter held Eric so tightly to him, he might have

managed to break some of Eric's bones. But Tony wasn't going to tell him off about it. "You can't take him from me," Hunter rasped through a throat that sounded like he'd been screaming.

"I don't plan on it," Tony promised. He didn't know how he was keeping it together. It didn't make sense. The only explanation was that between him and his wolf, they realized they needed to stay calm. Hunter couldn't, and Tony wasn't about to let them both fall apart, not when this might be the only chance they got to bring Eric home. "But we need to get him to the car, sweetheart. We need to get him over to Moondale so Rus can do her thing."

"She'll bring him back?" Hunter looked up at him, finally, *finally*. His eyes were bloodshot, his face a mess of tears and sweat. He looked impossibly young like this. Small and frail. Tony wanted to gather him close and never let him go again. To protect him from anything and everything.

They'd have to talk about that, eventually. Sit down and work out how the three of them were going to work together if Hunter decided he was willing to date Tony too.

But first—

"She's going to bring our boy home."

CHAPTER 34

HUNTER HAD no idea where Ava and Vanessa had gotten a cow on such short notice. Nor how they'd gotten it to Moondale without an animal trailer. *Nor* how they'd gotten it into the coven house for the Coven of the Forgotten at 154 Mourning Moore. And to be quite frank, he didn't care. It didn't matter. Nothing mattered outside of Eric's dear face, pale from blood loss, littered in crimson stains from his and Tony's fingers. Markers of their love for him. Of their desperation to keep him.

Maybe they should wash him before they did this. Would Eric be freaked out if he came to covered in his own blood? At least it wasn't someone else's. But still.

"Should we give him a bath or something?" Hunter asked. His throat was still raw from screaming and crying.

"He's just going to get bloody again." Rus hadn't sat still since they arrived at the house. She was too busy setting up candles, drawing out a circle with untidy characters scrawled around it, and throwing around instructions. A flurry of movement.

Hunter wished this were happening under different circumstances. Then he'd have the mental bandwidth to appreciate all the work that went into the ritual, all the intricacies. As it was, he was numb to it. A distant observer, blindly going through the motions as he and Tony laid Eric carefully down a short distance from the cow.

"Did you tell Meiling where we were?" Rus shot the question to Azure, who was helping Vanessa herd the cow toward the array Rus had marked off on the plastic sheeting in the middle of the overlarge living room at the front of the house.

Azure nodded. "Nesta and Cagney have also been informed. They plan to keep Greer busy."

"Good. The fewer people who know about this, the less likely the board finds out I did necromancy on Moondale lands." Rus seemed to wince at the thought, then shook her head and went back to mashing together ingredients with a mortar and pestle.

Ava snorted, rolling her eyes. "You're a necromancer, what else do they expect you to do?"

Rus shrugged. "Sit quietly and mind my business."

Hunter wanted to laugh. It was a little funny. But he couldn't. The sound got caught somewhere between his brain, which recognized the joke, and his tongue, which lay like a dead weight in his mouth.

"It's going to be okay, sweetheart," Tony murmured from where he'd settled behind Hunter. He'd let Hunter lean back against his chest. Held him close. Pressed his face into Hunter's temple. Kept Hunter from falling apart.

Another thing Hunter wished he could better appreciate. He doubted he'd ever see such tenderness from Tony again. He should really take the time to soak it up. But he couldn't. Not when Eric's skin was so cold under his hands.

"You're going to have to step away from him," Rus said after what felt like a small eternity. "I'm sorry."

Hunter's hands tightened in Eric's shirt without his say so. He couldn't let go. He didn't want to. What if this didn't work? What if Eric was gone for good? What if it did work and the Eric that came back wasn't *their* Eric?

Tony made a soft rumbling sound of comfort in his chest,

just for Hunter to hear where his ear was pressed to the bone, and carefully peeled Hunter's fingers away from the material. "Come on, sweetheart, let's let the lady work." He settled Eric gently onto the floor, his hands shaking. "Let's let Ashthorne do her thing."

Once Hunter lost his grip on Eric, it was like he lost his grip on reality. The only tether keeping him from floating off entirely was Tony and his soft murmurs, low and slow, his hands overly warm as they brushed careful circles into Hunter's back. His world narrowed to those things, just those. Everything else—the blood, the noise, the burn of magic in the air, the way Eric struggled against Rus's hold as she tried to force his spirit back into a body that resisted, the violence of this act—it all disappeared.

Until Eric gasped awake, coughing and sputtering and reaching for the newly stitched wound on his throat.

Tony and Hunter both took a giant step forward, ready to rush in and scoop him up. To never let him go again. But Rus raised a hand to keep them from getting any closer.

"Where am I?" Eric whispered, fear making the question wobble.

"Take it easy," Rus said gently as she helped him sit. "Slow, shallow breaths. That's it."

Hunter's heart was in his throat. His fingers were so tight in Tony's shirt that he swore it would tear. Neither of them moved—neither of them *breathed*—as they watched Rus coax Eric slowly back to himself.

"Where am I?" Eric asked again, his voice raspier than it had ever been.

Something passed between him and Rus in that moment. Rus answered the lost look on Eric's face with something like understanding, like kindness, but Hunter didn't understand it. And he didn't care. Eric was back.

"Oh," Eric said after a moment, his face doing something Hunter couldn't parse. His eyes flicked to meet Hunter's and

Tony's over Rus's shoulder. The smile that lifted his mouth was slow and strained, but it was honest. "Can I get a hug?"

"You're home," Tony whispered, a little disbelieving. Then, "You're home!"

That was all it took. Hunter and Tony rushed across the floor and tackled him, heedless of injuries and sickness. Uncaring of the hardwood beneath them or the blood that dampened their clothes. And Hunter . . . Hunter breathed for the first time in what felt like hours.

"It's temporary," Rus said as they all crowded around the kitchen table of her home next to the coven house at 157 Mourning Moore. Eric sat between Hunter and Tony with Ava's chair pushed so close to Hunter's that she was practically in his lap. Vanessa was beside her, though she kept a more respectable distance. Azure piddled around the kitchen, making tea, while Rus faced them with a grim expression.

"What do you mean *temporary*?" Tony snarled, and only the pressure of Eric's hand in his stopped him from leaping across the table at Rus.

"I mean, I bought you six months." Rus scrubbed at her face. She looked tired, haggard. She hadn't had to spill any of her own blood for the spell, but that didn't seem to matter. Dark circles ringed her eyes, and her skin had gone a shade paler.

"I don't understand." Hunter's voice was quiet, lost.

"Necromancy is about balance," Rus explained, her fingers threaded together on the table as if she needed to keep herself still. "It's hard to explain, but the easiest way to understand it is that it's about possibility. People like to think of it as a life for a life, but that's not really how it works.

Every life has its own cosmic value. One isn't better than the other, but—" She paused, sucking in a breath. "Think of it like stones in a stream. Some stones displace more water than others. Some take up more space than others. And some can divert the current entirely to erode the shore. In order to keep the stream flowing as close to the way it had been before to keep rip currents from forming, and damage from being caused, for every life I bring back to the world, I have to remove another that's almost exactly the same."

"A cow wasn't enough," Tony grumbled.

"No. A cow wasn't enough." Rus shook her head. "The only creature that would have been close to equal value was another Venator. And as there are so few of them, and I don't think you really wanted us to go out and murder—"

"No," Eric said. His throat felt a little better now that he'd had some water, but it still ached like he'd run miles and miles in the cold.

"Then what do we do?" Ava whispered. She hadn't looked away from Eric this entire time, like she was afraid he'd disappear right before her eyes. They all were doing that.

"You're going to have to cheat death." Rus's mouth ticked up at one corner in a smirk.

"How?" Hunter's hand flexed around Eric's, his rings digging into Eric's knuckles.

"Easiest method? Go find a vampire and have Eric turned. Given the nature of being a Venator, I'd suggest finding an old one. The older the better, in fact. Less likely your Venator blood will attack the virus and just wipe it out." Rus reached into her pocket and pulled out her phone. "I'll put you in touch with Bat. She might be able to help you find someone."

"Okay," Hunter and Tony said as one, nodding their understanding, grave determination lining their features.

"Tell us what else we need," Tony mumbled, his phone already in his hand, finger moving quickly to take notes.

Eric slumped back into his chair, did his best *not* to tune out as the chatter continued around him, even with his mind screaming, his bones weary, his every joint stiff, and his heart thudding slowly in his chest. . .

A steady reminder that he would never again know peace.

Goddess. He was so tired.

ABOUT LOU WILHAM

Born and raised in a small town near the Chesapeake Bay, Lou Wilham grew up on a steady diet of fiction, arts and crafts, and Old Bay. After years of absorbing everything, there was to absorb of fiction, fantasy, and sci-fi she's left with a serious writ-ing/drawing habit that just won't quit. These days, she spends much of her time writing, drawing, and chasing a very short Basset Hound named Sherlock.

When not, daydreaming up new characters to write and draw she can be found crocheting, making cute bookmarks, and binge-watching whatever happens to catch her eye.

Learn more about Lou and her future projects on her website: http://louinprogress.com/ or join her mailing list at: http://subscribepage.com/mailermailer

facebook.com/LouWilham
instagram.com/lou.wilham

ALSO BY LOU WILHAM

The Witches of Moondale
    The Hex Next Door
    The Ghost of Hexes Past
    Home is Where the Hex Is

The Hunters of Ironport
    Overkill
    Fresh Kill
    Kill your Darlings

The Fae of Eventide
    An offer Fae Can't Refuse

Sanctuary of the Lost
    Of Loyalties and Wreckage
    Of Love and Ruin
    Of Hope & Blight
    Of Blight & Ruin

Completed
    The Tales of the Sea Trilogy
    Villainous Heroics
    The Clockwork Chronicles
    The Curse Collection
    The Heir To Moondust
    Benvolio & Mercutio Turn Back Time

ACKNOWLEDGMENTS

I always start these things but thanking the reader, and this one is no different. I want to thank you—whether you're a returning reader or Lou is new to you—for picking up my little indie published book, supporting my dream, and following along with Tony, Eric, and Hunter on their journey. Without readers, I can't do what I do, so I greatly appreciate the support.

If you loved every moment of Eric, Tony, and Hunter's story (as I hope you did) please leave a review, follow me on social media, or give me a shout out. I love hearing from you guys, it's really the best part of writing.

Next I'd like to thank my family who supports me in this weird journey I'm on to become an established author. They show up to my signings, they listen to my rants about my characters, they look at my covers and tell me when they're complete shit (I design my covers FYI), and they're the best people to have in my corner, no joke.

Then there is the small hoard of beta, and sensitivity readers I had look at this bugger to tell me if any of it actually made sense, and if I'm as funny as I think I am (turns out I am). You guys provided so much helpful feedback you don't even know.

And of course my editor, Brenna. Who loves these idiots as much as I do, and it shows!

And last but certainly not least, thank you to my small writing family. Tiss, Elle, Whitney, and Nancy—without you there would be no Lou.

MORE BOOKS YOU'LL LOVE

If you enjoyed this story, please consider leaving a review.

Then check out more books from Midnight Tide Publishing!

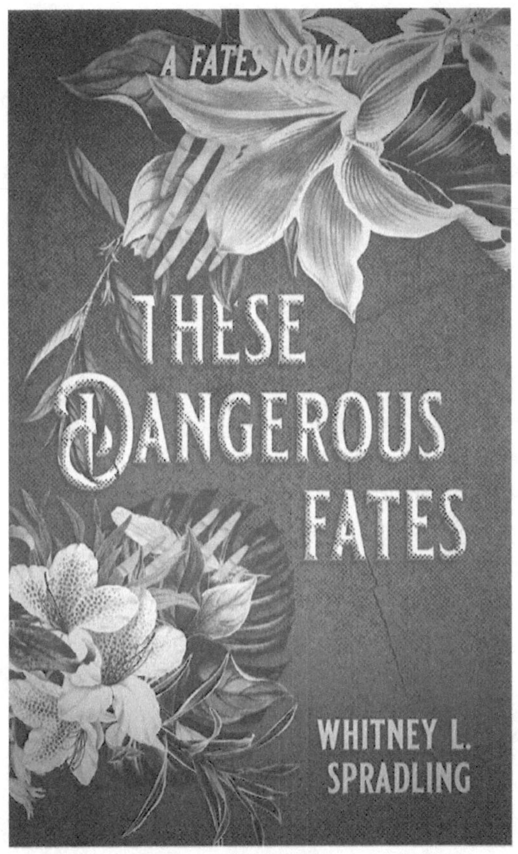

These Dangerous Fates by Whitney L. Spradling

I live in a magical world. A world filled with vampires, shifters, and mages.
Mysteriously, I was born without powers.

After living the past two years in a personal hell, enduring abuse from a fiance I didn't choose, I finally snapped. An act of self-defense against my fiance angers my father, and in retaliation for my actions, he creates the ultimate contest.

One that only the most powerful magicals can compete in to win my hand in marriage.

It sounds bleak, but anything has to be better than my current situation. At least, I thought so, until *they* appeared in the middle of the night to whisk me away.

A vampire prince.
A wolf without a pack.
A powerful mage.

My three captors do everything they can to win the contest, and as the attraction between the four of us grows, so does their desire to keep me safe.

When the mystery of my birth comes into play, we begin to question everything I thought I knew about my life. Am I just a human with no magical powers? Or am I something else entirely? One thing is certain, if my captors cannot keep me safe, more than my heart is at stake: my life is on the line.

Available Now

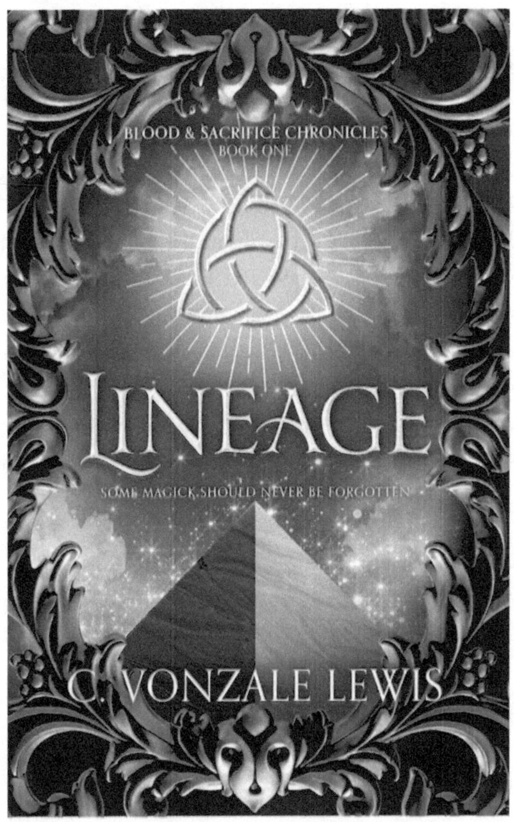

Lineage by C. Vonzale Lewis

On Tulare Island, Magick is a way of life, but for smart-mouthed Nicole Fontane, it's a curse to be avoided at all costs. Yet the legacy she was born with and her failure to live up to it isn't so easy to bury.

With less than two hundred dollars in her bank account and rent looming overhead, Nicole is forced to take a job at Tribec Insurance. Corporate, stuffy, and nothing like what she wanted for herself. It doesn't help that the company's proprietors, the Stewart family, harbor a morbid fascination with the Naqada, a mysterious pre-dynastic Egyptian society.

Between the eerie atmosphere, heightened security, and the stench of blood wafting through Tribec, Nicole suspects the Stewarts are dabbling in a dark art she never thought she'd encounter:

Blood Magick. Deadly. Forbidden. Unnatural.

Despite spending a lifetime avoiding Magick, Nicole unwittingly becomes a pawn in the Stewarts' nefarious schemes. To save her home and those she holds dear, she must confront her troubled past with Magick and unlock her latent abilities, even if she's terrified of the outcome and what it might spur.

The way of life Nicole shunned is her only lifeline—one covered in thorns—but it's all that stands in the way of an Old God's resurrection.

Available Now

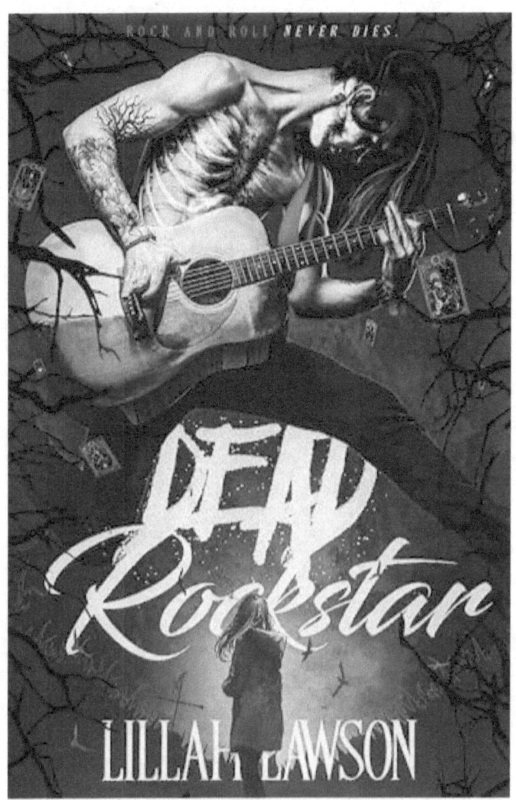

Dead Rockstar by Lillah Lawson

Stormy Spooner is at her wits' end. Careening towards bitter after a nasty divorce, she sometimes wonders what her life is becoming.

After unearthing a cryptic set of lines from a dusty album cover, Stormy tries the impossible: to resurrect Phillip Deville, enigmatic former frontman of the Bloomer Demons. Stormy's love for her favorite dead rockstar knows no bounds...but it was all supposed to be a joke.

When she answers a knock on her door the next day and finds herself face to face with the dark-haired rock god of her every teenage fantasy, her entire world is turned upside down.

Turns out, she's awakened more than just Philip, and Stormy will have to do battle against a cast of strange characters to keep herself and her new undead boyfriend safe.

Available May 15, 2024

www.ingramcontent.com/pod-product-compliance
Lightning Source LLC
Chambersburg PA
CBHW021031310726

48969CB00006B/1615